Find
Sam

Find Sam

Debbie Ann Ice

Bink Books
Bedazzled Ink Publishing Company • Fairfield, California

paperback 978-1-949290-20-2

Cover art
by
Chip Goldsmith

Cover Design
by

Bink Books
a division of
Bedazzled Ink Publishing, LLC
Fairfield, California
http://www.bedazzledink.com

To Daisy and in memory of Dora

Acknowledgements

Thanks to my brother, Chip Goldsmith, for the great cover art. Thank you Francis Coppola for creating Zoetrope studios where many writers like me were able to learn, workshop, and meet other writers. Thank you to the following writers who supported me either with encouragement or tough advice or inspiration: Avital Gad Cykman, Thomas Jackson, Lisa Lieberman, Beverly Jackson, Alicia Gifford, Len Joy, David Toussaint, Susan Henderson, Pia Ehrhardt, Tiff Holland, Mary McCluskey, Ellen Meister, Maryanne Stahl, Barbara Milton, Lydia Theys. Thank you to two friends who are always there for me: Jaynie Spector and Harriet Whelchel. Special thanks to my patient husband, Bart Ice, and patient sons, Thomas and Jimmy—who put up with me. Thank you, Bedazzled Ink, particularly Casey, for accepting my work and helping me on this journey.

Thanks to everyone who helps find lost dogs, rescue lost dogs, or adopt lost dogs.

And, finally, to all those brave souls who find our special needs population in a world that all too readily loses them . . . hang in there!

Chapter 1

Marcy
Losing Sam

MARCY THORPE IGNORED the muted TV—now displaying Charlie Rose's tired face—and contemplated the rest of her day as Sadie, the bulldog, snored and farted and Henry, the pit bull stray, licked her arm. She slowly rose, did a few yoga stretches, then headed toward the study. The Nelson hallway's too white walls were festooned with family pictures, lined up according to the time line of school—ending with graduation, all the kids appearing relieved to rid themselves of the town. The study was large and, like the hallway, too bold, with cherry red walls and shiny black file cabinets. Elizabeth Nelson's tedious memoir was still on the screen. Marcy saved it in on her memory stick in a folder marked noneofmybusiness.

Distant rumbles were now louder, more persistent. Leaves tapped the upstairs windows, the house creaked. Marcy had forgotten to check the weather but recalled hearing mention of a storm on the radio. It made her nervous because she had parked the car at the nearby park, let the dogs run it, then walked here. A seven minute walk in light rain was one thing, in heavy rain and wind quite another. She could easily stay in the house for its duration, of course, which would give her time to complete her latest editing consulting project, now two weeks past due. It would also give her time to snoop around the Nelson's emails, something she hadn't done in a while since Elizabeth's memoir had absorbed most of her time. But then again, a walk in a bit of rain never hurt anyone.

Sam, the Welsh corgi, jumped up on the chair, placed his paws on the table, and stared at the memory stick.

"Sam, there's nothing there worth your time, boy. Her writing sucks."

Sam barked, still staring at the stick. She pushed his paws gently until he dropped to all fours again. Before she could reach for the stick, she felt her phone's vibration. The iPhone screen revealed a panting golden retriever with the name Elizabeth underneath it.

Marcy's hello was soft, almost a whisper.

"Marcy?"

"Ms. Nelson?"

"I'm just calling to check up on Nellie. We've heard about the storm. Are you out in it?"

"I'm doing OK." Marcy went to the door, cracked it to let in the sound of wind blowing through trees. Max, the Wheaten, barked, setting all of them off yet again. "Could you hold on a sec." Marcy turned her head. "Sam! Control!" Sam nipped at Max. Silence. "No problem."

"Are those dogs I hear?"

"We're doing fine."

"I'm coming home early. I heard about the storm and thought maybe I'd make it home just in case trees fall. I'm sure you've heard the warnings on the radio. This is supposed to be a bad one. You may want to take the dogs home now."

"OK. What time do you think you'll get back?"

"I'm taking off in a few minutes. Why? Where are you?"

"I'm heading back now, walking to the car."

The tapping now sounded more like pounding fists on the ceiling.

"Is it coming down hard now? Are you out in the rain?"

"I'm near my car, parked on Battle. We've been at the park."

Now her unreasonable lie made her sound like a reckless dog walker.

"Whatever. Drive safely. I'll be home soon. Just wanted to tell you what was going on."

"OK. No problem."

Marcy shoved her phone into her back pocket, picked up Sam, ran to the den, and quickly began clean-up. The place looked like hell, with the paw prints, mud, dog beds scattered about. She had a lot to do, and she had to do it fast.

SADIE, THE ENGLISH bulldog, sat like a bullfrog in the wagon, the rest of the dogs trotted ahead on leash—except Sam, who assisted in keeping other dogs relatively organized. Marcy walked way too many dogs—eight, including Henry, the pit bull stray she found and kept at her mom's house until she located a pet friendly apartment complex. Most of her clients thought she walked four other dogs, but she needed to eat and buy clothes and, OK, a new iPhone. Then there was wine. She had other income, just not enough other income for her needs. The publishing company that had laid her off gave her part-time consulting work. This allowed her to define herself as an editing consultant working as an ostensible full-time dog walker. However, she usually snooped more than she worked and lay around houses more than she walked dogs, which made her, in reality, a full-time nothing working as a part-time liar and computer hacker/snooper. Life depended upon perspective.

A weak flash of light, followed by a distant crack, then another boom. More rumbles. Sam circled the wagon, ran behind the Wheaten, then returned to her side again. All the dogs now ran ahead of her—making Sadie look as if she were enjoying a ride in an Alaskan dog sled. Marcy considered sitting in the wagon with Sadie, but the sky flashed and she started to trot with the dogs. She counted between flash and sound to estimate the distance. She made it to ten before the crack, which indicated the storm was about ten miles away. Or was it two seconds per mile? She could never remember formulas. Still, she figured she had time to make it to her car. A few cars slowed then passed, the drivers shaking heads at the crowd of dogs the way everyone shakes heads at bunched up bikers on busy roads.

The vibration started up again in her back pocket. She quickly retrieved her cell phone, thinking this was Elizabeth again, now panicked because of the storm. But, no, this time the screen revealed a picture of a young man with tired eyes and scraggly beard.

"Hey, Edward. I got to get the dogs back to the car, so I'm kind of busy. Storm, as you know. Everything OK?"

"Hey, sis. Mom says you have to come over. They say this storm'll be bad. Ground's wet, roots soaked. Trees are going to fall. Trees. Down."

"Don't worry. I can handle a storm. Tell Mom, I'll call later."

"We think these big storms are global warming storms, but no one has looked into weather manipulation. No one. Russia has been doing this type of thing for years."

Marcy gently pulled a wet string of hair from her eyes. The rain was now coming down harder, more consistent. Her shirt felt heavy, the dogs were looking thin and clean. Wet dogs always look thin and clean in a rain, whereas Marcy looked swollen and dirty. She thought about this as her brother talked, because his talking could rarely be tolerated unless one thought about something else.

"Marcy? Are you there? Russia is working our atmosphere, don't you agree? I asked a question. It's a big one, too, this time, my sis."

"Edward, is Mom worried about the oak tree out by the den window again? She always gets nervous about that tree. Tell her it's survived several storms."

"That has nothing to do with my question. And Mom is OK with the storm, Marcy. She is OK with everything. Too OK. Too complacent."

"Did you take your meds this morning, or just some? Tell me what you took and what you didn't."

Breathing. Silence. Marcy's mother's voice droned in the background. " . . . wet . . . fired . . ." Or maybe her mother said "tired," not "fired" and Marcy was thinking fired because that was what was going to happen to her if she didn't get all the dogs home.

"Edward?"

"Sis, I think what you and Mom do is change the subject. I'm talking about serious things here. I am not lost. And is Henry with you? He may be scared of storms."

A distant boom. Two dogs barked.

"Henry is not scared of anything. Look, no more phone calls. I've got to walk the dogs back to the park, get my car, because, like an idiot I parked my car next to it."

"Are you saying you were like an idiot when you parked at a park? Or, are you saying parking at a park makes you like an idiot. I would have driven to the house."

"I was thinking a run in the park, a little walk, may be good for the dogs."

"Not in a storm, my sis. Not in a storm. If you had a weather app, you would know when to walk and when to lounge. Me? I simply follow Russia."

"Bye, Edward."

Marcy shoved the phone in her back pocket and tried to concentrate on walking fast and efficient. She usually liked this walk in the Nelson neighborhood, not just because she always took a pit stop to work and snoop through Elizabeth Nelson's private life, but also because the homes were massive, their hedges and gardens bucolic. Many were set back on generous open land, unlike other neighborhoods where mansions were huddled behind ramparts of stone walls or verdant hemlocks. Instead, these large estates were unobstructed. She thought that said something about these rich people, something decent and sociable. She imagined they waved at passersby, tossed balls to dogs. But she didn't like this neighborhood today, the storm made the homes appear lonely, the passing cars rude.

It happened fast. Rain, then pounding, forceful water. Buckets of water. The wind rose in tandem with water volume. The air pushed at her chest. It made noises she had never heard before. She had to constantly steady herself with the wagon handle.

"This will be over soon," she said in her head, or maybe she said it out loud. She was always talking to the dogs, which probably indicated craziness, but only if she told someone. "This will be over soon."

She could now make out the park's huddled trees swaying with the wind. Her car was parked on Battle Avenue which bordered the park. Just a few more moments and they would be in a dry place.

"Dogs like being wet, anyway, right? It's kind of like swimming."

Sam looked up at her as he trotted. She figured Sam was the only dog who knew humans were not supposed to actually talk to dogs, and if they did, they were actually talking to themselves, similar to dogs growling at their tails.

The crack this time was strong and felt right behind them. The clouds were no longer billowing in the distance but covering the entire sky. When she finally approached her van, the dogs started barking, pulling on her leash. Marcy did what she always did when the dogs went wild—cuss and scream—hoping perhaps that the dogs would interpret this as leadership and obey. Sam ran by her side and sat. But the others continued to pull on her leash and bark. She slid the door open, reached inside her van, grabbed a box of liver flavored biscuits, and raised it in the air.

"Lots of fucking food!" she screamed. A crazy woman was one thing, but a crazy woman with food was quite another. It didn't take long to shove them all into the van.

After all the dogs were in, Marcy reached into her pocket. That was when she noticed it. Her pocket only contained her keys, which was OK because she needed keys but not OK because what was always next to her keys was her memory stick. It was not in her pocket because it was back at Elizabeth Nelson's house, probably right on top of the keyboard where she had left it, sitting in full view, as if asking Elizabeth to please pick it up. She imagined Elizabeth plugging it in, looking through its contents, clicking on noneofmybusiness folder, because that is what people do, right? They see something that is none of their business and they go right to it. Isn't everyone a voyeur? Marcy thought the answer was yes, because if it was no, that meant perhaps something was wrong morally with her.

She considered her options as she started the car and felt the weight of her wetness. She was not only heavy with rain water, but also painfully hungry. She hadn't eaten breakfast and the dog biscuits were looking pretty good. She wondered if one bite would give her some bacterial infection. An intermittent gust of wind rocked the van, and thunder rumbled again overhead. The dogs panted heavily, which added another foul odor to the air already filled with the smell of wet fur, dog farts, urine, and something metallic. She wanted them home and her back in her apartment, maybe in her bed with a good book. But she had to at least try to return to the Nelson's home. There was a chance Elizabeth had not left work yet. She would have to try to beat her there.

Lightning flashed and a crack came within two seconds, a bad sign. The bulldog started barking, followed by the herder, then Lab. Soon, all dogs were whining or barking.

"Shut the fuck up!" Marcy screamed.

More barking. Another gust of wind rocked the van. Behind her, a dog shook, spraying more wet dirt around the car.

"I need cooperation here! So, here is the deal everyone."

The bulldog barked. Sam snipped. Growling ensued.

"Enough. Hey! I've had it. This is an emergency!" she screamed.

Silence finally. At some point, crazy humans scare dogs into silence. She had reached that point.

A ripping sound now, then a thud. A few hundred yards, a tree lay supine across the road.

Marcy put her van in gear, raced down the street, took a turn onto Langley Avenue, which would route her back to Anderson Road, which connected to Armory Street, where the Nelson's lived. But there was a problem. A police officer, dressed in yellow rain gear, was cordoning the area. In the distance, a large white pine lay on the road, its branches and twigs scattered around contiguous property. At least the dogs were now sitting quietly, a few lying down. Marcy checked Google maps, which revealed only one other route back to the Nelsons—unfortunately it went through someone's back yard. She could simply drive around the cordoned area, over the small branches and twigs, and cut slightly through the property that edged the street. Of course, the police officer presented a problem, and that problem was now approaching her car. She rolled down the window when he tapped on it.

"You can't get through here, ma'am. Got to turn this around." A foul weather jacket covered his frame; its hood flopped over his head loosely, stopping right at his eyebrows. Marcy only saw his sharp blue eyes and reddish beard, a penumbra that looked two days old. His eyes, beard, way of being, seemed young, perhaps a few years older than Marcy, which made her consider flirting her way around the tape, but then again, she was a soggy dog walker who now smelled like dirt and dog fart.

"That pit bull yours? It doesn't have a license tag."

"Why are you asking about my pit bull? You see pit bull, you assume a woman cannot own it? Or do you assume it's dangerous? That's called profiling, you know."

"Are you going to answer my question?"

"I've got to get home, so I'd like to chat about dogs, but no can do."

"You're going to have a hard time getting home. Trees are down everywhere and some are still falling."

"So what do I do?"

"I don't know. I just know you can't get through here." Henry for some reason barked. He always remained quiet next to her when she drove. But now he decides to bark at a police officer. "Why doesn't that dog have a collar? Where's his license tag?"

"His name is Henry. I accidentally pulled off his leash getting him in the car." Edward lost the collar, but she was not about to get into Edward with a cop.

The officer stared at Henry, Henry barked back. Could a police officer arrest a dog? Could he arrest Marcy for having a pit bull that barks?

Marcy said, loud, "Hey!" She poked Henry's shoulder, but he didn't budge.

"Can you step out of the car for me," the officer said.

"Can you tell me why I have to step out? Are you charging me with something?"

"I need to check the license of your dog."

"It's not my dog. And it's raining."

"You're not going to get out of the car?"

"And you're not going to protect and serve? There's a huge storm going on right now. I've got to get these dogs home. I think your profiling of my pit bull is distracting you from real police business."

"Great advice. That is quite a mouth you've got on you."

"I am wet and dirty, and I've got to get this dog you're concerned about to his owner."

"Let's see. Just give me his owner's name and I'll follow up later. Make sure he's properly licensed."

Henry stood and barked again. Sam barked, then the Lab started up.

"Hey!" Marcy shouted. "You're going to get me arrested."

Henry and Sam stopped. The Lab whined. The rain picked up again. Henry barked.

"Oh forget it. Just turn this around and drive," the officer finally said, then dropped his flashlight and turned away.

Marcy backed up slowly, turned her car, then, because she had no other alternative, because she suspected there was no other way back to the Nelsons, and because she had a tendency to behave badly when panicked, she sped to the right, around the cordoned area, across the corner of a yard, through a space between the supine tree and the edge of woods. She didn't look in the rear view mirror, only in front of her. She imagined the police officer wondering whether it was worth a chase, but deciding, no, who cares. She kept her thoughts and car moving forward, operating on instinct. But now her rear view mirror flashed color—red and blue. She jammed down on the accelerator.

Marcy was no longer simply an unemployed dog walking voyeur. She had metamorphosed into a criminal, a stray dog owner, pit bull stray dog owner with no proper papers, and someone who was on the run. She would be charged with reckless driving, stealing strays, trespassing, talking sassy to an officer. He would probably beat Henry, maybe even shoot him, because why not, who wouldn't understand an officer shooting a pit bull? He would say it was self-defense. She would have to get it all on her iPhone video. Now she would not make it back, and Elizabeth Nelson would arrive home, see the memory stick on the keyboard, then notice her cell phone voicemail alert—which would be the police informing her the dog walker was in jail for sassy talk, running away and owning a stray pit bull. He would say the dog jumped him so he had to kill it. Elizabeth Nelson would inform the officer that she just discovered that the dog walker had read her memoir, so there would be another charge—reading memoirs without permission. Marcy would probably have to spend at least three years in jail. But most importantly, Henry would be dead. A dead profiled pit bull. All of these thoughts flooded her brain within seconds.

Another crack of thunder. And then another crack of something else—something heavy yet fragile. The rear view mirror revealed the officer, out of his car now. It was hard to tell but there seemed to be something in his hand. She leaned close the mirror. A gun. He had a gun drawn?

Marcy screeched onto the next street, then another, then the Nelson's street. In the distance she could make out the fallen tree a few yards past their driveway, but no cordoned tape yet. When she reached the house, Sam hopped over the far seat, put his paws on the top of the passenger seat back, then craned his head around it to view Henry, who sneered at him but didn't bite or even growl, as if he knew things had gotten crazy. Tails stopped wagging. There was a strong fresh urine odor. Someone peed. The Lab had a talent for peeing in small spurts.

"No. Everyone stay right here. I'll be back." She hopped out, ran to the back door, tapped in the security number, opened the door, oblivious to any noise except the thunder overhead. Of course if there had been no thunder, if she were not still agitated by the police chase, if she were not wondering if any minute a police car would be pulling up the driveway, she would have noticed the BMW's windshield in the garage's pane glass window she passed en route to the back door.

After taking off her shoes, she entered the basement, glancing immediately over at the dog bed expecting to see Nellie, but not seeing Nellie. It was when she opened her mouth to yell Nellie, that she heard it. The footsteps. Then the door at the top of the stairs opening. Marcy crammed her body into the coat closet, closed the door, dropped to the ground, and pushed herself into a corner, fully expecting the door to open for a coat.

"Come, sweet cakes. Come see Mama. What a storm, right, Nell? Are you scared, muffin? You are such a good girl, yes you are, yes you are."

Marcy couldn't decide what was worse, being forced to listen to inane dog baby talk, or her growing fear that the voice would move down the hall to the computer room where it would change from dog baby talk to cussing and screaming after the memory stick was noticed then inserted into the computer. Marcy could of course open the door and distract her, tell Elizabeth she had been hiding as a joke.

"Sweet girl, you stay. Mama has to turn on the generator so we can watch TV."

Marcy talked to her dogs, too, but only when stressed, and Sam seemed to get her. Elizabeth was not stressed and Nellie was not getting her, so the talk appeared psychotic. Any minute the dogs back in her van would bark. Why weren't they barking? Thunder again. Now she heard footsteps moving to the back of the room. The generator was stored in a shed at the other end of the house, reached by another door in the basement. If Elizabeth went to the shed, Marcy would have time to run to the computer room, snatch her memory stick. She could now hear the far door creak open then close. Marcy opened the closet door. Nellie was right there panting.

"Hey, girl," Marcy whispered, slipping herself out. She reached in her pocket, pulled out a liver treat, and jammed it into Nellie's mouth. Nellie inhaled it.

As she brought one foot in the direction of the computer room, the far door creaked again, which created a situation where an immediate decision had to be made. Memory stick or escape. Marcy chose escape.

It was a quick, panicked decision based upon complete terror. She stuck another liver treat in Nellie's mouth, opened the back door, ran to her car, noticing the open door but car full of quiet dogs. In fact, half the dogs were sleeping. Thunder again, but now another noise, like a loud buzz saw. Elizabeth had started the generator. She was probably standing next to it, which meant the generator noise would provide the cover needed to start her car and leave. Which she did.

IT TOOK FORTY minutes to make it out of the Nelson neighborhood and to the other side of town where five of her dogs lived. Downed trees, cordoned lanes, and slow traffic all contributed to miserable driving. Misery was also enhanced by Marcy's fear of all things police. She assumed they were all aware of a wild woman with dogs, including a pit bull, driving around cordoned streets and ignoring police officer orders. Any hint of police activity resulted in immediate rerouting.

She didn't notice it until after she dropped off Margaret Wilder's lab. The Wilders commuted to New York, which made their home—a 8500 square foot monstrosity with comfortable leather upholstery and a huge high definition TV—one of Marcy's favorite lounge spots. Marcy turned off her engine in the driveway and considered waiting out the storm here. It had been a while since she read Margaret Wilder's memoir anyway (She was in Elizabeth's town library writing group, apparently). Margaret was a good writer, better than Elizabeth Nelson. Her memoir was not purposefully edited into quotidian boredom, but rather wryly written and unapologetic. Intimate descriptions of delicious affairs, dysfunctional extended family, wild parties with unstable social celebrities. Its progress was slow though, and sometimes one chapter didn't quite follow the previous, as if Margaret had forgotten what she had written. The disorganization was probably due to Margaret's benzo addiction. Marcy had found three bottles in the bathroom cabinet. She had poured a few into her purse.

She noticed it when she opened the door to let out Margaret's dog. She realized her crowded van seemed just a bit less crowed than it should have been at this point. There was one yap missing. One smell gone. One less nip.

"Sam," she said. Nothing.

Henry barked. The Australian herder jumped over the front seat and sniffed around. Marcy crawled into the back seats, bent over, looked under the seats, as if miraculously the corgi squeezed his long body under them.

"Sam!" she screamed. "Sam! Sam!" She stopped screaming as the reality hit her. She laid her head on the steering wheel.

LIFE NEVER CHANGED gradually. One did not lose a job over a year. Well, if one had paid attention, the dead-end direction of a lost job would have been apparent. But for those who never paid attention, the metamorphoses of life happened in a breath. You breathed in and you were just a regular dog walker—who, yes, had a mouth, and, OK, snooped and hacked on occasion, and admittedly didn't walk dogs as often as required—you breathed out and you were the infamous town dog walker (wanted by the police) who lost Sam.

Chapter 2

Sam
The escape

THERE ARE BOOMS in the sky that are extraordinarily annoying and add to my present discomfiture. If I were not running and in a more tranquil state, the constant bursts of rumbling would not bother me but would instead, perhaps, lead to a pondering of the metaphorical significance of this unraveling in the dark sky above us.

I am running a bit obsessively because I seem to be unable to stop running. I was in the house earlier, and the booms were not as annoying, but now I am not in the house, I am wet, uncomfortably so, and booms are distracting, to say the least. Did I mention I am running? Running makes my world view quite limited. Wet dirt, stumps, grass, weed. Stump, grass, weed, tree. My scenery rushes by me, a verdant wet blur, if you will. Another boom, a flash of light, a tree, weeds. Oh dear. I seem to be unable to stop. It's a corgi trait—running, discursive thoughts, limited attention span. A genetic proclivity of sorts.

Let me back up and elaborate a bit. I am running in part due to several booms in the sky, which I understand results from storms. I am not an idiot. I am not a clueless dog who thinks explosions are occurring in the air, mind you. I realize we had a storm. We had a storm, then a car ride, then some rather strange human, a "chosen" one, in a long yellowish coat and yellow-ish cap (my spectrum is limited, mind you, but color is not necessary to my understanding of the world, and actually allows for a more unbiased approach. But that is beside the point), chasing us until we ended up at Nellie's house where Bosslady went crazy. I do not believe Bosslady is crazy, although there have been moments when the word unstable came to mind. While I am a dog, I am a corgi dog, so human words do not evade me. Unstable humans are allowed to roam free, and these humans can be quite functional. Bosslady is a very functional unstable human. But today, Bosslady went a bit batshit crazy. Excuse my language. She parked the car, opened door, left said door open, which in my world is a clear invitation to follow, so I did. Once inside, I ran down the hallway to the room she plays in often. I jumped up on a chair and it was then that I finally noticed Bosslady was not behind me, and in fact Bosslady was not anywhere. Bosslady had disappeared. After I noticed Bosslady had disappeared, I noticed another smell, a sweet smell this time. I started to trot out to greet this sweet smell, but I heard, "Hey, sweetcakes . . ." Baby talk. Insulting, mind numbing baby talk. Rubbish. I froze in place, deciding it best to avoid the baby talking human, whom I assumed was the one Nellie believes is her real "mommy." I heard more baby talk, more chatter, which made me wonder if perhaps most humans were a bit unstable, like Bosslady, all talking to dogs who could not possibly translate because they were not born with the corgi gift.

So, during all this chaos, I noticed Bosslady's miniature stick laying on the table by the machine toy she played with. So I put tiny stick in mouth. It is what dogs do. Put stick in mouth.

She liked this tiny thing. She liked to take it out of her treat box where she kept it and play with it on the big square machine. But today she didn't play with it as much, as she was too busy dealing with all the impertinent ones. Mind you, I am not usually this judgmental. But in order to do my job, I have to call the world as I see it. Dogs, other dogs, tend to be a bit impertinent at times. It's a trait a bit more obvious in certain breeds. I am not a bigot mind you. I am quite the progressive!

So I was comfortable because, while no Bosslady was in sight, and Nellie's "Mommy" seemed strange, I had stick in mouth. I suddenly received a generous whiff of Bosslady, then a door opened and closed. Then nothing. No smell of Bosslady anymore, so I trotted out into the den.

The stick did not taste sweet or even bitter. It tasted like that shiny coin I almost swallowed once. I did not love this taste, nor the tiny stick, but what can I say? When there is confusion, I go for stick. I just do. So, I sat in the middle of now empty basement with stick in mouth, contemplating my existence, or our entire existence here among the human material possessions, all while outside great winds tossed the earthly possessions, which made a profound metaphorical statement. Sticks keep me in the present, and the present sometimes brings on existential thoughts. Anyway, I digress. So, I sat there a while pondering, because I do that when in the present, particularly when with a stick. I pondered why Bosslady carried this puny stick around in our treat box and then when we were occupied, shoved it into the table machine? I pondered this as I sucked on it. I also pondered why anyone would make such a small stick, one that fit quite nicely in my mouth.

Suddenly, Nellie's mommy opened the back door, causing me to run back to the far room then back to the den. Nellie, now on the dog bed, lifted her head to observe my active body, then plopped it back down. See, I was with stick! And when a human opens a door and us dogs are with stick, game is on! I ran around the sofa, then back to the computer room, then heard angry human talk. I kept stick in mouth, ran under table, and lowered my body to the ground, which, mind you, took limited effort as I am already quite close to the ground.

"Goddamn generator's almost out of gas, Nell. Fuck that. You'd think Larry would at least think of gas. He never remembers anything. Sweetcakes, you stay here. I'll be right back." Footsteps. Door. Nellie standing up. Silence.

So, I figured the human left because of the necessity of gas, which I found strange. When life is not regular, one cannot predict human behavior. So, human prediction is close to impossible during storms, booms, human fights, or any number of sudden accidents. Actually, I must say, in my opinion, (and this is controversial, mind you) humans are unpredictable most of the time, unless you are predicting the behavior of one of the so called "anal" humans. (I learned "anal" from one of my dog friends. It does not mean lovely smell, it means overly bossy and organized.) Bosslady is not anal. I like Bosslady. My mom, or owner, is anal.

I digress again.

Let me continue. I realized at this point that I was in a peculiar position, because I was stuck in a house that was not my own. I dropped the stick, ran to the door, put my paws on it, and bounced, but the door was shut and there is no opening a door once shut. Just cannot be done. My thinking was distorted and I found myself drifting into a sort of panic, which I am ashamed to admit. I am usually a calm dog. Progressive and calm. I looked down at the stick on the floor and wondered if I should just leave it there. It was too small. It tasted bad, smelled like Bosslady sweat with a touch of dirt, nothing at all special or appetizing. It was basically worthless, but it was Bosslady's stick and Bosslady was an exceptional human. She did favors for us, fed me junk food, put me in charge of the pack, talked to me. So, what the hell, I kept it in my mouth, figuring I would bury it somewhere for her, keep it safe.

Then it occurred to me, there with stick in mouth, that I was not simply stuck in a house, I was stuck at Nellie's house. I was now living with Nellie! Would I now be stuck at Nellie's forever? Nellie and me always here? Not that I didn't like Nellie. Goldens are OK, just a bit too eager to please for my taste. *What do you want to do? I'll do anything you want to do. You want to play. OK I'll play. You want to sleep. I can do that too.* They're not hyper, so that's good, but they're just too happy. I can see why the humans like them. They are a bit naïve. Most all goldens I've met think the humans are their real "moms." It's quite embarrassing. They don't listen to reason. This loyalty and naiveté make humans feel warm and loved. Corgis make humans feel dumb. I've been told this.

I decided I could not live with a golden forever. Mind you, I am not a bigot. Truly, I am not. It's just that it is not a good time for my life to change that dramatically. One must sieve through life's options.

"Look, Nellie," I said, "I need to get out. I need to find the Bosslady who for some reason forgot me."

"I don't leave the house, ever, unless Mommy lets me out, and then I can't go anywhere because of the sting air near the road. You can't leave the yard because if you cross that wall? Your neck is fried."

"Nellie," I said, slowly so she would understand me. "It's the collar. The collar with the box attached to it? If you can determine the proper way to remove this attachment, you will not feel the discomfort of a sting."

She stopped panting to consider my wisdom. She looked at a place on the wall, then lay back down, as if contemplating my theory was too tiring. Deep thoughts are painful for breeds who are eager to please. Again, please know I am not a bigot. This is simply a fact.

I said, "Look, Nellie, if you really have to leave—if your mom is in danger and you have to leave to find her and get her out of danger—

what do you do?" We all know how to leave a house. We pretend we don't know. Like at my house? I can get the patio door open. Owner rarely bolts it. In a panic I can do it.

"If I really have to leave, I just jump out the window in Mom's room, but you'd break your legs. No offense, OK? I am not trying to insult you, Sam. Don't get mad. But those legs cannot take too much crashing around. Don't get sensitive about this."

"My legs are of no concern of yours, Nellie." What the hell? The dogs were always getting on my ass about my legs.

"When Mom's friend came over with one of those hotdogs, he got out here," Nellie said, still looking at the wall. She slowly got up and touched the window over the sofa with her nose. She put her paws on the window, and it popped out. "It's never locked."

The rain flowed through the window and onto the back of the couch. Nellie's paws got wet so she jumped off and licked them. The back of the couch turned a darker color. Nellie rolled over on her side, and I leapt up on the sofa, then out the window. After burying the stick in the garden real quick—under the bush that smelled like rabbit, a touch of Nellie slobber, and fox pee—the booms startled me. The startle triggered a bit of panic, which is unusual, as I have told you, very unusual. But these booms were very loud, and cacophony contributes to temporary discomfiture, which is a major reason for all the wild running.

I am still wildly running. I cannot stop. I have tried, but I cannot stop running. Rain pounds my back. Ice bounces around the ground. The air shakes, the ground moves. Something from the sky explodes. The trees bend, a large branch misses me by a few feet. Light falls down in front of me. Sparks glitter around me. At the edge of one yard, a big tree falls on a house. Then another one falls. More booms in the sky. I keep running. Pee, a touch of vomit wafts to me. There is also some sausage with lots of garlic in the air. These whiffs come and go and come and go. They are driving me nuts.

Another loud noise. Another crack. I run.

This is not normal rain. It is thousands and thousands of garden hoses in the sky, all turned full force. It is wind and branches at my feet.

I try to calm myself down. I say, "Sam, stop, make it to a street and stop, you can't just run, you have to cease all motion, ole boy, stop, think where you're going. Stay in the present, Sam. In the moment." But I cannot listen to myself. I can only run. I am on one street, then another, then another. I never see Bosslady's car. I never see anything but wet ground, bushes, bark, limbs, fences, pavement.

I realize I do not know where I am running. This isn't like the times I wondered away from my own house and came back. That was my neighborhood, so I always knew where I was in relation to my house. But now I am not in my neighborhood. I am in Nellie's neighborhood. I have no idea where I am in relation to anything.

Basically, I am lost. And it is loud. And I cannot stop running.

Chapter 3

Marcy
Lies

MARCY HELD HER iPad in one hand as she paced her den, back and forth, back and forth. She and Henry were taking a quick break before heading out one more time to look for Sam. The break was needed to establish plans. Lie plans for the inevitable phone calls concerning the missing dog. Movement helped concentration, and she needed concentration when immersed in lies which inevitably grew like vines on a trellis. Each lie on her trellis was critical because it had to be backed up by other lies, which branched into yet more lies, then more, depending upon questions asked by outside parties. She stopped walking and sat down, leaned over and rubbed Henry's back.

The storm had ceased, all dogs back at their warm and cozy houses. She had driven around the circumference of Nelson neighborhood twice, careful never to pass in front of the house or Langley, where the dreaded police incident took place. Several roads were littered with downed trees and branches, making driving treacherous. She stepped out of the car a few times and yelled, "Sam!" But nothing. When she had finally returned to her apartment, her superintendent was standing by her door all self-righteous and eager to lecture her about the no dog rule again.

"We allow exceptions in emergencies for people such as yourself. I am not evil, Marcy. I know you think we're evil for putting our foot down about this rule. But dog smell gets into these apartments and is hard as shit to get out. We can't rent stinky apartments." He gave her a few more hours, but then Henry had to leave. She had lied and agreed. She needed Henry more than a few hours because he was critical to finding Sam.

God, Sam. She could not stop thinking about Sam. He was a herder, and thus loved to roam, which meant there was no telling where he had wandered off to, but she was hopeful he would remember how to get back to the park, where she usually took the dogs for a quick run. So, that was the next step—go to the park, let Henry run around sniffing, until he found him, maybe under a bush or something. Or Sam would see them, run out, bark. Voilà! Life back to normal.

Marcy led Henry back to her car and managed to make it to the park entrance after taking several detours due to downed trees and branches. She parked on a side street, let Henry out and watched as he ran about the park's circumference, sniffing at the wet grass, lapping up water from dirty puddles. The air was crisp, slightly cool. The storm had altered the park's appearance, blanketed the baseball field with limbs, twigs, leaves. There were several trees supine across the land, a few with their massive roots ripped from the earth. Their thick intransigent trunks, so majestic when alive, now looked defeated and sad. The tendrils of ripped up roots hanging loosely from the trunk's muddy ends exacerbated the already macabre and depressing post-storm atmosphere.

"Sam!" Marcy screamed. "Sam! I need you! Now! You gotta come. Now. I will feed you! Wanna treat?" Her screams only brought Henry back to her, as if he figured running somehow was a good thing that led to treats. She walked toward a grassy knoll that edged the baseball field and screamed again. She ran to the building and screamed Sam's name at the crawl space. She yelled at Henry, "Go get Sam, Henry. Go get Sam!" Henry wagged his tail, ran around in a circle and came back, jumped up on her, grabbed her sleeve and pulled. She shouted, "Stop!" Nothing. He jumped on her again. She said no. He barked.

She yelled at Henry again, then took off jogging around the park, thinking there was a chance she would simply run around and find Sam because he would sense her hysteria and run toward it. Sam was very good at sensing her hysteria. While Henry seemed to understand they were looking for something, the name, "Sam," didn't seem to trigger any recognition on his part. She couldn't recall teaching any of the dogs the names of other dogs. They only knew their own names. Of course, how does one teach another dog the name of a friend? Still, Henry did seem to understand something was lost, because after he sniffed everywhere, he looked pleased with himself.

It would have helped if she had been sharp enough to have remembered something that had belonged to Sam—an old collar, old toy, anything to inspire their olfactory senses, but, no, she had brought nothing; she had not wanted to call Ellen Maher's house to retrieve anything because she was practicing the one skill she had perfected as an editor—avoidance. She had simply left a message on Ellen Maher's land line voice mail. She didn't even text her, because texting would have resulted in an immediate phone call, which she wasn't ready for. She wasn't prepared to hear Ellen's voice.

After what felt like hours, but in reality was about fifty minutes, Marcy decided there was no hope at the park. Sam could very well still be in the Nelson's neighborhood, but surely Elizabeth would have called her by now if he was found outside. And it was best to stay away from the neighborhood for a few days to avoid the police officer who had chased her. She couldn't stop thinking about the cop pulling out his gun. It was so unbelievable, she was beginning to wonder if it was not a real memory, but, instead, an image created by hysteria and panic.

Marcy gathered Henry, now wet and muddy, put him in the back of her van, and drove back to her apartment. She left Henry in the car while she walked around her parking lot periphery, then slipped into the apartment complex to make sure there were no people, no superintendent, in the hallway, stairwell, or elevator area. By the time she made back out to her car, opened the door, a familiar Taurus arrived and parked next to her van. The door opened and Lorene quickly stepped out. Her tall, gaunt body was wrapped in a tight black suit today, and her thin bleached blond hair was neatly removed from her eyes in a hair sprayed wave. She pulled out a cigarette and stuck it in on her upper lip, where it hung like an appendage, then searched her purse until she found a lighter. When she lit up, she looked toward Marcy's van. Marcy pretended to pick up something from her car floor, but when she lifted her head up, Lorene was at the window, plumes of smoke rising from her nostrils. She motioned for Marcy to unlock the passenger door, then carefully slipped into the car and exhaled a long sigh of tobacco filled vapor without bothering to apologize. Marcy didn't allow smoke in her car—a rule Lorene had been told on numerous occasions.

"Hey, Lorene."

"Hey. Where's my cutie-pie?" Lorene moved the cigarette to her right hand and leaned over the seat to grab Henry. "Marcy take you for a walk in this storm today, you sweet thing? That must have scared you out of your mind. Come here, give me a big kiss." Henry appeared startled every time Lorene approached; however, despite Marcy's lukewarm reception of Lorene, he allowed the woman to smash his nose against her mouth. "You been out with the dogs, Marcy?" She let go of the relieved Henry and turned back, slightly cracking the door to blow another jet stream out into the world.

"You know I don't like smoke in the car. But that's OK I guess. I'm about to leave the car."

"With Henry? You going into the building with your pit bull? Super's not here, but you better hurry. I saw him take off in the truck earlier. I'm only home a few moments, to pretty myself up for a drink after work today. Touch up the ole make up. Finally got Linny to pay attention to me."

"The one that works in the cubicle near the stairwell?"

"That one, indeed. Maybe it was the storm. Everyone calling home, all nervous about trees falling on their houses. He has a house, you know. Left the wife, like I left my husband, but kept the house, didn't sell it like my asshole did." When she sucked the cigarette her cheeks fell in, giving her a sallow, weak appearance. Marcy could make out the beginnings of age marks just forming on her cheekbones near the edge of her face. Her makeup was too thick, so with the added moisture it looked like oily brown paint. Marcy wondered how old Linny was, if he smoked, or drank. Lorene was in shape though, not just thin but sinewy. She attended at least two aerobics classes a week and jogged every other morning. Then smoked all night as she drank wine.

"I may try to keep Henry a while. Park's a mess. And I lost a dog today in the storm."

"You what?"

"Yeah, I know. Lost a dog."

"You didn't lose the Nelson's dog did you? Elizabeth's chairman of the Board of Education, you know. Kind of one of the town influentials. You may have to leave town if you lost her dog."

Marcy had a quick image of Elizabeth looking at her memory stick, pondering the illegality of her dog walker's snooping.

"No. No. Nellie's safe in her house. It was the corgi. Sam. My favorite dog."

"Oh no. What a shame. Corgis are so cute." She sucked long and hard, cracked the door, blew, then dropped the cigarette. She closed the door and still smelled of smoke, which had more to do with the accumulation of cigarettes over her lifetime than the one she had just consumed. "Poor thing out there lost and alone. Such great dogs, those corgis. I can't help you now, but give me a few days and I'll go out to that neighborhood with you. We need signs. Signs, pictures. And something that smells of the owner. Does the dog love its owner? Is the owner a good one or just one of those Connecticut owners, you know, that decorates their house with a dog?"

Marcy imagined Ellen Maher, her trim, professional body always neatly attired, a designer handbag stuffed with work and iPad. "I doubt Ellen Maher kisses dogs on the mouth, Lorene, but I don't know what kind of owner she is. She calls herself his mommy, something I am sure you approve of. So maybe her smell will bring Sam. God, what have I done?" She dropped her face on the steering wheel.

"Well, don't you worry. Corgis are smart, right? Smart dogs know their way around. And everyone will notice a stray corgi. Not like cutie-pie back there." She pointed to Henry with her cigarette. "So many mutts wondering around, no one pays attention to them, right, Henry?"

Chapter 4

Marcy
Altering lies

MARCY TOWELED OFF Henry and gave him a treat. Soon, he was curled up on his dog pillow in the bedroom. Sam's owner, Ellen, would be returning home about now from her job, ready to bend over and accept the small corgi in her arms. She will click on the voice mail and hear Marcy's long message. She will become upset, flustered, then immediately call Marcy. So, Marcy needed a lie, a good one. A good lie about the lost corgi. It wouldn't be a horrible lie, it would be close to the truth. She couldn't just say she lost the dog, as she did with Lorene who didn't ask any further questions. She had to go into detail with Ellen Maher, who was one of those professional types always in need of details.

She would start by saying, Sam ran away. Yes, that's it. The lie would start that way—the corgi ran away. That would be truth. Nothing wrong with that. The reason would be the lie. The reason would *not* be that, after a police chase in the storm, her car stuffed with several dogs—because she had lied and was actually walking twice as many dogs as everyone imagined—she had gone back to the Nelson's house because she needed to retrieve a memory stick that had a folder, nonofmybusiness, that contained other peoples' business that she didn't want Elizabeth to find, but then she had to hide in a closet, then escape, because Elizabeth had returned home, all of which was done while her car sat in the driveway, it's front door wide open. Allowing Sam to escape.

No, she could not say all of that, not even begin to say that. She would say Sam had run away at another point in the day. Sam was scared of thunder. That was it. He was scared of the thunder and had run away near the park. Ellen would want to know when. When. When was the thunder the loudest today? She thought around noon the storm had peeked, but was it noon the police chase had peeked? But when was she chased? When was the police chase? She had to calm down and think about time. The lie had to put Sam somewhere away from the police chase because she had to be nowhere near that area at the time the officer reported the chase. But, then, when did Elizabeth Nelson call her earlier? She had to lose Sam after the phone call somewhere away from the Nelsons. Hadn't she told Elizabeth she was out near the park? And when was that?

Henry's snores ceased and Marcy could see him through the open bedroom door. He raised his head, as if hearing Marcy's thoughts. Strips of light slipped through the window behind the sofa and stretched across the hardwood floor, highlighting loose bits of mud on both of her vinyl lazy boys and leather sofa. Her upholstery was all dark so dirt blended in nicely. She also had no rugs, which made life cold in the winter but also served to hide dog dirt. Everything smelled like a huge wet dog fart, but at least the dirt was hard to see.

Henry was now up and sniffing around. He stopped at the far corner where a tennis ball seemed to be hiding from him. He sucked the ball into his mouth and went looking for something else. Henry, like most dogs she knew, enjoyed several items in his mouth at a time, just in case one fell out. She rose slowly, still thinking about Sam's escape, went to the kitchen to retrieve dog food, lots of it. She would stuff Henry because a full stretched stomach would keep him satisfied, and a satisfied dog stays quiet. She didn't feel like driving him back to her mom's house.

She poured grain into the bowl, her mind still on lies, good ones. There was a possibility she would have to think of new lies, of course, when Mrs. Nelson discovered the memory stick with her memoir on it. There was a chance Mrs. Nelson would assume the memory stick belonged to one of her sons. Maybe she would plug it into the computer but not click on any folders. Sometimes people respected the privacy of others, so there was that small glimmer of hope. Marcy tried to hold onto this glimmer while she retrieved a can of dog food.

The kitchen was small and cluttered because she had brought friends home the night before, fixed omelets, and left water in the pans. She put the last dish into the dishwasher, poured in detergent, closed it, and pushed start. The pans were now in their place. The counters were wiped.

Henry sat. Marcy sat. Both waiting. Henry for play, Marcy for the inevitable phone call.

When her cell phone sang a Grateful Dead song—"Truckin"—a golden retriever face appeared. There was a chance Elizabeth Nelson was not calling to discuss the memory stick. There was a chance she had found Sam and was calling for her to come over and leash him, take him back to Ellen Maher, his "mom."

"Hello," Marcy said, quickly.

"Marcy?"

"Yes."

"I'm standing here with Nell. Me and Nell. I'm in a state of amazement. Just amazement."

Shit.

"I mean, I don't know what to say? First, is everything OK with you?"

Is everything OK with you is a question one carefully asks crazy people.

"I'm fine. Why do you ask?" Henry whined. Marcy put her phone on mute and said, loud, "Hush. Hush. I mean it Henry or I will kick your ass."

Elizabeth Nelson was chirping on the phone. Marcy held the phone away from her and willed all of the chatter to disappear, willed Elizabeth to go away. She looked at the screen, then put it to her ear.

" . . . damage, water damage, trees limbs."

Marcy put the phone in her lap again. Elizabeth chirped into her lap. She put it to her ear.

" . . . at one time. So many. I just cannot imagine how the town is going to operate with all the streets closed like this. The schools have damage too, so I will have to convene the board. More money that of course we do not have. So, I will be in need of your dog walking services. Hello? You aren't answering me. Are you OK? How did you get home? Marcy?"

"Oh, sorry, I was distracted. It was a nightmare. The storm came up on us fast. I don't believe I was even able to do much but let Nellie in and leave." And now would be about the time Elizabeth Nelson would mention the memory stick. Marcy waited.

"Well, you're a hero. I emailed all my friends about how wonderful you were, making sure the dogs were protected and brought back home.

I noticed I left on the computer, and it wasn't plugged into a surge protector. I could have killed the entire computer, wiped out all my content."

She forgot to turn off the computer!

"Well, you're lucky," Marcy said. "That's for sure."

"And so are you. So are you."

The line clicked. Another caller. A corgi face appeared, underneath it, Ellen Maher. Marcy considered avoidance. But no, not this time. She asked Elizabeth to hold on.

"Hello."

"Marcy? Is that you? Where is Sam? Do you have Sam? I cannot find him anywhere. At first, I thought the thunder and all scared him and he was under a bed. I looked everywhere, my bedroom, the kids' bedroom. Everywhere. He's simply not here." Her words came out as if attached to each other. Ellen was an avid coffee drinker. "Marcy, are you there? Do you have Sam?"

"No. I don't have Sam. Did you not get the message I left on your land line machine?"

"No. What message? I forgot I still have a land line. Why didn't you call my cell? Where is Sam? What happened?"

And the lie and all that followed would be the ending of life as she knew it, and the beginning of her ignominious nightmare—the Find Sam movement.

Chapter 5

Sam
Hunger

DARKNESS DOES NOT persist, I always say. At least one ray, falling from a place of many rays, will push aside obsidian space, open up a small path. All we need is that small path.

We lose trees, yes, but then again we gain cavernous spaces, which, mind you, are perfect for tucking the ole body away and out of sight. Of course, one must share these spaces with other creatures. Mice, if you will. I smell their asses everywhere. A nice smell, actually, a touch of fecal matter, soil, nuts, bird seeds. I could eat them, no question. I am not saying I will eat a mouse, however. My taste is tad more epicurean. I am not planning upon metamorphosing into a slovenly homeless animal running after rodents. Although, I may run after rodents, mind you. I may reach that ravenous state, yes. But I don't have to eat unsanitary animals, dead ones for that matter, not yet. I believe there are a plethora of eating establishments for the homeless with decent noses. Places where I can sneak a bite or two. I am well equipped to find extra food, because I am an expert at discovering human food hideouts, which allowed me to formulate a plan long ago. I have always had a backup plan. Any smart dog has one.

Let me explain this backup plan. Us dogs pride ourselves on having excellent observation skills, which have allowed us, particularly me, to understand idiosyncratic human behavior patterns, which we then use for the backup plan. For example, I know that humans donate food to other humans. Donation trucks arrive at the human abodes to take containers filled with donations away. I have seen this human phenomenon, studied it, actually. This is how it worked back at my owner's home. On certain mornings, one of the humans would stuff two large, lovely smelling buckets with donations. One is filled with paper donations, the other food donations. They place these donation buckets at the end of the driveway where the containers stay all morning. The entire street has these donation containers, all lined up, one next to the other, waiting to be picked up by other humans in trucks. After a while, sometimes a long while, a truck arrives. The first truck has humans standing upon a protrusion attached to the back. They leap off intermittently, pour food donations into a deep cavernous compartment. Another truck comes, men leap out and grab the paper donations and repeat the process. These trucks travel down roads, until they are filled with donated food and items, then—and this is an assumption—they deliver these donations to other humans in need of food. The buckets are rolled back to the homes where they are stored and filled with the next week donations. I have always found this extraordinary gesture, for humans, otherwise, have trouble parting with cherished items. But food is different perhaps, because, while we cherish food, humans are not that attached to it.

So, my backup plan has always involved these donations. I realize that pilfering from humans in need is not a respectable survival strategy, but my body only needs to steal a bite here and there, maybe more than a bite at times. Maybe a bag or two. OK, look, I was raised in a free market world (A human concept I learned by listening to Mom and Dad debate). If I am hungry then the poor humans will have to suffer a bit. I cannot start feeling guilty. This is my backup plan and I am sticking with it. Maybe Canadian corgis have nicer plans. Well good for them!

Up ahead I see a crowd of humans wandering like me. But when humans wander, they stay with each other and lumber, like Sadie, the lazy slob bulldog Bosslady pulls along in a wagon.

I hide behind a limb to observe the lumbering humans. A man shakes his head at the scene before him—a rather large tree that has landed on a house. It is, most definitely, a depressing sight. I am hoping the house had no dog, and if there was a dog that it was not a bulldog. If the house had a bulldog, it is now a dead bulldog. Lab, setter, golden, or any dog like me, would smell that tree coming, get out of the way. Bulldogs have no nose, only holes smashed into their head.

There is trash in the street, wires littering the area, one lying across a stone wall a few feet in front of me. It looks alive, sparks spitting around it in a wild halo. I have seen loose wires before and have noticed how humans react around them. All the humans appear to understand the wires are not a positive sign, except one woman talking on her small box as she walks around. Humans like to do that—walk whilst talking into small boxes.

Now, a big yellow truck arrives, stops by the tree. Men jump out with yellow tape so they can mark an area to stop the lumbering, mindless humans. These are the "chosen humans." I have noticed over my short life time that certain designated humans, special humans, if you will, are required to mark off areas precluding entry of other, regular, or less special, humans. "Chosen humans" are required because the vast majority of regular humans are incapable of predicting danger. Danger surprises a human because they have no foresight, no sense of smell, no ability to listen intensely. So, when danger appears, they are shocked by it. Therefore, other humans, chosen by "leader humans" (those are similar to us herders, the ones with the unenviable task of organizing entire populations of clueless, or "regular," humans), travel the area to designate areas of danger so the clueless majority can understand where to go. I've seen this all before.

After humans mark this road with yellow ribbon, no cars or other humans can enter it. Which I certainly appreciate. Marking areas as off limits to humans is always a positive development. I don't wish to engage with "stranger" humans. Or let me reword that—I do not wish to engage with a human who has not been properly vetted. Humans are unpredictable and one must always be cautious. You can end up with a human who has a baby human. Baby humans are allowed to do anything they please. I have spent countless hours whilst baby humans smash my head through holes in various cloth formations. Then my paws go through holes. Soon the talking boxes come out and there are flashes. The baby human pinches me and puts small fat arms around my neck, which makes me feel suffocated and paranoid. I have learned to suppress true emotions around baby humans, because calm, appropriate behavior—which results from suppression of true feelings because true feelings can cause cussing when smashed into cloth formation—is critical if one is maintain the elevated status that assures security, food, and a warm bed with humans.

I digress again, let me move forward with my exposition. I have decided, due to risk of "stranger" humans, that I will be the one to announce my presence, if I indeed ever decide to announce my presence. I will not wait for them to announce theirs. I know, I know. I am beginning to sound like a human profiler. I do not profile. I am quite the progressive type. I understand humans, so I don't have to categorize other humans. I've been walking with the Bosslady long enough to have learned the art of normal human interaction and so can distinguish between normal "stranger" humans and abnormal "stranger" humans. Normal human interaction has a mild, sweet smell. Bosslady smells a bit sweet when interacting with dogs and sometimes with human, unless life becomes complex in the way life can always become complex with Bosslady. Then Bosslady's smell then changes. She used to meet up with friends at the park, sometimes male humans. Once, the Bosslady mated with a male human while the rest of us snoozed at my house. Right there on the sofa. Not that we minded that much. Hell, we all mate at the park, so it is not out of the ordinary. It's just that my mom human never mates. Not even at night when she sleeps. She and her male spend nights in different rooms. So when the Bosslady mated, I was a bit taken back at first. No one else paid attention, except Henry, the pit bull, who gets all horny and starts humping a sofa pillow. Really, the crew I am forced to socialize with are beyond embarrassing sometimes.

The lady is now precariously close to the wire and continues her discourse with her box. She is expressing extreme emotion, and she apparently has not noticed the yellow ribbons put up by the chosen humans. This is not too surprising, as lumbering, emotional humans tend to ignore "chosen" human warnings, which can lead to disturbing conflicts. The crying leads me to conclude the woman lives in the house which now has a tree lying upon its roof. She smells awful—sour, bitter. She has stopped right by the tree trunk I am using for cover. I suppose I could go out and jump up on her leg. I do that with my mom when she expresses extreme emotion, because jumping on the human leg whilst engaged in extreme emotion sometimes forces their mind off themselves for just a split moment, and the emotion subsides. But there is a risk involved in jumping upon a human not vetted. She would probably be surprised, then curious. A surprised, curious human can behave impulsively. She may attempt to pick me up without allowing the obligatory sniff, so I would be forced into her arms without the necessary vital information, such as pet owning status. Then there is the risk of her engaging in baby talk, always a bad sign. One cannot discount the chance of being hauled off to a dog prison—something we have all been warned about, mind you. Then, of course, she could simply take me to her human home, where I would live the rest of my life, something that would be a positive if she had lots of food, but negative if she had bad food. And there is always a chance she was a bad "stranger" human. There are bad "stranger" humans in the world. I know this because I've seen them hitting dogs, yelling at dogs, cramming dogs into cages in their cars. I've seen dogs panting in hot cars out amongst other cars, no one around to set them free. There in hot car, knowing their life was ending. What if she did that? What if she locked me in her car in a parking lot?

I ponder all of this as I watch her cry, talk, and walk toward the dancing wire. I'm thinking she will surely step on that wire, which of course will cause all kinds of commotion, inspiring "chosen" humans to bring in more 'chosen" humans. She talks, cries, moves closer to the wire. My protection instincts are bigger than my fear instincts. So I yell. Humans call our yelling, barking.

She stops and looks around. I step out from behind the tree and yell again. Her foot is right by the wire. I run and nip at the foot. That is how you move them when they don't pay attention to yelling. You nip at the feet. She dances back and says something into her talking box, taps it, and puts it away.

"Hey, sweetie. Aren't you a cutie," she says.

Baby talk. Very bad sign.

"Come here, cupcake." She leans over and holds out her hand.

I step forward just a bit so her foot will move in my direction not the wire. I put my head down so she knows I am not a bad guy. She moves forward. I do not move. Then, real quick, she tries to grab me. I jerk away, but she has my hair. My hair, for crying out loud! I am a corgi! My hair is one of my most outstanding traits besides brains and language development! Do you know how long my grooming takes? Do you know how long my mom brushes me! The woman grabs my hair? I whine but she won't let go. I cuss, "What the fuck! This hurts!" I cuss when stressed. Cussing comes out as a growl in human world.

She lets go and jumps back as if my warning indicates she is now dealing with a common criminal. She moves away, then runs, screaming and waving her arms at the "chosen" ones behind the yellow tape. She then runs to other men who are carving up the tree in the street. No question dog prison is on their minds. There is no way to explain my intentions to humans because, while I spent years and years learning their language, they have not spent one second trying to learn mine. Thus, when misunderstandings like this happen there is simply nothing to be done but run. One simply must run when humans are confused and language impaired.

The world passes by me in a blur again. The ground is wet and a few times I stumble over weeds and roots. Weeds, roots, bark, twigs. Lots of death, piss, crap fill my nose as I try to stay in underbrush and trees, away from human homes. I make sure my paws only hit wet leaves, never pavement. In the distance I see something that looks like a ditch, which makes me think water. A very good find, not just for thirst, but for directions. Water flows near places with food. I know this. It also flows around donated food. I have always smelled the direction trucks take food donations. They head south to water.

My fur is cluttered with twigs, leaves. My paws are all mud. My belly, which does not drag on the ground but drags on weeds, is wet and soiled. I do not stop running. The world is weeds. The world is roots. The world is wet leaves. The world is branches. The world is a small animal escaping my paws.

I am panting but I am not tired. I cannot stop. The hysterical woman may be behind me. She could now be with many "chosen" ones.

I see through two tree trunks in front of me. In that space is a street and houses. Lots of houses. Too many houses to be safe so I stop by a tree and decide to do a bit of reconnaissance before taking the risk of entering the world of streets and houses.

The sky is blue, the sun warms my nose. The clear street sits before me. No downed trees here. A small car passes. Another car. Another. The street has houses that are medium sized, not as big as my mom's house, but not too small. There are no people, only houses, all darkened at the windows. I picture humans sitting in their dark homes unaware of me out here, alone, in the light but also in the dark. A deeper, inner dark. I feel as though I could wax poetic any moment, but I hear a noise behind me, several hundred yards behind me. A rustling movement. No voices, just movement. I do not smell human, I smell something else.

Something with urine on it. A bit metallic. I decide to step into this neighborhood. I cross the street.

The car that screeches and stops has a man in it. He is talking into the talking box, too. This is something humans do quite often and I find it annoying. They are always talking. Yet, humans do not like it when we talk. It's apparent they don't notice that when we talk we aren't simultaneously performing other tasks, which makes our talking more efficient, to the point, and focused. Their talking is always rather breathy and distracted. Inefficient.

I yell at the tires, because that is what I do with cars, yell at the tires. It's the only thing I see and tires are scary at close range, particularly when the car has a driver talking into talking box. I do not stay there yelling too long because the man is out and he does what the other woman did. He bends down and says something like, "Hey, fella. Where you going?" I want to say, I am moving away from your tires because you are talking and driving and therefore at great risk of squashing sentient beings like me. And now you, who almost squashed me, want to entice me into your thick arms? Do you think I am an idiot?

It is quite amazing how many humans immediately try to catch you when you run.

I yell.

He moves toward me.

I say, "Fuck you!"

He stands, steps back, and I run.

I run through a yard, which smells like onions and candy, chocolate maybe. Baby humans live here. I look over at the house, briefly. A boy looks out the window. I am gone, gone, gone.

I run in and around houses, across several more streets, until I find a very small house that is half built. It is dark on one side because that side has a roof, the other does not. There are trucks and machines in the yard, which is only muddy gravel. The wood is yellow and pipes run along the sides of walls, around the top, then down and around the bottom. One section in the back does have a roof. But most important, the house has a large cave under it. And by this little cave is a large box filled with sticks, boards, nails, and something else, something that smells salty. Dairy product. I smell a dairy product. I am intimately familiar with this scent. I jump up on a few boards and sniff the air. It doesn't take long to figure out how to push a few things here and there so I can climb to the top of the big steel box and retrieve the bag. Bread, lettuce, meat, cheese. Lots of cheese. I finish this fast and lap up some water in the puddle by the hole that leads to the cave.

I am safe. I am wet and rather soiled, but I am not opposed to wet and soiled. In fact, I appreciate wet and soiled. Now that I think of it, I have to say, what I really appreciate, more than anything, is freedom.

Chapter 6

Marcy
Embellishing altered lies

MARCY'S HANDS TREMBLED so much when she listened to Ellen, that the first few minutes of the conversation was filled with intermittent pauses so she could switch the phone to her other hand, which did no good as both hands were trembling. She then stood and paced while talking, which helped to some degree, but also gave her a breathless personality. Ellen's questions came out at a staccato pace.

"Where was he lost?"

"In a neighborhood near the Elizabeth Nelson, well, not very near, kind of more near the park actually."

"Why were you in that part of town?"

"We went to the park."

"When was this? Like what time of day?"

She forgot about time and place. "During the storm. The storm came on so suddenly." Think, Marcy, think. When exactly was the storm? When exactly did the police chase occur?

"Yes, this was a long storm, though. You must have been out walking right before it hit. So, when was that? Noon? Didn't the storm him around ten, or started raining at ten?"

"I suppose. I can't remember."

"When you say you were walking back from the park, can you be more specific? Which street were you on? And exactly where were you on that street? Do you remember any house numbers nearby as you walked? And what exactly happened."

Marcy switched the phone to her other hand and stood, leaving the silence there in the phone, while she gathered lies. She was thinking about noon. No, not noon. She was on the phone with Elizabeth Nelson around what, eleven-thirty? Then there was the police chase, and she needed to place herself far away from that, just in case he actually reported it. Did he report it? Could she find that out? The chase occurred during the storm. She tapped her iPad, Googled weather.com, started reading as she talked to Ellen.

"He was frightened of the thunder," she finally said. "Then, he took off so fast. So fast. Really fast. He jerked the leash out of my hand."

"And this was where? And when was this?"

"I was near about the middle of Battle Street. Yeah, middle."

Marcy stopped pacing and tapped her iPad on the side table. The weather site outlined the storm in detail, putting it at their town around ten-thirty. So, noon would not really work, since that would mean she was out walking the dogs during the thunder storm which would be irresponsible and of course the reality of the situation.

"I just don't recall house numbers or anything," Marcy slowly continued, talking without her mind, as she always did when she read her iPad. "But, truly, it was raining and the wind was picking up. All I was thinking was making it back to my car."

"I am having a hard time with this. So you left your car where? At the park? The Nelsons? I thought you always left your car at my house just in case you had to take Sadie the bulldog home. Why did you take the dogs to the park? Or were you at the Nelsons?"

"No. The car was not at the Nelsons. Actually, the car was at the park. I took the dogs to the park." Her lies were coming so fast she didn't have time to stop and connect all of them. Of course she had told Ellen she always walked from her house to pick up the other dogs, and she should have stuck to that lie. But that lie would have put her dog in her neighborhood and Sam was a smart dog who would have obviously not been as lost as he probably was now if originally lost in his own neighborhood. She wanted Ellen to search the right area, but not too right as that area had been a place with police complications. She knew her lie was a dangerous one, because it nudged the truth.

"Did Sam run off scared? And when was this? You said the thunder scare him? I ask because he has never been frightened of thunder before. Of course, I have always been there with him, at least during most of the bad storms, and dogs behave quite differently under stress when with their mommies."

"I think this storm was beyond just bad thunder. Trees were falling around us. I've never seen so many trees fall. I saw one actually drop on a house. I guess the roots had been rotted out by all the rain lately."

"Did you call? Sam always responds to calls. Even in the storms. Again, I know you're not his mommy, but he probably sees you as a surrogate."

Marcy simply waited for the chatter to stop, hoping Ellen would forget her questions delivered like shotgun pellets.

"I guess I need to first call the papers," Ellen said. "Or maybe drive out there? I will drive out there and walk around a bit, yell his name. Have you tried this yet?"

"I went back to the park after the storm. I called and called but nothing. Nothing. I've been busy dropping off the other dogs. It happened so fast. He was there then gone. It happened so fast."

There was a moment of silence as Ellen probably struggled with her nascent grief. She was most likely extremely mad with Marcy, frustrated with the situation. She figured Ellen blamed her, because of course Marcy was wrong, but then again, Ellen needed her to help with her dog retrieval. Ellen probably knew Marcy was feeling guilty and anxious so there was no need to punish her. At least those would have been Marcy's thoughts if Sam had been her dog. Ellen's sniffle was a Connecticut sniffle, one that allowed only a slight revelation that a crack had formed on the surface of her carefully contained composure.

"Well, Jim will be upset about this, too. It's a good thing he's out of town. Hopefully we can find Sam before he returns." She stopped talking a moment as if to consider her husband out of town. "Sam will be around there somewhere. He'll be wanting food and water. And he has never been scared of people. He'll just run right up to the nearest person. Everyone knows everyone around here. I'm sure he'll get picked right up."

"I'll meet you at the corner of Battle and Wesson," Marcy said. "We can walk around. Do you have something of yours he can smell? Maybe if you brought an undershirt or your pajamas, we can place that out with water and food. Email me a picture and I will put together a sign on my computer."

Ellen said she would bring her running shorts and a box of Sam's favorite treats. They would meet at six and have about one hour or so before the light slipped away. When Marcy hung up, she closed her eyes and dropped her head in her hands. This was beyond awful. She knew a bit about strays from Henry, who was a stray she had found a year earlier at the park. She had trained him to walk with her pack, and he now lived with her mom and Edward, at least until she found an apartment that allowed pets. She had looked online, put up notices at vets and dog missing personal notices, but her attempts at finding his owner failed. She never took him to any shelters because three years earlier she had taken an emaciated mutt she found behind a restaurant to a shelter that insisted no dog was put down. But six months later when she returned, the thick-waisted, tattooed handler had shaken his head. "They find a few homes, but they mostly kill dogs here. It's not like those TV shows." The paid labor always told the truth.

Marcy knew from her research back then that losing a dog was complicated, particularly if it was a working dog, like a herder. Herders roamed. Herders were smart and creative. They survived because they were clever and understood how to manage the land. If this had been the bulldog, Sadie, she would have been concerned about different things. The need for hydration, food, energy. Sadie could have died of a heart attack if she became dehydrated or too anxious. But Sadie would have been found. She would have been found in a yard prostrate, asleep, snoring. She would never have made it out of the neighborhood. All anyone had to do with Sadie would raise a cooked chicken in the air. But Sam was no longer in that neighborhood. Sam was alive, yes, and he would stay alive. But Marcy knew finding him would be very difficult.

After Ellen emailed a picture of Sam, Marcy got to work on a homemade poster. The picture was of Sam sitting on Ellen's lap, his little triangular ears sticking up, eyes alert as if he was about to talk to the person behind the camera. His fur was golden with small white puffs of fur scattered on his chest and forehead. He looked like a child, actually, a smart, sassy grade-schooler, the kind of child who was always trying to pull one over on the mother. Ellen's smile was the smile of an owner who was proud of her dog. Marcy's eyes burned, but she didn't have time to cry or become filled with guilt or drama. They had about two hours before sundown. She cropped the picture on Sam's body only, then typed up the quick facts.

If you have seen this dog please call. . .
He is much beloved. . . . last seen on Battle Street.
He may be frightened. Please call if seen.

No, maybe she shouldn't say he could be frightened. She deleted frightened. Sam was not frightened. She knew in her heart Sam was not frightened. And frightened when attached to a dog usually meant threat. Scared dogs bit, and if anyone thought a dog would bite, they would not attempt to capture. So, Marcy changed that line to: "*Friendly, loves people. He will come to the name Sam.*"

After printing up a few copies, Marcy retrieved her staple gun from her kitchen closet and headed for the car to meet Ellen and figure out how to end this nightmare.

MARCY DROVE AROUND until she spotted Ellen's Lexus. Ellen's head was down, probably busy with her smart phone, typing texts to her husband about meeting up with her idiot dog walker. Or maybe she was posting rants on social media—tweeting about her incompetent dog walker. There was no escaping mistakes of small business people in the twenty-first century. If Sam was lost for good, Marcy could basically hang up her dog walking business. Her rankings on Anna's list would fall. Facebook postings and tweets about her horrible incompetence would travel around the world. Nothing was more disparaged on social media than incompetent care of dogs. What made the situation worse was Ellen's celebrity status. Ellen was a well-known public relations executive who handled popular cases—politicians involved in scandals, actors on drugs etc.

Marcy parked behind the Lexus and sat for a moment, breathing slowly as she took in the neighborhood. Debris littered yards. Downed tree trunks blocked driveways, their severed limbs tossed around the yard—a tangled mess of wood and leaf. No one was outside, not even dogs or squirrels. The houses, hidden behind littered lawns, their windows blackened, looked as depressed as Marcy felt.

Marcy got out and approached Ellen's car. She stood at the window. Ellen was no longer typing, only reading, which made Marcy want to lean in and view the message, but that would have been impossible. And it was best to at least attempt to be calm, confident. Sure, she lost the dog, but she had good lies explaining the loss, and so far her lies had been believed. Dogs cannot talk, so no one would know the truth. And the chances of running into the police officer, given this horrible storm damage as a distraction, were slim. OK, maybe that was not true.

Marcy tapped the window. Nothing. She tapped again. Ellen continued reading. She banged the window and Ellen jerked her head up. The window pane descended.

"How long have you been there? I'm sorry, I never saw you park. Are you ready?"

She tapped off her smart phone and opened the door.

"I just arrived actually. I've got everything. Posters. Staple gun. Ellen, he's around here somewhere. I think we'll find him quickly."

Ellen barely listened. She tapped her smart phone then locked her car doors. She reached out, indicating she wanted to look over Marcy's posters, then stood studying them. Her eyes narrowed, as if disappointed in Marcy's work, then she quickly looked up, handed the poster back, and marched forward without saying anything.

"These are simply preliminary posters. I will obviously touch them up later."

Ellen walked fast, stopped at the intersection, and stared at the fallen tree, the yellow tape. "He is terrified. Look at these trees. Sam saw all of this and is terrified." She looked down at the poster in Marcy's hand. "Yes, that isn't the best we can do. But it will do for now. Let's put them up and see. I brought a pair of running pants. But where do we leave them? And will Sam be able to find them through all of this with his nose? He could be miles away from here. I just don't know."

Ellen kept walking. Marcy clipped behind her, anxiously aware Ellen was headed in the direction of the dreaded Langley Street, where the police incident had occurred. They stepped over branches, twigs, a few large trunks, occasionally pausing so Ellen could scream, "Sam!" Marcy stapled the posters to trees and telephone poles every block, keeping her eye out for any police. Eventually there were signs of life—a few people wandering around yards. One asked about their poster, but for the most part, the wandering people seemed too distracted and disoriented to care about a lost dog.

After a while, they approached Armory, the Nelson's street, and Marcy couldn't help but tense up. By now, Marcy figured Elizabeth had discovered her memory stick. Perhaps it was under something at first, which is why she had not discovered it before. It was probably in her hand, or worse, back in the computer and she was perusing its contents. Elizabeth would realize that her memoir had been copied, stolen. Was there any evidence the stick belonged to Marcy? This particular memory stick was new. It only had a few folders, one for contracted work, the other for snoop. Marcy tried to remember what was on it as they walked.

"Sam!" Ellen yelled again, jolting Marcy back into the present. It was more of a scream than call, a terrified scream. "Sam! come here boy! Good boy. Good boy. I got you a treat!"

They were about two hundred yards from the Nelson's house, about a mile from the intersection where Marcy escaped the police. She remembered him chasing her, gun in hand, pit bull by her side. Any minute something horrible was possible—the police officer would appear, or Elizabeth Nelson would appear, one with a gun, the other with a memory stick.

Ellen screamed "Sam!" again.

"I'm not sure Sam is going to come to you right away," Marcy said, thinking the hysterical screaming would only attract humans she didn't particularly want to see, like Elizabeth and wet police officers.

"Why wouldn't he come? He's probably desperately looking for me."

"Yes, but maybe just say his name softly. And it's best to think nose," Marcy said. "When lost, he will resort to the nose. It all depends on where he is and which direction the wind is blowing. Yelling does less good than smells. Just don't leave food. Food will attract predators and raccoons. Mean things."

Ellen raised her brows at the mention of raccoons.

"Sam is a tough dog, though," Marcy quickly added. "I would not mess with Sam if I were a raccoon."

"Sam will come to me. I know my dog."

This is the kind of confidence that made Marcy realize why Ellen was a good public relations representative. She imagined a conference table with union officials on the take, or state legislators caught in FBI sting operations, or someone like Jimmy Mallon who had been caught out drunk with some woman. There they would all be, sitting at a shiny mahogany table, shamefaced, while Ellen kept them moving forward, like she was doing now. Except now they were moving forward in the wrong direction.

Ellen jerked to a stop, and shouted again, this time with both hands cupped around her mouth. "Sam, come to Mommie now, Goddammit!" The image of the conference table with shamed faced famous people vanished. Ellen began to cry.

"Hello." The voice was behind them. "Marcy? Is that you?"

Elizabeth Nelson had on baggy jeans and a very clean, crisp red collared T-shirt with a small yellow logo over her left breast. The T-shirt looked new, actually, not one wrinkle, as if she had just lifted it off the hanger at Macys. Maybe she had. Maybe she had gone to the mall and shopped for storm wear, so that she would look appropriate. Her memoir mentioned an incident in her neighborhood once, a fire in her neighbor's garage. The entire neighborhood chipped in to help them clear the rubble the next day. Elizabeth had purchased rubble cleaning clothes. Marcy wasn't surprised she would do that, only that she would actually put it in the memoir.

"Hi, Ellen," Elizabeth said, in a way that suggested she and Ellen were more than simply acquaintances. "Marcy's my hero. Got the dogs out of the storm and back home. What's up with Sam?"

"I wasn't a hero for Ms. Maher. Sam got away from the pack when lightning struck near us. "

"She lost him around the park, not far from here. Sometime around eleven to eleven-thirty."

"Oh, I'm so sorry to hear this. So sorry. Eleven?" Elizabeth looked at Marcy now, her brows furrowed, her eyes moving up above Marcy toward a space in the air reserved for people who think too much. Elizabeth was thinking too much. "No, Marcy, it must have been later. I called you around that time. Remember? I know because I was in front of my computer screen when I called. It was eleven-twenty? Or around that time. And you were heading to the car I believe? Or in the car. I can't remember. I do recall you were at least near the car."

Ellen studied Elizabeth, then shifted her eyes around the neighborhood, before allowing them to land upon Marcy, who remained quiet, but of course her mind was in high gear, desperately racing through the new time schedule, so she could redo her lie.

"Right, I was in the car at eleven-twenty. But I had just started toward the car when you called. So, I guess I was walking. I don't wear a watch. I get times mixed up. And who looks at their time in a thunderstorm?"

"It's not your fault, Marcy." Elizabeth touched Marcy's shoulder, as if Marcy were a friend, not just a dog walker, a voyeur, a hack, a memoir thief, and someone who engaged in a police chase—which was probably a felony of some sort. "The storm caused all this damage. I can't even imagine the terrified dogs."

Marcy's eyes burned. She moved her fingers quickly under them.

"I'm sorry. Look, don't worry," Elizabeth said. "We'll have the entire neighborhood looking for him. Can you give me a picture?"

Marcy handed Elizabeth the homemade poster. She squinted the same way Ellen had squinted. "What a cutie. I love corgis. And no way will he go unnoticed. Corgis will be recognized."

Ellen forced a smile. "Oh, I know. I'm just a bit worried, that's all."

"As you should be. You know, I had a friend a few years back who lost her Lab. She did the poster thing, too. But she found this dog detective. The detective was famous, used to go on TV shows. Like that Dog Whisperer man's show? Anyway, she had a great track record. Uses this software GPS program to track the stray. She also has a pack of dogs with good noses to track the lost dogs. All of the trackers are rescued dogs."

"Strays?" Marcy said. "She uses strays?"

"Rescues."

"But they used to be strays."

"Why do you ask?" Ellen said.

"I don't know. Just wanted to clarify. I think Ellen and I will find him soon. She brought her shorts. We may just set them out somewhere, then hope Sam smells them."

"Nope, nope. You can't do that. According to my friend, a dog goes into survival mode fast. They are not thinking about finding owners, only surviving. You really need someone who has studied this working with you."

Ellen held her running shorts tightly and seemed to carefully consider Elizabeth's speech.

"I'd put your shorts down someplace," Marcy said, carefully. "Like over near the edge of the woods."

"I'd contact this detective," Elizabeth insisted, who had obviously not visited her computer yet so still thought of Marcy as simply her dog walker, not someone who read her personal memoir and emails. Marcy figured within twenty-four hours, after discovering the memory stick, Elizabeth would morph into something different than what was now before them, something hot and enraged, talking furiously into her phone with a lawyer or police officer.

"Just drop the shorts here," Marcy said.

"I've got her number." Elizabeth stepped closer to Ellen, ignoring Marcy.

Ellen looked at her choices: follow Elizabeth, a nice friend with good clothes, or Marcy, the dog walker who lost Sam and couldn't remember what time she lost him. She went with Elizabeth.

"OK. Well, I'll just leave these posters around then call that detective woman. She's probably expensive, but it'll be worth it."

Elizabeth helped them put up posters on telephone poles and trees near the edge of the woods. They all drove back to the park and walked around, this time not yelling, only looking. More posters on more trees. By the time they finished, it was dusk and they figured Sam would probably find safety for the night under some bushes, maybe a shed.

Elizabeth stayed with Marcy after Ellen drove away. They stood listening to the fading chirps of birds, the beginning of cicadas' nightly serenade.

"Be careful with Ellen," Elizabeth finally said as Marcy turned toward her car. "I remember when my friend lost her Lab. She never got over it."

"If he doesn't show up tomorrow, we'll get the detective, so, I'm not too nervous," Marcy said.

"She was great. I think her name was Debbie Serendon, and her company was called something like Best Dog Detective Service. I'll text all this information to Ellen. The detective had an amazing ability to know the psychology of dogs, where to look for them. And they almost got him."

"Wait. What do you mean the owner never *got over it*. They *almost got* him. They never got the dog?"

"The detective was still good."

"Where is the dog?"

"Probably down in Texas. They all go to Texas."

Chapter 7

Marcy
The lies to protect lies

THE PHONE ALARM blasted Grateful Dead's "End of The Line" at seven-thirty a.m. Marcy tapped the screen snooze and closed her eyes. She had been up all night, Googling Detective Serendon, clicking around the Best Dog Detective Service website. There seemed to be a few success stories, but most of the dogs had been found by people who saw the picture of the lost dog at the vet's office or grocery stores.

The song came on again and Marcy stared at her ceiling. There was still a stain from the flood a year ago when her neighbor's child left the bath tub running. The repair left a rusted color that looked vaguely like blood. She assumed one day the landlord would get around to repainting the ceiling. Or she would get around to moving to a place that allowed dogs, and finally she could adopt Henry, although it would not be an adoption, not really.

She tapped the alarm off right when the phone rang. She let it ring, imagining it was Elizabeth holding her memory stick, preparing to yell into voicemail. Or maybe she was planning some smart, passive aggressive comment that would come out in a voice that had the tension of a cork jammed into the opening of a tea pot filled with boiling water. But when she checked her voice mail, it was not Elizabeth's voice.

"I can help with the dog. It's one of those little ones right? Long and little? I've been out looking already. Dogs follow me all the time. Henry follows me as you know. But others do too. They only thing that stops them from following me and Henry out walking? Is the invisible fence. But I saw a dog run right through the fence to get to me. Marcy, hold on." Edward took a sip of something. She hoped it was coffee, not beer. *"And they go for garbage. Me and garbage. Haha. Mom says call her, by the way, cause she*

wants to talk with you about a job she saw in the newspaper. We both think you should get out of this dog walking business. No real future in that."

She stopped listening and called him back. "Edward? It's seven-thirty in the morning." She kept staring at the ceiling. She would definitely paint the ceiling today, then send a bill to the landlord. "I've had a bad day or two. I need my sleep. So, how did you and Mom find out about my situation?"

"One of your dogs is in the paper."

"Marcy, is that you?" Her mother had picked up the other phone and joined them. She often jumped on the phone when Edward called, then Edward would hang on so he could interject intermittently. "And they actually said your name. Didn't they, Edward? Your sister's full name in the local papers delivered to all the surrounding towns. Of course, I suppose losing a dog will not be good for business."

"Mom," Edward interrupted. "I am going to find the dog. No problem. I've got a talent for this kind of thing. Finding dogs and such. I know the secret."

"Apparently." Her mother ignored Edward. Everyone ignored Edward. He was twenty-four years old and everyone ignored him, unless he stopped taking meds, then everyone in the world paid attention to him. "His owner is some big deal P.R. rep for like Jennifer Ranniston? Did you know this? Her house is tremendous. Of course, all your clients live in big houses, I guess."

Marcy sat up and threw the covers off, ran her hand through her hair. "My name was mentioned? Like how? Did they simply say I was the dog walker or did they give details?" She desperately tried to recall exactly what she had told Ellen and Elizabeth. Where she lost the dog, what time. Why hadn't she written the lies down? "Did it give times?"

"I don't know. Yeah, I think. I can't remember."

"They suggested you lost the dog at Battle Street," Edward said. "Times are irrelevant. Dogs wander. They wander around looking for food and shelter. They are forgotten by the world because they are homeless. They are homeless and if found? They go to jail. Everyone thinks the homeless belong in jail."

"Marcy," her mother continued. "I don't have the paper with me right now. I just thought it was so interesting that your client worked with Jennifer Ranniston. Do you think Jennifer Ranniston will visit your town to help with the dog?"

"Mom, no, no I don't. And you know? Edward, I think I can find the dog myself. And I really have to go. I have so much to do today."

"I don't think you will be walking dogs today, because of the storm clean up," her mother said. "Have you heard about the trees? So many streets are closed. Have any of your clients expressed concern over your dog walking now?"

Marcy stood and walked down the hall to the kitchen. A few dog food pebbles pushed into the soles of her feet.

"Marcy? You still there?" Edward said.

"I'm ignoring you two. I don't know if my clients are concerned. I suppose Ellen has fired me. Of course, my services are no longer needed until she has a dog again."

"Oh, now, sweetie, there's a good chance they'll find the dog," her mother said.

"You've got to look on the positive side," Edward said. He took another sip of something Marcy was hoping was coffee. "Did she put out something with a familiar smell. Like a toy?"

"We were going to but then this lady said you aren't supposed to do that because the smell may actually scare the dog away. You're supposed to put up posters and wait for phone calls. I think she's getting some detective."

"Detective? Like dog detective ? How much do they charge? I bet you'll have to pay for it," Edward said.

"That may be a good business for you," her mother said. "Do you think this detective would be hiring part-time help?"

"I could help her," Edward said. "I know this area. I have great ideas about dogs. It's all about—"

"I know. Look, later, OK? I'm going to hunt down Sam today. I have to find him. It's very important."

"Come on, sis, you're getting a bit too sensitive. And you are nervous. Dogs can smell that. Gotta stay calm. My meds help me. Maybe you should take a few meds during these stressful times. I've got extra Ativan. I never need them."

"Yeah, I guess. Look, I kind of got to go. I'm going to try to put more posters up. Anything else in the papers I should know about besides my client's famous job and lost dog?"

"Well, the damage to your town is pretty significant, more than the damage to our town," her mother said. "Seems the highway is closed. Train service delayed. So, stay safe. When can we expect you for dinner?"

"I'll call."

"I'm going to join one of those groups to look for the dog," Edward said. "The paper said they were forming teams, so I already called."

Marcy had a sudden image of Edward attending dog hunting groups. There, at table with the detective leading a discussion, her brother with his avocado body and unshaven appearance, coke in his hand, rambling on nonstop about his various world theories.

"No. No need for you to do that, Edward."

"I think it'll be good for him," her mother said. "Edward has a good understanding of animals. Remember that rabbit he caught?"

"Oh, please, can we not talk about that rabbit." The rabbit was dead now.

"OK, then, we're off. Please let us know if Jennifer Ranniston comes to town."

The click was sudden. Edward didn't say goodbye.

Marcy finished her coffee, took a shower, then looked over her timeline she had created last night. She realized it was silly to worry about the police. They were certainly preoccupied with closed roads and storm cleanup, and the officer probably had been too distracted to concentrate on her car or license. He did look right at her, though, right into her eyes. Did he see Sam? She couldn't remember if Sam had barked. One of the dogs had barked but she thought it was only Henry. Sam was so small and crowded in the back with the big dogs, probably hanging in the way back

Marcy had constructed a truth time line and lie time line. The truth time line was positioned above the lie time line for easy comparison. The truth time line had the storm beginning mid-morning, probably about ten. She was at Elizabeth's house around eleven. She had the police confrontation after the call, sometime around eleven-forty-five to twelve. She then hid in Elizabeth's closet, which was when Sam probably jumped out of the car and ran off. When, she was not too sure? Twelve-thirty? That seemed too fast, but maybe trauma accelerated time. Under this time line was the lie time line which placed her far away from the area of the police chase or Elizabeth's house when she was not supposed to be there hiding in a closet. That fictitious time line had her walking around the neighborhood, ending at the park where she walked the dogs until the phone call some time after eleven.

She had already told Elizabeth she was at the park at eleven, so she had to stick with that. She had told Ellen she walked all the dogs at the park, so that lie had to be kept. Once one travelled down a particular lie path, one could not make a detour. One never knew who talked with whom and which lie path everyone was on. That was the most important rule in lying. Always assume everyone talks with everyone. So, the lie time line put Sam's loss at around eleven-thirty to eleven-forty-five near the park. She lost him, then looked and called for him, but no Sam, so took the other dogs home. That would be around one. Truth loss twelve-thirty, lie loss at eleven-thirty. Close enough.

Now she simply had to keep her face and the pit bull, Henry, out of the papers, which reminded her—newspaper! She needed to read the local news.

THE DELI DOWN the street still had a small pile of the Windhaven Dailies left. The front page was all bold font—STORM DEVASTES TOWN. At least four pictures of huge trees lying prostrate across major avenues covered the first page. Marcy bought a coffee and whole wheat bagel with butter and scanned articles about various tree accidents. Several houses had been damaged. Cars wrecked. Wires down everywhere. The power would be out for three days. One article suggested the wind shear had reached seventy-five miles per hour. Sam's picture was on page six. It was a different picture than the one she had put on the poster. He was sitting on a couch, tongue out, panting, which made him look amused. Sam always looked like he was laughing at you. As Marcy stared at the picture, she felt her stomach tighten, appetite subside. She couldn't even sip her coffee. The article didn't mention the time he was lost, only that the corgi ran off during the storm when he was with "his dog walker, Marcy Thorpe." She stared at Sam a few more minutes, then closed the paper without reading the other articles.

When she left the deli, she noticed Lorene's car. Lorene's head was down, as if she were reading. Marcy decided against her usual routine—strolling by as if she didn't notice her, or waving a quick hello like she was too busy to chat. Lorene was a very kind person, just annoying, and she asked way too many questions. However, today was different, today Lorene was someone Marcy needed.

Marcy tapped the window and waved. Lorene smiled as the window descended.

"Hiya!" Lorene said. "You OK? Have they made any progress with the lost dog? You're in the paper. You saw that, right?"

"Yes. No. Yes."

"That no was the dog."

"Yes. I'm very worried. Have you heard anything about it? Are people talking about it?"

"I don't know what anyone is saying about anything. I've been working. Storms keep insurance companies hopping, hon. Look, don't worry, sunshine, I'm going to help you find that dog. I've got to go to work today but I'll call when I get home. We'll brainstorm. Maybe you can retrieve ole Henry and he can help track that corgi. He knows what the little guy smells like. Think positive. I know this is going to guilt you out, but you got to think positive. At least a tree didn't fall on our apartment. Or us! Did you read about that police officer that had some tree fall on him while chasing some crazy person?"

"Police officer? What do you mean tree?"

"I guess it was a branch. Yeah, it's in the paper. A big branch fell on some police officer. He was in pursuit of someone who was giving him a hard time. What the heck is someone doing running from a cop in this kind of storm? He's got some major concussion. Can't remember anything but that he had been in pursuit of someone. They found his gun by him so apparently he drew the gun. He only remembers running."

Marcy opened her paper, ignoring Lorene who kept talking, no longer about the storm and her work, but something else, something about Linny, her latest "special friend." Marcy found the article on page three. How had she missed it? POLICE OFFICER INJURED IN STORM. And there he was, in his uniform, smiling at her, although he was not smiling at her yesterday. *"Doctors expect Officer Willard to make a full recovery. Memory sometimes takes months to return after a major concussion. "He'll recall details of the chase," Sergeant Cooper assured reporters. "It'll take time but the perpetrator will be captured."*

Marcy wondered who would be caught first, her or Sam.

Chapter 8

Marcy
The dog detective

THE NEW "FIND Sam" signs started appearing a week after Ellen Maher hired Detective Serendon. They had a picture of Sam panting. "Lost" was in bold letters at the bottom of the page and in smaller letters the date and where he was lost and a phone number to call. "Please don't try to capture him, simply call." Ellen hadn't called Marcy to help with the volunteer efforts. She hadn't even invited her to the first organizing meeting of dog searchers. Ellen was probably still traveling through the stages of dog loss grief, which Marcy assumed began with rage at the dog walker.

Even though Ellen ignored Marcy, Detective Serendon did not. She contacted her because she needed information. She also unfortunately wanted a walk through.

"A reenactment of the actual trigger event," she said over the phone, her voice slightly raspy and officious.

Marcy imagined her husky, maybe even overweight, or muscular, built like a rock. The detective had that kind of voice. While her name was Debbie, Marcy got the distinct impression the woman would prefer to be called Detective Serendon. She had introduced herself quickly, rambling on about her credentials, a verbal resume of all her police work and recognitions while employed at the Kansas City Police Department.

"I was there twenty years, and—I'll just tell you this—I had one of the best arrest records in that part of the country. I could catch them better than anyone. I use the computer. Apps, maps, tracking models. Once the guy was on the run, they'd call me in."

Marcy tried to excuse herself from the walk through, because she was not quite ready to walk and lie. Lying while walking was always more difficult than simply lying while sitting and talking on the phone. And if this woman was a good detective, she was probably particularly good at detecting lies in a face and body—the slight blink of the eye, the distracted focus, the hand gestures. When Marcy lied, she always played with her hair. It was a habit she had a hard time breaking. She had tried all her life to hold her hands, place them in her pockets, but, no, when the lie came, her hands went to her head, then hair, always tucking strands behind her ears, or combing a piece from her eyes with her fingers.

The detective would not allow Marcy to back out of the walk-through and insisted she meet up with her at the park. So, Marcy pinned her hair on top of her head after she tapped off her phone, closed her eyes, and imagined herself telling the fictitious story. She went through this inner monologue over and over while sitting perfectly still with her eyes closed. She learned this mind control strategy back when she played high school volleyball. Imagine the event, imagine your action, repeat it over and over in your mind. It worked for sports, dog walking issues like dog fights, sex, and lying.

DETECTIVE SERENDON WAS not large and boxy, but lithe, with wisps of brown hair that lightly curled into her face. In fact, the hair didn't seem to budge even in the soft breeze. She wore heavy cargo pants, the kind advertised for construction workers on TV in commercials that had bulldozers running over them to prove their value. The pants swallowed her small frame. She wore a very clean bright yellow sports shirt underneath what looked like a hunting vest, but instead of slots holding bullets, it had small pockets filled with dog treats, whistles, and other various a sundry of dog detective equipment. A small camera hung around her neck and she looked down at the Google map on her smart phone as she talked in short bursts of words, quickly delivered, as if she didn't have time to talk, because no moment could be wasted.

"Let's go through exactly where you were, exactly what you witnessed, precisely how this dog behaved. I am going to ask you questions, OK, and then you are going to answer the question, succinctly, to the point, OK?"

"I wrote down exactly what happened, thought it may be of help, because I know when . . ."

"That's good. That's real good. I will just take that." Detective Serendon stared at Marcy's sheet—her fictitious time line—for a good ten minutes, then tapped her Google map, then stared at the sheet, then tapped the map.

"Of course, I can still walk you through it."

Detective Serendon lifted her hand, palm out. Marcy stopped talking.

"OK. Sorry to interrupt you. I find it important for the conversation to be one way in the beginning. Me ask, you answer. I find that in the beginning emotions run high on these lost dog cases. We get enormous front-ended emotion on these cases. It's best to allow the professionals do the talking. I am going to ask questions, but, yes, eventually, we will have to walk through it quickly." She glanced around, then looked back at her iPhone.

They were standing in front of the Bradley Park gate, where ostensibly Marcy had lost Sam. She stared through the gates toward the road, then off to the field. Marcy was terrified this woman would spot something wrong with her time line, something obvious Marcy forgot. Detective Serendon's tracking dogs were now running back and forth sniffing the ground, as if they already smelled something interesting. Probably a skunk. The detective glanced at the park but didn't appear to want to enter it, only walk around it. Probably because the dogs didn't appear to want to enter the park.

"So, based upon the weather history, I see the storm began at ten. And you say you started the journey from the park to the Nelsons' at what time? Eleven?"

"You know, I was not at all looking at my iPhone or anything. So, keep that in mind. Exact times are hard, but I know Elizabeth Nelson called me after eleven. I was not really walking at that time, just . . ."

"The rain started at what, ten-thirty. Light but rain. That's my understanding. Why were you walking the dogs when you knew a storm was coming?"

"I got delayed in the park."

"But when did you begin the journey from the park? It must have been raining. You talked with Elizabeth before you walked from the park? Or after? It was raining?"

Why had she told this to Elizabeth Nelson? Why had she volunteered any information? Now she was stuck with this stupid walk in the rain. The lie put her away from the crime scene and stupid.

"What are you looking for, confession of stupidity?"

Detective Serendon looked up from her map, reached out, and squeezed Marcy's arm lightly. "Sorry. I'm sure you feel guilty enough already. And look, Ellen's anger at you is normal. They all blame the last person seen with the dog or near the dog. I have had clients blame trucks for scaring their dog off a leash. Shit happens."

"Well, thanks. It was my fault and I shouldn't have been out in the rain, so I don't blame Ellen for being furious with me."

"So, you started here and walked how many blocks? Why don't we walk, I find movement helps a person's memory." Detective Serendon stuffed her iPhone in her back pocket and began to walk. Her walk was feminine for someone in baggy cargo pants and a raspy voice. It even had a sway and rhythm to it. Her two dogs were mutts. The one that looked like it had a mixture of hound dog, Labrador, and terrier ran free. The second one—that looked like an Irish setter managed to mate a beagle—was on a flexi leash. The beagle mix ran to the left, then right of the road, sniffing every five feet. Detective Serendon strolled slowly.

"I notice that you already put up new signs even though you hadn't received all the details from me," Marcy said.

"This is a herding dog. Doesn't matter exactly where you lost this herder, it will wander off. Herders wander." She stopped abruptly, looked around, as if she heard the dog. Her mind seemed as fast and distracted as her words. "That's what herders do when lost. Roam. Sniff around one place, then roam again. So, the most important thing to do is put up signs. Fast. Get those mothers up. And this is how you make a poster. She faced Marcy. "You got to have, one," she held up a finger, "face." She put up a second finger. "Two. Facts." She paused with two fingers in the air, staring at Marcy. Then came the third finger. "Three. Phone number. Face. Fact. Phone number. That is what you have on all posters, and you get those mothers out fast fast." She released her fingers, turned, and walked forward, as if knowing Marcy would follow in order to hear her. "Gotta have signs everywhere. Get the picture of him, the phone number out there. That. Is. Key. Now, for me to track?" She turned her head slightly to make sure Marcy was in her blind side.

"I need this walk through. Chances are my tracking will not find the dog. What will find the dog is someone seeing the dog, then calling us, so we can set the trap fast. What we don't want is anyone approaching the dog, trying to feed the dog, calling the dog, playing hero. We don't want heroes. We want everyone calling that phone number and letting the professionals do the job."

Marcy was so caught up in Detective Serendon's speech she had forgotten her lie story, exactly when she was supposed to be in this vicinity, exactly what route they took. She was hoping this was not that important now since the detective had talked a lot about the dog wandering.

"How far do herder dogs wander? Do you know? I mean could Sam conceivably be in the next town by now, making this walk through a bit moot?"

Detective Serendon turned abruptly and faced Marcy. "Nothing is moot if the dog is still alive. The dog is in survival mode now but will tend to roam in circles around a general area. His wandering will expand concentrically. I need to set a center then try to go from there. So you say it was here, say, about eleven-twenty, or around then? Where did the dog escape, kind of close to this park?"

"I think. Yes."

"What do you mean think? You mean think like you think it was eleven-twenty, or think like you think it was near the park? Because where you lost him is important. Time? Not so much. Where? Important."

"Yes, here, definitely is where the thunder scared him. Here on Battle."

"So, did he run off with the leash on him?"

Marcy had told someone this, but she couldn't remember who, probably Ellen. Why had she said that? Probably because obviously if she were walking the dogs, the leash was on all of them. She wouldn't be walking one dog off the leash. She brushed a few strands of hair that had come loose then crossed her arms over her chest. "It was right about here, right around here he ran off."

"Did you intend to avoid my question or do you avoid questions when thinking." Now Detective Serendon crossed her arms as if imitating Marcy or perhaps trying to emulate her body position in order to create a more trusting atmosphere.

Marcy had participated in conflict resolution seminars when she worked at the publishing company. Dealing with conflict was quite common, all new hires had to take the course. Once in a while they had to meet with writers and conflicts over their poorly constructed sentences were inevitable. What they were trained to do was subtlety emulate the body positions. If the writer crossed legs, the editors were to eventually, slowly, cross their legs without drawing attention to themselves. Crossed arms were a bit harder as that screamed imitation to the observer. Detective Serendon obviously had attended a similar conflict resolution seminar when on the police force.

Marcy uncrossed her arms and shoved her hands in her front jean pockets. "I'm just thinking on it a moment."

Detective Serendon uncrossed her arms but didn't put her hands in her pockets. "That's an important fact. If he's on a leash, we have a dangerous situation. There is a risk of course of entanglement, even strangulation. And then predators have easy prey. There are predators out here. We have coyotes, foxes, probably some bobcats. Of course, he could figure out how to get out of the collar. Lots of runaways get out of the collars."

"You know, I do remember saying he was on a leash, but now that I think of it, I had let the dogs run some in the park, and I let Sam help me get the pack going. I do that sometimes with Sam. He's good at keeping dogs in line."

"So he was roaming in the park during a storm? The dogs were running around at the park in the storm?"

"This was before the storm.'

"The storm started to roll in, at least the light rains, according to my research, sometime after ten to ten-thirty, so if the dog was off-leash, then he was off-leash in the rain."

Well, that all sounded bad, allowing a dog to run off leash in a storm. Ellen may not only fire her but kill her. Of course the alternative was supplying bad information. If she said the dog had a leash, everyone would be terrified Sam was hanging from some low lying branch. Maybe another smart predator grabbed the leash and yanked him into their teeth.

"No, not off leash. Let me regroup and think. I have the leash, so obviously it was not on Sam. I had him on the leash, after the thunder, of course. I took him off leash for just a moment."

"I see. Well, at least he may still have the collar on him. Ellen told me she never put a microchip in him. This is why you have to microchip dogs."

"Sam is a smart dog. I don't even need him on a leash. He follows all of us. Actually, we all follow Sam."

"Yes, those corgis have quite a bit of personality. So, well, the leash was off him, that is all we need to know. That and the vicinity. He was around this area when he ran. Did he run fast in any particular direction?"

"I can't remember actually. It wasn't back toward the park. Maybe it was a bit at a diagonal." Marcy pointed toward the Northeast, in the general direction of the Nelson's neighborhood. "I'd think he would be far from here now, and I am not sure where he was running would matter but it was in that direction."

"You'd be surprised how important the first direction is. They go feral fast. Survival instinct kicks in and they're almost like a wild animal. OK." She clapped her hands. "I'll go back, get the rest of my tracking dogs and we'll do a quick run around. We have a few items for scent. I think that should do it." She smiled at Marcy. "Anything else you think could help us?"

"No. That's about the story. I think your best bet is with trackers. Dogs are amazing. I bet they pick up Sam's scent fast."

"OK then." Debbie touched Marcy's shoulder lightly. "Don't go worrying about Ellen. She will soon get focused on getting her dog back and forget about this grudge. Grudges go away. And, look, I'm going to do a public call-out for volunteers on social media. The public loves cute dogs. Generally, when you do a public call-out, you get a lot more volunteers. You're welcome to join us."

"I think I may. And if you need help with newsletters or any writing, I'm a retired editor."

"That's nice to know. Yeah, we will need some write-ups. This process is harder than you think. You don't just put out food and a poster or two then hope for the best. We just found a pug after three months of hard work."

"Oh, God. But at least you got him. How did you capture him? A trap?"

"Someone found him in their backyard. Playing with their Labrador."

"I thought they went feral after a few days."

"He was feral. The Lab just appealed to his feral playful side."

Chapter 9

Marcy
Gathering support

TODAY'S WALK WENT smoothly. Sam's face was omnipresent. Every telephone pole had a panting corgi plastered on it. His picture sometimes appeared with Ellen, his owner, sometimes alone, always accompanied by the number to call and a small map showing where he was last seen. Every quarter mile, there he was, announcing to the world Marcy's incompetence. Most of the rubble had now been cleared, and piles of logs dotted the back yards and woods. Construction crews were dispersed at various broken homes. Trucks with extension arms dangling buckets of tired men were now only an occasional presence on streets. There were only fifty homes still without power, located predominately in less affluent towns contiguous to Windhaven. Marcy's power had been back a week, so she had finally been able to read with a lamp, not a flashlight, take warm showers, keep wine in the fridge. Most importantly, there were no longer cordoned off areas guarded by police, which always caused her to back away, head off in another direction, thinking any day the officer she had escaped that dreaded day would appear again by yellow tape with his memory returned and vivid.

She hiked with the dogs through the back woods behind the Nelson's Street because Eric, the herder, loved the experience, and she was hoping he could pick up Sam's scent. Sadie, the bulldog, was miserable in the woods, so finally lay down under a large beech tree, refusing to budge. Marcy screamed Sam's name several times, even though she had been told not to yell his name. There of course was no response, no trace of Sam. She didn't quite know what a trace of Sam would look like. Small footprints? A collar? The dogs never barked, never seemed to be alerted to a familiar scent. No, Sam was far gone by now.

Marcy had stopped snooping at the client's homes, and she no longer allowed dogs to roam empty houses, gallop in the park, sometimes swim in the Long Island Sound—like she used to do on hot days. She behaved herself now and simply walked dogs, most slightly anxious, as if knowing a pack member was in trouble. Only Nellie appeared oblivious to the missing dog and altered team dynamics. Marcy still had no clue what became of her memory stick. Elizabeth's housekeeper hours changed to correlate with pick-ups, and the housekeeper greeted Marcy at the door every morning. This of course prevented any attempt to enter and check out the computer room, but Elizabeth had not mentioned it. So, Marcy assumed Elizabeth found it, figured it belonged to her husband or maybe one of her sons, then tossed it in a drawer. Only middle-aged people would ignore the contents of some strange memory stick that suddenly appeared by the computer. Marcy wondered if after she reached, say, forty-five years old, she too would cease being curious.

She had an urge to toss one of her socks around a yard, by a tree, see if her smell would attract Sam. She had a half-eaten sandwich in her car, which she could toss down too, but no one was supposed put out food or toys or clothing. These instructions had been delivered with force by all local radio announcers and local news reporters. "Find Sam" Facebook posts and Twitter feeds emphasized no action other than calling in a sighting of the dog. Pictures were allowed but nothing else.

Marcy only read about it, because she hadn't yet attended any Find Sam meetings. The whole Find Sam volunteer effort was full of drama, and Ellen and her dog were now local celebrities. Ellen wore fame comfortably because she dealt with it in her job. She appeared on all the local TV stations. Her picture was on the front page of Windhaven Daily News, holding her panting Sam looking happy and loved. She was interviewed on local radio talk shows, her voice somber yet professional. At first, Marcy assumed Ellen would spread bad information about Marcy's dog walking service, causing the entire town to question her competence. But, no, the opposite happened. No one seemed ready to blame Marcy, instead, they felt pity for her, which, OK, was worse, but pity did not take away client revenue. And ironically, Elizabeth Nelson had praised her to other clients. Margaret Wilder told Marcy that Elizabeth had thought Marcy had done an amazing job keeping the dogs together given the circumstances.

"Don't pay too much attention to Ellen," Margaret had told her. "It would look bad if she blamed it all on you. Besides, we'll find Sam, then she'll forget it. That much I know." But it had been two weeks. Two weeks of front page articles, local news interviews, posters. And nothing. Nothing.

AFTER SHE DELIVERED all dogs back to their home, Marcy returned to her apartment to sit, stare at her wall, and feel sorry for herself. Another day that would merge into evening with no plans with friends, just TV and food. She opened the fridge and regarded the apple, a black shriveled avocado, and a loaf of bread, all clinging to each other on the middle shelf. There was one tomato and a head of Romaine lettuce, which now resembled something alive, albeit barely, in the vegetable bin. She closed the refrigerator door, opened a bottle of wine, and poured a full glass. The knock came after her first sip.

Edward looked nicer than usual. His black jeans seemed to actually fit and his T-shirt tag was not in front. His green eyes were rimmed with a very white sclera, signaling no beer consumption or lack of sleep.

"I do not have Henry, your dog. No dog, as that is against the rules and I am following rules. Unlike Russia, my sis. Russia is now bombing Aleppo, and let me suggest, just in case you've missed it, Russia does not care. I repeat, does not care about citizens of any country." His stream of words came out as he walked into the apartment. He turned and kicked the door shut.

Marcy returned to the couch, picked up her wine as Edward started again, his soliloquy, all monotone deliverance of news, primarily concerning Russia, gathered from Breaking News reports on cable TV He disappeared into the kitchen. The door opened with a soft sucking sound, then closed.

"You never have beer, so I cannot imbibe in spirits with you. Wine's too much like vinegar. And, it's best to stay away from alcohol until I completed dog hunting volunteer work." He sat like an old man in the club chair, his body deflating. "Today at the dog finding group at the park, not one person around my side of the table knew a Russian missile almost destroyed a hospital. Pitiful."

Marcy closed her eyes as she took a sip, the image of Edward there on the back of her lids, talking with women clad in khakis and sports shirts, warning them all about Putin.

"Please don't get involved in this because of me. You don't have to do this. I'm fine right now. I'm figuring it all out, right as we speak."

"You, my sis, are drinking and not participating. Here you are alone and you have not turned on the news, which indicates you are removing yourself from not just this sad situation but also from the Middle East. Russia. And no one complained about you. We all sat around a table with the owner and talked to a face on an iPad. A big talking head and no other information. What is she wearing? Is she wearing anything? Of course Ronda Maddack wears jeans, not just on Breaking News but all the time. We see more of her, though, not just the face."

"Edward." Marcy put down her wine. "What are you doing here?"

"I'm in my planning mode now. I walked Henry and did my usual study of the nonverbal dog. I do that, study the face, which involves mostly eye study. The word that came to me today was escape. Escape. That is the what we have to conquer in order to know where to begin. Henry's eyes consider escape at all times. We train them not do to this—consider escape—but they consider it. I see it. I see it in all of them at the park. It is an impulsive thought. What would happen if I just leave? the dog thinks to himself. The dog stares at the woods, sniffs a strange butt, then the thought happens again. Escape. Not lost. But escape." He looked down at his thighs spread out on the chair. "Escape."

Marcy considered the word, but didn't say it out loud. Sam was not escaping. Sam jumped out of the car because she left the door open, then maybe something scared him. Of course, maybe he felt the tangles of life around his neck, the way it suffocates you at night before you drift to sleep, there in the back of your mind every day, tempting you, nudging you to the airport, where you would buy a ticket, maybe a cash purchase, to Colorado; you would grow marijuana and live off the land, no credit, no bank account, cash hidden in the walls.

The knock, then jiggle of doorknob, yanked Marcy out of reverie and caused Edward to sit up, readjusting himself for that sudden merging of his intimate world, shared with his forgiving sister, with the potentially less accepting public world.

"You're drinking alone during the day. I can't allow this," Lorene said to Marcy who opened the door, wine in hand. "You may be depressed." She stopped when she noticed Edward. "Hi, Edward?"

"Lorene." Edward nodded but didn't stand. "I don't stand because that's sexist. Some men do that. I don't insult women."

"You are one progressive man." Lorene headed for the kitchen. "I love a man who understands the dangers of Putin. And how condescending a woman makes her feel."

The cabinet door creaked open, then came a ping and quiet cork pop. Marcy sat down.

"What kind of wine is this? Oh, Pino Grigio. Great." Lorene reappeared. "So, now that you are not drinking alone." She looked at Edward, took a long sip. "How's the pooch?" She sat too close to Marcy, their hips touching.

"I assume you are referring to Henry," Edward said. "Pooch is not the word. He's a canine, a pit bull canine. That would be like referring to Putin as a minister or potentate, or even president. Putin, as you know is a dictator."

"This man is something else."

"Yes, he is," Marcy said, her mind racing through the list of other topics to keep Edward off Russia. "I haven't snuck Henry here in a while. I'm a good girl for a while. I may go to Mom's tomorrow, make sure he's OK, take him out for a run. The detective uses rescues to track. Makes me think Henry may be of use."

"Yeah, well, you should have seen those dogs. I did a walk through with the detective a few days ago." Lorene held out her hand to check her manicure, then put down her wine and opened her oversized purple Channel purse.

She pulled out a large wallet, hair brush, small notebook, iPhone, several red and white mints, three packages of gum. She turned it over and shook the remaining contents out onto the coffee table, then rummaged through everything, which appeared to mostly be tissue, coins, and pens. A small nail file was hidden under the iPhone, which was apparent after she moved all the items around each other over and over again. Edward leaned over to study the items with her. He put the remote back on the table.

Nail file in hand, Lorene seemed at ease, slumping back and beginning on her left index finger with such intense concentration and vigor, Marcy assumed the dog meeting discussion had been forgotten, that the nails now took precedence and they would simply sip wine and do nails. She looked down at her nonexistent nails. There was no polish, and one finger's cuticles were dried and cracked in the corners. Her nails were weak, easily chipped, which made her think there was something seriously wrong with her health. Or maybe nails reflected stress and dog management. She remembered when she had manicures, polished her nails, wore tight pants with stilettos. Back when she was a real person with a real job, back when people actually bought books and before management investigated what an angry editor does in her spare time when mad at management and knowledgeable about hacking techniques.

"So, her tracking dogs look like they've been treated like dogs," Lorene said suddenly. "They're ratty looking, but well-trained." She stopped filing her nail and blew on it. "And this detective. What's her name?"

"Detective Serendon," Edward said.

"Yes, I knew that. Temporary blip that comes with the first sip of wine. That, mind you, I am drinking in the day only to keep you company. Keep you company so you are not drinking alone."

"How many people showed up for the walk through?" Marcy asked.

"I'd say there were maybe eleven, twelve. Mostly friends of Ellen. With all the publicity, there'll be more. There was one guy who read about it in the paper. Then me, who knew you. I didn't see you, Edward. You've only been to the organizing meetings, yes? I remember you at one. I couldn't make the one today."

"I'm in my idea stage, as you know. And, Marcy, I didn't tell anyone I knew you. As far as the table knew, I was a walk on."

"You can say you know me. What's wrong with knowing me?"

Lorene glanced at her quickly.

"They went around the picnic table and everyone was encouraged to introduce themselves and discuss their experience with rescue dogs. It was kind of fun," Edward said. "I said my first name. Didn't advise them like I did at the meeting you saw me at, Lorene."

"So, was Elizabeth Nelson there?" Marcy asked quickly.

"I'm not sure," Lorene said.

"Don't know names. Names of humans evade me," Edward said. "There was a dog there called Nellie, a compliant golden."

"Elizabeth Nelson was there then. The Windhaven Board of Education Chairperson. Short, chemically treated hair, conservative attire, probably black pants, and like a soft colored T-shirt of some sort."

"My sis, that is quite amazing. You would be a good FBI informer. Even the speculation of soft color was accurate."

Marcy slowly stood and walked to the kitchen, opened her lap top, checked mail. A few editing clients were there, one with a large attachment. More work, a good thing since she needed money.

"After the meeting, I got to knock on doors, ask people if they've seen Sam," Edward said to Lorene. "Then ask if I could put up the poster on their tree. We are forced to emphasize they are not to call the dog, nor chase the dog, only call the number on the poster."

Marcy scrolled through the potential job. She had to keep these odd editing jobs because she could never pay rent, utilities, and gas with just dog walking fees. She had to work on it right away. If they never found Sam, there was a chance the ill-will related to his loss would bleed into her business.

"Actually, I had a moment of dog study today and have some other ideas about catching Sam, having to do with how one plans escape. Escapes have a planning feature to them," Edward said. "I didn't go into barking recordings, as I suggested in the meeting I was in with you, Lorene."

Marcy looked up quickly. "You suggested barking?"

"It's OK. Not bad advice actually, and have you heard Edward imitate different dog barks?"

Marcy closed her lap top, hard, as if to stop conversation. Edward rose on cue.

"You don't have to go," Marcy said.

"I've got an appointment with Breaking News, actually. I just wondered by and thought I'd stop in, make sure you're OK, tell you about Aleppo. Lorene, Marcy can fill you in. Russia is making gains in Syria, changing the dynamics of our intervention, altering the Middle East."

"That is the last thing I want to do is keep you from your appointment, and don't worry," Marcy walked to her door and opened if for him, "I'll tell Lorene everything."

"Lorene," Edward said, stepping outside, turning his head only slightly. "I will not be at the cocktail meeting tonight, although I do like cocktails, beer cocktails, but not tonight. I attend day meetings for now. I think my sis will be attending, though."

The door closed, and Lorene looked back at her nails. "Getting involved in the hunt will make you feel better. Make you less guilty."

"I don't want to piss off yet another person whose angst could impact my business. If I lose all my dog contracts, I'd have to move back with Mom and Edward in Darlington."

"At least you have a family, a safety net under you."

Yes, but Marcy's mother wouldn't exactly welcome her into the household if it came to that. Marcy hadn't been an angelic teenager, and her college years were no better. And now, her mother's life with Edward was volatile, filled with unexpected hiccups—a wrecked car last month, a dead rabbit a few months before that. Edward hadn't meant to kill the pet. He never means to do anything. It simply happens. He rarely got into serious trouble.

"Life works out," Lorene said, as if knowing safety nets had holes in them when a sibling like Edward existed. "Edward's doing OK at the meetings I've attended, by the way. The barking was funny."

"OK. Whatever. I'll go. But I'm assuming I can go off on my own a bit, walk around the neighborhoods. No one has to know."

"OK, but check the website, at least get an idea of where he's been sighted." Lorene picked up the nail file again and filed vigorously.

"Yes, I've seen the page. And I've read all the articles. You know people beyond just our town, our state, are talking about it. My second cousin in Alabama read it online and called about it. He's a lawyer, so offered his services. He said the owner would probably sue so advised me to stay away from the entire thing, keep a very low profile. Not that that is the reason I'm staying out of it all."

"Sue? No one is going to sue. He's wrong. Start going to meetings. You'll meet people who may give you some business."

Marcy was now staring at Google Earth, studying the Nelson's neighborhood, where she had hiked with the dogs today. The woods behind their house abutted another large four lane avenue, which hopefully Sam avoided. To the north, about two miles north, a small creek slinked behind houses and street. She knew this was a piece of the Connecticut River, a small branch of it. It eventually emptied into a pond, which became another stream and emptied into another pond. Streams into ponds into streams until the water finally found the Long Island Sound. Once near the Sound, the water turned brackish, then salty and undrinkable. The further north, the fresher the water. The closer to the Sound, the saltier. So the best place to start would be northwest, toward the Connecticut River.

"We need the Hawking machine," Marcy said.

"The what?"

"Hawking was on the Charlie Rose show. I was watching it with the dogs right before the storm actually. The machine kind of reads his mind. Or his eyes. Or something. I really don't know how it does it, but it speaks for him. Amazing. Here is this crippled man, who looks shriveled and pitiful, but the machine talks and out comes funny comments, intelligent insight. If you took guesses at what he was thinking based upon his look, his expression, you wouldn't even come close. Not even close. I was thinking if we could have that for the dog, we'd hear thoughts we never dreamed of."

"I think there was a cartoon movie with a machine like that. The dog said things like squirrel, squirrel."

"Yeah, but that is a writer's idea. Writers always put themselves into everything. Some writer thought his dog was obsessed with squirrels because the writer was maybe obsessed with squirrels. It's called projection." Marcy sipped her wine. "Hey, why are you home anyway? It's too late for lunch, too early to quit for the day."

"I took the day off after a few claim adjusting visits. Everyone thinks I'm on a call."

Lorene put down her nail file and picked up her wine, took a sip, then exhaled loudly. A door slammed in the parking lot. Keys jangled as the footsteps arrived then faded. A robin chirped, a blue jay screeched. Most residents hung bird feeders on their patios. When an apartment complex bans dogs, people gravitate to other creatures.

Marcy said nothing, just sat with her and stared out the window, thinking about their disparate worlds. This forty-something woman she had passed every day without really knowing, although she knew her more than she knew most neighbors. Still, she wasn't her best friend, but now she was taking the time to stop by, drink wine, and just be with her. Marcy figured it had to do with her appearance—the lack of detail in her attire, un-manicured nails, wandering mind, all outward signs of a devolving state. Lorene was worried in the same way Marcy worried about her brother. Maybe this is how her brother felt when he stopped his meds and his persistent communications suddenly stopped and became something else that inspired Marcy to call, visit, ask too many questions.

It was nice to have someone reach out. But once that hand reached inside, it became a mirror, talking to you the way mirrors do. "This is who you are, so lost, we're all trying to find you." This made her think of Sam, out there, no hand reaching in. He was a dog, of course, so it was different. His thoughts were all survival and instinct and dog related.

Chapter 10

Sam
When corgi roams, corgi ponders

I AM TRYING to sleep in leaves, a situation not to my satisfaction, to say the least. I find myself cussing, and I usually do not like to cuss, but there is so much out in this world that causes me great trepidation. Like, for example, these leaves. I don't appreciate leaves covering me. And I don't appreciate bugs that live in the leaves.

There are times I wish I wasn't a midget. Times I wish I could see the world from a higher point of view. This is one of those times. All I see are trees, leaves, fecal matter, bugs, mice. Everywhere I look there is fecal matter and mice. The smells were interesting at first because they overcame my olfactory senses intermittently. Small zephyrs of scent. There, then gone. But now they overwhelm me.

I've been on the move too much to contemplate my appetite. I can barely run before being interrupted by yet another street filled with asshat cars, or asshat "stranger" humans trotting around, talking too much. Most of these "stranger" humans smell questionable. They do not smell bad, just questionable. I have had experience with "stranger" humans with questionable smells. They used to congregate at Mom's on occasion. I was shoved into rooms, into crates, told to hush, given really bad treats, forced to suffer through baby talk. So I understand enough to be fairly discriminating. As I have said before, the smell tells. There are humans and then there are humans, and then, there are sentient beings that only appear to be human, beings you simply do not want to become entangled with.

I wouldn't mind finding Bosslady. I suppose I would also appreciate seeing ole Mom, too, although the times with Mom were not the best of times. And not the worst of times. (Yes, I love Dickens! Mom watched his creations on TV a few times.) Anyway, there was always something about the mom, something I didn't quite trust. Hard to put my paw on it. But, now, Bosslady? She was a pretty decent character, albeit quite flawed. Bosslady, I noticed, was not at all straight up with her species. Certainly, if I were a human, I would have kept my eye on Bosslady. But I am not a human, I am a dog, and we forgive humans who are not quite straight up with their kind. As long as they are straight up with us. And Bosslady was straight up with us. She understood our unique ways. She was also progressive, introducing us to the homeless dogs, who, I will add, taught me many life skills critical in my current emergency of sorts. For example, Henry, who by the way was a pit bull—not that that means anything, mind you, as, again, I am not a bigot—told me that it was important to stay near water at all times. I instinctively understood this, but it was his anecdotes about problems he encountered when away from streams that brought it home. He also suggested we stay far away from the raccoons, something I believe I would have concluded early on in my adventure, anyway, but it was critical advice. Anyway, Bosslady's progressive world view allowed us to interact with these homeless creatures and learn from them. You need to see all types as individuals with varying assets and liabilities, because, Lord knows, one never knows when one is going to end up in the same shape one day. We all can end up homeless. All of us!

But enough of that. I cannot lie here always reflecting upon my past, my dilemma. It's a waste of time, and I do not have an extraordinary amount of time. Days pass fast, then I have to find shelter, like here amongst these leaves, where I am forced to sleep. Once I wake up, I have to trot back to water, then hunt down morsels of food.

Night is approaching and night is a difficult time. I am not nocturnal, and will not become nocturnal. I have to sleep, avoid raccoons who, like Henry said, are mean, talk in hisses, and think dogs are wimps. Nasty teeth and claws. I would have some claws too if the mom hadn't forced me to lie down whilst she used that horrid cutting machine.

I tuck myself in, stop all my thinking. But then I am thinking, well, ole boy, what will you do when you vacate these premises before dawn? Do you even remember where you are in relation to where you were? I can't lie still, so I leave the leaf-infested log and run around a while. I don't know why I do this, I just do. I keep the log in the center of my universe, which allows me to remain in the general vicinity of original designated sleep area. My leaf-filled log is by the creek, which connects to a pond, which leads to another small river, then the big water.

As I trot, now deep in the woods, my feet occasionally become tangled in underbrush, my thoughts drift once again. My mind leaves my body when I drift like this. I cannot stop the drifting and when I do it, I always end up lost again. It's quite frustrating. So, after this drifting and trotting, when my mind comes back to body, I realize, once again, my wandering has extended too far beyond my original log. I am now in a bad place, behind a big building with lots of cars. The building is in the general vicinity of the fast street. The cars are quite dangerous so I try to keep my distance. Raptors hang out on the poles, looming over everything like black angels. But, while this is a bad place, because of its close vicinity to the bad, fast cars, it has huge metal boxes in the back, some of which smell quite lovely. Donated food! They have donated food!

These metal donation crates are much larger than the buckets my mom rolled to the street. These are as big as twenty, thirty twenty dog crates. Every now and then a human walks out and dumps one of his small boxes into this big metal box. I am amazed at the plethora of donations—the incredible generosity of these humans in this location. And I cannot imagine rolling this donation box to the street.

I am so amazed at this metal donation box, I decide to hang around it for a day or two. Up until this moment I had forgotten about the donation buckets, and this discovery, as well as grumbles in my belly, have reminded me of the backup plan, which I forgot to ponder about. So I find a place in a bush nearby and ponder.

Here is what I think. Humans donate food, which is transported by trucks, like the ones I used to observe at the end of my old home's driveway. The donated food travels here and there, eventually landing in these larger containers, like the one near me. These containers do me no good, because I cannot reach the top.

While I think through this, something extraordinary happens.

A monstrosity arrives. It smells like dead leaves and rotten fruit. There is a bit of fecal matter in the air near the monstrosity as well. This metal monstrosity is similar to a truck, but it is immense and it has arms! Arms emerge from its ass and pick up the huge donation metal crate. It proceeds to pour all donated food, every morsel of it, into its ass. It's quite amazing. So remarkable! Then it drops the metal crate and takes off. And that is that!

So, I am assuming, this is not the final destination of donated food! There is yet another large donation center out there somewhere. So, I have to re-ponder my original pondering. So, I do this.

Here is what I now think, after re-pondering. Humans donate food, which is transported to other larger centers, where it is then picked up by these tremendous creatures with arms in their ass! These travel to God knows where until somewhere "chosen" humans arrange for distribution to humans in need.

The complexity of human food donation transportation system is beyond belief! And why? Why do humans transport donations here and there? It would seem easier to simply walk out to a street and hand out the food donations to the less fortunate humans. The donation system is so convoluted, one would think the humans would get tired of it all and simply throw food away. But no one in their right mind would do that! Oh, the thought! Dear Lord! No, they probably have a complicated donation system because hungry, less fortunate humans are complicated. Yes, that's it!

I ponder this over and over until the pondering—a soporific activity at night, mind you—results in sleep.

I WAKE UP early and leave, trotting back toward human homes, then up and down streets. I am in search of donation buckets. That is the key. I need to get to donations at their place of origin. I cannot handle huge metal donation crates, nor large monstrosities with arms in their asses, but I can tackle the small donation buckets. I see a few humans walking to their cars, a few walking with dogs, some running. But no donation buckets.

I am hungry. I am focused. I am determined. No more digression. No more wandering. I have a goal, a glimmer of hope. Donation buckets!

Chapter 11

Marcy
Collective action

FIND SAM! week 4

Facebook page: FIND SAM!
Total friends — 3. 1k

"Call, do not try to make contact. It's important to realize, the dog is now feral. Sorry we only give areas of sighting, not location. We have to watch out for those who wish to find the dog for nefarious reasons. . ." Detective Serendon

New Comments:
Lisbeth Elderack (picture of moon over ocean at night): *I was out in the park and saw what looked like a small nose peeking out of a log. I didn't do anything, just took a picture. If you look closely you can see the black nose. (picture of log with hole and small black furry object, possibly a rat). So excited to think the dog could have made it up here to Maine!*

Dottie Williams (picture of two toddlers in swim suits): *We are all pulling for y'all! On the look out down here in Mississippi. Dogs usually migrate south, y'all. Just like New Yorkers. haha.*

Henry (picture of pit bull standing on map of Russia): *All dogs are lost, even in our homes they are lost.*

Mary Johnson (selfie of young woman wearing shiny sunglasses) *Well, I certainly hope the dog walker is helping out. Anyone still hiring her? Sheez! Walking dogs in a storm.*

Twitter @FindSam
Followers 2.3k
#FindSam #WeloveSam #windhavenlovesSam
#hugyourdogforSam #dogwalkersfromhell

Excerpt for NYT regional article:
It's a mistake most of us would never make. A storm is coming, a particularly severe one with forecasts of hail and high winds. Windows are shuttered, patio furniture put away, cars tucked into garages, dogs safe inside, some in crates due to anxiety produced by thunder. But Marcy Thorpe, Windhaven's popular dogwalker, was out doing her job—walking her dogs. When the storm hit, Ms. Thorpe was at the local park, desperately trying to round up her dogs for a dangerous trip back to their homes. She did eventually make it to back to most homes, but she made it back without one owner's beloved corgi, Sam.

"I guess I lost track of time," said Marcy, a petite young woman with bright green eyes, tangled hair, and a wry expression that hinted at her rather defensive and sarcastic personality. Marcy and the now galvanized community spend hours and hours looking for Sam, organizing their efforts into what has become a social media phenomenon—the FindSam! movement . . .

MARCY SHUT HER lap top hard. "Defensive and sarcastic? What the fuck does that mean? My hair is tangled because they ran after me while walking dogs. Who doesn't have tangled hair when they walk dogs?"

She wished she hadn't said yes to Lorene about the Find Sam cocktail party tonight, but after the disastrous *New York Times* interview, in which she kind of lied about being involved with Find Sam (although she had planned to eventually get involved) she had to do something. Ellen had officially forgiven her, because she had suggested on a local radio show that she could never get mad at a dog walker who was simply doing her job. "Anger is a waste of energy." So, Ellen had to include Marcy due to a radio talk, and Marcy had to show up at meetings due to the *New York Times*. Thank you media!

Marcy had actually been doing her own private searching, which consisted of obsessive searches while driving her car in Elizabeth's neighborhood, obsessive studies of Google map, obsessive readings of Facebook posts and Twitter feeds, and obsessive Google searches of news articles about Sam or her. Her obsessive private searches led to obsessive fantasies—*there he would be, behind a large maple tree, anxious, a bit feral, but he'd see her and run, tongue out, eyes alert. She'd be the one to return him to Ellen, who would forgive her in earnest. Everyone would embrace her. She'd get more calls begging her to be the dog walker. Marcy Thorpe, the new brand of hero—guilty, complicated, redeemed.*

She had tried to find distractions that would ameliorate her obsession, but she still couldn't stop staring at maps, thinking, analyzing, searching. She rationalized it away. It was a grieving process, a guilt induced energy. Friends called, but she rarely spoke to them, preferring texts and emails over voices. She listened to their voicemails, imagining their faces with worried expressions, all feeling sorry for her. She could handle anger, but the pity bothered her.

She had figured Sam would show up by the third week, and then that week passed, and now here she was in the fourth week. The attention given to the Find Sam movement was not waning, it was growing. News outlets were still publicizing Sam's disappearance. Radio talk shows mentioned him almost daily. And the volunteer base had expanded beyond town acquaintances of Ellen. There were now about six different groups organized to hunt for Sam, each in different neighborhoods, a few forming in different towns. Marcy had joined Elizabeth Nelson's dog search sub group, a risk, but a calculated one. It covered the neighborhood where Marcy knew Sam disappeared.

Marcy did not look forward to the cocktail party, which included a lecture by Detective Serendon, but at least it would provide an opportunity to search for the memory stick, that is, if Elizabeth Nelson had not already discovered it. What would a journalist ask her about that? Then, there was the police officer whose memory was improving. *"The dog walker no longer looked wry, but tired, as if loaded down by her plethora of illegal activities, betrayals, and lies."* #criminaldogwalkerfromhell

The tap on the door was loud and persistent. Marcy took a breath and slowly stood. The tap came again, louder.

"Marcy?"

Lorene was fifteen minutes early. She stepped in as soon as Marcy opened the door, then leaned over and kissed her on the cheek quickly before heading to the kitchen. The refrigerator opened, a cork popped, the cabinet door opened. "You want a glass too?"

"No, I've got to appear professional and competent. Sober."

"I'm going to ask you something," Lorene said after her first sip of her half glass of wine. She sat down, put her foot on the coffee table.

"Is this like an opinion?"

"Do I have to first give you a category to introduce my question?" Lorene crossed her feet, as if she were going to stay for a while. "I realize this dog walking is a side job. You got projects and such you are working on. But you gotta want to get a steady paycheck. You gotta want to stop this dog stuff. Don't get me wrong. I love dogs. Love those strays. But when are you going to simply get a job? I can check around my insurance agency. You'd have to be trained to do what I do. Claims adjusting requires training, you know. But insurance companies can always use a good writer, editor. That would not really include too much training."

"Have you heard something at these meetings? Are you preparing me for clients laying me off?"

"You've really got to forget that. I doubt anyone cares anymore. In case you haven't noticed, the movement has become a force of its own."

Marcy looked down at her iPhone and didn't say anything. She was used to people wondering what someone like her, someone with a college education, was doing walking dogs.

"OK, I won't talk about it anymore. I get it. I get it. But if you want me to say anything, just let me know. Hell, life is tough enough living on our own, here in this shit apartment complex. I'm just saying. I know you love dogs but you truly may want to think on it."

"It's more than just wanting the time and loving dogs. Half the reason I'm not as dedicated as you about this group hunt for Sam is because I feel no one understands what a dog is thinking. I've wondered if we all underestimate dogs. We underestimate anything we do not fully understand." Marcy fell quiet a moment. "It's all guesswork. I think I get them. Kind of. Plus, whatever I do, they still forgive me." She looked down at her nails. She had meant to polish them, but forgot again. "But, look, thanks. For everything. I don't know why you're so good to me. I'm not a good person."

"I've lived a lot longer than you, sweetie. I've learned what good person means."

Marcy stood.

"Hey, by the way, there was a sighting three blocks from our apartment," Lorene said. The cigarette bobbed then fell to her lap. "It's like he's looking for you. You think Sam is looking for you? Maybe he smells you or something."

"No, it's probably a coincidence. He's roaming. Or they saw a fox, not Sam."

"He's only gone on your walking route, right? Seems he would try to find his own house, a place that is familiar to him."

Marcy looked down at her iPhone. She tapped his Facebook page, then the detective's map. Small red dots indicated Sam sightings. Of course, she had taken all the dogs to her apartment a few times. She had taken them to almost every house, or every house that had basements where their presence could be covered up. That would be most of the dogs. Could Sam have remembered where her apartment was?

"Marcy? You ever take the dogs to your apartment?"

"Sam is probably all over the place. A good thing. At least he's still in town. Lots of lost dogs roam to other towns, other states. Hell, I read many head south in the fall like migrating birds. It's why there are so many strays in places like Alabama."

"I just figured when they get sick of dogs in the South, they just let them go."

"You do know I was born in Alabama, don't you?"

"You're here aren't you?"

"Doesn't mean the South was a bad place. Well, not really. Once it was certain how Edward was turning out, we got the hell out of there. I was thirteen. Dad had already left a few years earlier. Mom spent months researching the best states for special needs kids. She read all these reports that graded states based upon funding and quality of care for the disabled. The entire southeastern corridor received either a D or F. So, we left. Just like that. Mom has always missed her friends, and she complains constantly about the cold personalities in New England. She loved the South."

"The South just didn't love boys like Edward."

"Well, no one does. There are just other regions that will pay to help him. The South wouldn't."

Lorene stood, drank the rest of the wine, placed it on the coffee table, and headed for the door. "I understand. You miss the South. You think we are colder, but spend the money. But I've always trusted money. Money flows where the heart goes."

"THERE SHE IS, my favorite dog walker. And, Lorene, nice to see you again." Elizabeth stood at the front door, raising her wine glass. When Elizabeth was entertaining, she wasn't just nice, she was effusive.

"How's Nellie?" Marcy said as she and Lorene stepped into the foyer. The house was one of those open construction designs, rooms demarcated by slight positioning of furniture. The living room area had been cleared and several aluminum chairs were lined up in front of a large projector screen.

"Missing you. You wore them out today," the voice chipper—no indication of hidden anger—inventoried, ready to come out at a later time, passive aggressive and viscous. No, this voice did not at all indicate the person speaking had found Marcy's hacked material on a memory stick. "I could tell. He's sleeping down in the basement. But I'm glad he was worn out, I got home late. Lots of Board meetings. I need him to sleep. Exciting news this evening,"

Elizabeth seemed intent on catching Marcy's roving eyes, but Marcy ignored her and looked over the crowed of dozens of women. In the distance, she could barely make out the door leading to the basement.

"Our wonderful detective has made progress."

Marcy looked back at Elizabeth.

"And, get this. Ellen, who, as you probably know is a public relations representative, is still out there getting little Sam national attention. NBC is planning to air a short segment on how the town has come together for this one dog. It's more about our Ellen and the town but it will get his name out there. We have a very famous dog."

Marcy moved her lips up in an attempt to at least display a mild body language alteration which would acknowledge agreement.

"Well, fame might help, I suppose," she finally said, then opened her mouth to add a mild caveat, but Elizabeth waved at a friend and excused herself, leaving them alone amongst a room full of well-dressed women who were excitedly contemplating fame. And possibly Sam, too.

Marcy hated fame. She had noticed that fame loved sin and regret, both of which she was full of, therefore, she tried not to think of fame, hoping it would go away soon.

The presentation began once everyone was seated. Detective Serendon was not wearing her usual cargo pants and tennis shoes, but instead black yoga pants with a loose flowing top. She stood, confident and in command, with Ellen, whose eyes skirted the room until they connected with Marcy's. She lifted a limp hand and waved, then, like an elementary principal, clapped her hands and nodded to someone in the back. The hall lights flickered twice.

After everyone was seated, Ellen began with a quick rundown on the progress made. There had been three verified sightings. Sam had looked healthy, according to the callers, and everyone calling in had followed the rules. Everyone clapped. Ellen emphasized she was very excited about Detective Serendon's work. The crowd's applause was loud and lasted a beat too long.

The detective waived.

"I am going to let our hero here"—More applause—"talk about the next step. But first I want to share great news on the PR front. Sam will be on NBC this Thursday night." Lots of applause and whoops. "I'm helping the crew put together a little PR segment about the town and Sam." The entire place thundered for a while. "Also, drum roll . . ." A pause for the crowd to chuckle. "Our Facebook page now has over three thousand friends. Visitors from all over the world. We even have a friend from Vietnam! I sure hope Sam isn't there." More applause. "I can't tell you how excited I am. We have started a Go Fund Me drive, and Elizabeth is working on a raffle, and we know how successful she had been raising money for so many benefits here in Connecticut. All this while she chairs our Board of Education."

Ellen droned on.

The detective was then called to the table. Debbie Serendon once again talked about her experience, her success rate, how she approached all projects. Then she put up the GPS map, the dog personality profile, the tracking locations, speculation on movement. "This work, as you see, is not really different from humans except for one thing. A dog is more predictable. A dog is a survivor and will go into a feral state quickly, meaning he will look for water, he will look for easy locations for food. What we want to do now, of course, is locate more feeding grounds for him. There has been some concern over our traps, so tonight I thought we'd discuss traps, how they work and how safe they are."

She leaned over and tapped the lap top. A large dog crate appeared on the screen. The crate had one door lifted in the air, which was of course the trap door. A chain hung down the side, attached to a hook. Once the chain was pulled the door fell down. The other end of the chain was attached to a plate at the far end of the long crate. Once a dog stepped on the plate, the chain was pulled, the door fell down. Smelly food was placed at the end of the crate, or trap, to encourage the dog to walk in, then the door slams down. A short video illustrated the capture.

After the video explanation, Debbie continued to talk a bit too long about the importance of not "being a hero. Let the professionals do the work." Questions followed. What food is put in the trap? Hotdogs. When is the trap set out? Early morning, or night, unless it appears the dog is roaming only at night, then they set up night cameras.

Marcy figured all Sam had to see was one wild animal go into the crate. One. That would do it for him. Lorene asked several questions, but Marcy slipped away to the foyer, then kitchen, then basement door. She slowly turned the doorknob until there was a slight click, then inched it open. The door squeaked, but the sound was covered by an eruption of laughter. Marcy clicked the door closed and was down the steps, three at a time. And there was Nellie all ready for a big fat bark.

"Hey, girl."

Nellie smelled her hand and started dancing and whining around Marcy's feet, then ran to her bed, crammed two balls in her mouth and brought them back. Marcy pulled a bully stick from her pocket and tossed it on Nellie's bed then flipped on the lights and hurried to the computer room. The table was cluttered—papers, bills, various gun and candy wrappers, an old coffee cup. Marcy didn't touch a thing, only looked around the papers, in the area behind the screen. She opened drawers. In the distance she could hear Nellie chewing. Then came thumping from upstairs, another roar of laughter, more thumping. Nellie's chewing stopped.

Marcy looked everywhere—under the desk, behind the computer screen, inside all drawers. The memory stick was nowhere. It had simply vanished.

Somewhere upstairs barking started up. Marcy wondered if that was Debbie's tracking dogs. Laughter again. More barking.

Marcy opened the file cabinet and looked the file marked "computer." Nothing. She knew she had left it on the keyboard. She remembered pulling Sam away from it. Just the thought of Sam made her realize what probably happened.

"Oh, shit, Sam!"

"Are you talking to yourself? And what the hell do you think you're doing?"

Lorene stood at the door, hands on her hips.

"You snuck up on me. Why'd you do that?"

"You're snooping in someone's computer room and you ask me why *I* snuck up on you?"

"I'm looking for a memory stick I left here a few days ago. No big deal."

"When did you leave a memory stick here?" Lorene stepped into the room and looked around the table. "So, you, what, come here to pick up the dog, but pause to work on your projects?" She picked up some papers.

"Don't pick up papers. She may recognize a disturbance. If we move anything we need to first take a picture then put everything exactly like it was."

"You seem to have this down to a fine art."

It occurred to Marcy the sound of chewing had stopped, the basement den was quiet and still. "Nellie?"

No whining, no tap of claws on floor, nothing.

"Nellie. Come here, girl."

Marcy ran into the basement den. Nothing. She noticed the open door at the top of the stairs. A voice moved closer to the door.

"She's so sweet. Hey girl. Oh, Elizabeth, leave her here, she's not bothering anyone."

"Lorene, you let the damn dog out," Marcy whispered.

"Hello?" Elizabeth peeked around the corner. "Marcy?"

Chapter 12

Marcy
When in doubt, rebel

"I'M SORRY, ELIZABETH," Lorene said quickly. "We just came to see the dog. I've never seen her. It's my fault. Love goldens. Marcy was just showing me how she picked him up each day. You know."

"Irene is supposed to meet you at the door with Nellie so you don't have to leave the other dogs outside. Is she not doing that?"

Marcy didn't look at Lorene. She flicked off the hall light and started up the stairs. "Oh, I meant when you guys were on vacation. Yes, Irene meets me at the door every day. Nellie is always ready to go. I'm sorry we let her out. Let me go get her."

"Oh, don't bother," Elizabeth said, following her. "Marcy, slow down, it's OK. She's lying down, not bothering anyone. Debbie's just brought out the trap. We're doing some more traps tomorrow. We got a lot of calls last week only a few streets down, near the Sound. Did you know that?"

"I saw the signs, but, no, I don't know details," Marcy said, pausing at an empty chair. Lorene was trying to catch Marcy's eye, but Marcy refused to look at her.

Elizabeth appeared confused but unconcerned, as if Marcy was someone to handle delicately now. Lorene continued to stare at Marcy.

"Well, I'll leave you two. Don't bother with Nellie. It's OK. Truly. I'm glad you visited her. Really."

Elizabeth hurried to the front of the room.

Debbie's strident voice was now saying something about her trap, which was in the front of the room, a volunteer inside, pushing down the panel.

"So, if a toy, or stuffed animal were near that door?" Debbie looked around the room, smiling, as if proud she had been proven correct. "See? The door would be jammed open. And it doesn't matter if you put the toy in the back, because a dog could easily sling it back in order to get at the food. So no pet toys in the trap. Got that?"

"Thank you, Debbie. You're amazing," said a participant sitting up front. "I would never think of this. Isn't she amazing?" All the women nodded in unison at the amazing detective.

"So, tie the toy to the back," Marcy said, loudly.

Debbie's smile disappeared.

"Tie it with something that belonged to the owner, like a torn sock," Marcy continued, looking around the room. "Dogs love smells and toys. And no raccoon is going to mess with a toy. Raccoons will eat all that food. I would also maybe put the owner's pajamas somewhere. You know, get that owner's smell in the cage."

"No. No toys, no smells. The dog is feral. The owner's smell could scare him. And"—Debbie Serendon smiled and leaned toward Marcy—"I'm sorry, I know we've met but I can't remember your name. I've met so many people."

"Marcy."

She squinted. "I also don't have my glasses. I don't know why I hate wearing them. I mean why be vain? I'm a dog catcher!" Everyone laughed. "Yes, Marcy. You're the one who walked the dogs."

"I lost Sam."

"No, you didn't. He ran away." Ellen looked at the other women, not Marcy.

"And that is something we have to not do," the detective said. "We have to not personalize any of this. We can't allow ourselves to feel so sorry for the dog, or guilty for what we did. It will make us act desperately. We do this methodically. We do this right. We catch the dog."

The audience fell quiet again contemplating this emotionless, yet dramatic adventure. Or maybe they were all contemplating the dog walker's guilt. Or the trap that did not look very inviting.

"So," Ellen started up again, softly. "I want to thank our wonderful detective for coming here to train all us future dog hunters. I will be sending out instructions to the teams, when, where to be. Marcy, you were out when we discussed the traps. We're putting up three more, one near here, another in the town of Norwich. We have three teams assigned to the new traps. We put you and your neighbor on the Waveny Street trap at the Johnson's house, over by the Sound. Lola Johnson said she saw him in the back, swimming. She said he acted like he owned the place. Just jumped right off the dock into the water, swam around a while and came out on the bank, like he had been there before." She stared at Marcy.

"So, it's time to go. You and I, like in the car," Lorene whispered. "And, sweetie," she leaned into Marcy, "you got some splaining to do."

"DO YOU THINK I'm just going to let this go?" Lorene said after Marcy had quietly driven for a few moments. "I bet you do. You think, well, I'll just change the subject and Lorene will forget I lied about that memory stick." She opened her purse, retrieved a small brush, and pulled it quickly through her hair. Next came the lipstick, which she applied after pulling down the visor and flipping on the mirror light. "You didn't leave your memory stick at that house this week. And you're welcome, for covering your ass. I've lived by you about two years now and while we've talked, even had dinner on a few occasions, I now realize I don't really know you. I guess I'll be getting to know you now with all this dog hunting. But, I'm not going to let you just keep this secret. It's only fair you let me in on what the hell you were doing sneaking through the Nelson's computer room. Don't you agree?"

"OK. I left the memory stick there the day of the storm. I don't know why I told you this week."

"The day Sam disappeared?"

"Well, it's like this. It started out with this project that I had to complete and some of the houses were always vacated, and Elizabeth's was particularly nice. This was back before the housekeeper started working mornings. She used to work afternoons, and since I walked the dogs in the morning, I had the house. So I brought work to do. It's a great place for the dogs to lounge. So, I don't know. I got bored. And sloppy."

"I don't think I want to hear this. What, you threw a party? Had a boyfriend over?"

"No. No. Never that. Well, not never. I did have sex with my ex at Ellen's house. So Sam has seen me in a certain way. A feral way."

"This is too much. Is this Chris? I thought you guys were just friends."

"Our generation views friendship differently."

"So what the hell did you do at Elizabeth Nelson's house when you got bored?"

Marcy had only one glass of wine, not enough to spill her life. It usually took that third glass for the usual verbal spillage, but when life turned terrifying, she sometimes divulged bits of herself. Lorene had been such a good neighbor, and now a good friend. And besides, if Lorene was going to help her find Sam, they would become more intimate, which meant flaws were on the table for discovery. If someone was going to discover basic flaws, one of which was dishonesty, it was best the discovery occurred early in the relationship. That includes all relationships. Hiding certain egregious flaws was the reason for Marcy's elimination from the publishing house payrolls.

"I kind of downloaded something of Elizabeth's. No big deal. Don't make that face. It's a boring job sometimes. And there you are in someone's house, all alone. The computer's on and so what the hell, you bring your memory stick and work a bit while the dogs rest or gnaw on their bully sticks. Then you see some interesting things, and you are an editor—you spend your life correcting, nicking this or that, trimming here, rewording there. So that is what you do. And, well, I'm so used to writing comments. Of course, when I worked in publishing, I made comments a wee more professional. I never said what I said on the memoir. I never typed in the margin, "This sucks so bad a trash can would reject it."

"You downloaded her memoir to your memory stick? You did that? And then you go and make insulting comments all over her personal, intimate life?"

"I just wanted to read it. I don't like her, so maybe I kept her personal crap on my memory stick because it gave me power. Oh for fucks sake forget that one. I don't know why I wanted it. I admit, I'm not exactly perfect."

"You want to talk imperfection, let's talk divorced three times. And I stalked my first ex. Stalked him. That's imperfection. Downloading personal data is something else. I don't know what, but it's illegal."

"Yeah, I know. You can drop out of the dog hunt and we can kind of just go on being acquaintances. I'm ashamed of myself."

Lorene cracked the window and lit a cigarette. "Don't say a fucking word to me about smoking. I get to smoke after this."

"Can you roll down the window a bit more?"

"No. Deal with it." Lorene's cheeks sank and the cigarette's tip brightened. She inhaled and leaned her head back. The smoke streamed out of both nostrils. "I'm not dropping out. I'm into this movement. I may even volunteer to hunt other dogs. I like this. It's not something I'm doing because I feel sorry for Ellen. She could buy an entire litter of corgies. I do, or did, feel sorry for you because you lost the dog. And Edward. I do admire how you take responsibility for him. I like the guy. Very lost and challenged. But interesting. Anyway, I thought your extreme guilt always had to do with that poor sweetheart out there alone and wet, scared. But now I know."

"I love Sam, and I do feel guilty he got away. I'm not evil, just dumb. And, OK, a little on the curious side. I think I lost Sam when I was putting them all in my car. And the woods back right up to the Nelson's house."

"You lost him at the Nelsons? You mean we all think the dog was lost on Battle Street by Bradly Park, and you lost him here?"

"I didn't want them to know I was there. There was an incident." She stopped talking.

Lorene groaned.

"It's a long story, and I am not getting into it. Sam isn't anywhere near here anymore. The sightings have been all over the place."

"Shit." Lorene took another long pull. Ashes flickered onto her lap and she brushed them off. "Well, the Johnson's house was a sighting. That isn't too far. He'll probably make his way back to the Nelsons."

Marcy made a quick turn into a driveway, backed up, then headed in the opposite direction.

"Where are you heading, back to the party?"

THE JOHNSONS LIVED on the Sound side of the street, but a bit further west from the Nelson's. It was in a neighborhood framed by large hedges and stone walls. It was unusual that an elite family like the

Johnsons would approve of a trap on their property. But the town was anxious to help, and Ellen had a certain pull with the community due to her connections with local town officials and celebrities. Everyone wanted a potential spot in some upcoming news segment. And there was a chance, if Sam continued to outsmart the detective, that famous people would come to their town for benefits to raise money for Sam and rescue operations.

After they passed the Johnson's estate, Marcy pulled over and parked on the street. She turned off the engine and stared at the hedges, as if waiting for Sam to stick his nose out from under them. She thought back on what the detective said about the Johnson's spotting a dog swimming in the water, as if comfortable with the activity. Did he remember Marcy taking all the dogs swimming in the Sound?

"Marcy? We're just going to sit here?"

Marcy didn't say anything, just kept staring into space.

"Look, I think I can overlook this one thing. You're an editor, you saw a story, your instinct kicked in. I'm the same way. I see a car accident and have an urge to pull over, look at the damage, and speculate about the claim. We can't help what our bosses have made us. The human mind is a strange thing. I've seen some weird minds in my job."

Marcy smiled but said nothing. She didn't snoop around only one client. Sam's owner, Ellen, owned two houses—one in Windhaven, CT, one in Cayman Islands. They paid hardly any taxes. The tax returns were not even stored in a password protected file on the computer. They were simply in the folder titled taxes. There was a password file—saved in a folder marked p-ssw-rd. And Margaret Wilder, the lab owner, tried to off herself four years back. One would think after that she would get rid of opiates. But nope, besides Benzos, she had Vicadin all over the place. The Rigardos both enjoyed porn, sometimes gay porn.

"Well, thanks," Marcy finally said as she cracked her window. The smoke was suffocating.

After one last drag, Lorene flicked her butt out the window.

"I'm kind of regretting that instinct. I was just curious, then it got to be this thing, like a hobby. I need to kick the habit. I think Sam may have the memory stick. God knows what he did with it. Maybe I'll be safe."

"Why would a dog take a memory stick? It's small and metallic tasting. I think it's probably there."

"I remember him there, sniffing at it, trying to paw it. It's the last thing I instinctively remember about Sam. Him trying to take the memory stick off the table. He probably thought there was a biscuit inside it. I have a little biscuit box I carry for treats. It's metal too. I don't know."

"Where do you think he put it? In the house? And I really don't think we should be sitting here."

Marcy opened the door and stood a moment, mainly to let the noxious smoke out. "Let's just walk a bit. I don't think the Johnsons would mind me wanting to check out where the new trap will be set, although hedges this big make the estate look like a fortress."

"Nope. This is stupid. You're obsessed. You also are not following the group's rules."

Marcy ignored her and walked down the street, dimly lit by a clear, effervescent sky and occasional lights of distant cars traveling on intersecting roads. Marcy stopped after about ten minutes and shouted, "Sam. It's me, boy. Come. Stop this right now. Come boy. I got treats!"

"Shush. We're not supposed to do that," Lorene said, now by her side. "This is not a good idea."

Far in the distance, way down past the Johnson's house, about five houses down, Marcy could make out a faint sound—a shuffling of leaves. Marcy left Lorene and trotted over to the driveway. Lorene called her, but Marcy held up her hand. Another rustle somewhere far off. She couldn't tell where it was coming from, which house. It was distinctly coming from near the Sound. She ran down the stamped driveway, which curved in a long "S" down a steep hill toward the Sound. The house came into view—a Tudor with a few parapets and mock masonry veneer. The backyard was greensward that slid into the ocean. Lorene called out to her again, but Marcy ignored her again. A car turned down the street, its headlights casting streams of light down the asphalt road, highlighting the yellow center line and Lorene, now frozen at the end of the drive. The car pulled over quickly, the lights went off, the door opened, someone with a flashlight stepped out and slammed the door. The flashlight moved down the driveway landing on Lorene, then Marcy, now fifty yards down the drive .

"Is that you, Marcy?" Debbie Serendon yelled. "Hello? What the hell are you doing?"

Chapter 13

Sam
The sound of humans?

THE SIGNATURES IDENTIFIED by the olfactory senses are always accurate. My vision is fairly decent, although devoid of a few colors on the spectrum. My hearing is superb—my discrimination of tone, inflection are fairly accurate, albeit not perfect, mind you. But I can detect a human with my nose with a high degree of accuracy.

So, let me inform you that, indeed, Bosslady was attempting to alert me. No question, she was calling me in her alarmingly high volume. Bosslady yells. It's her specialty. There were also pungent scents—sour, salty. Human anxiety is quite odorous. I was a bit confused about the significance of my name released into the air in such a manner, accompanied by anxiety smells.

Now, however, as I peek around the edges of a rather thick tree, I can barely detect the outline of the female "chosen" one, who has been roaming with dogs, obviously in search of something, or someone, which I presume could be me. I do not trust this "chosen one" or her dogs, and here she is—talking to Bosslady. Their voices grow, then I hear another voice. My mom? Too far away to get a good view, but yes, indeed, I do believe it is most assuredly Mom.

So, here we have it. The strange "chosen one" with the asshat dogs. Bosslady. Mom. Bosslady is talking a bit obstreperously to this woman with asshat dogs. This is what Bosslady does. She is impertinent and sassy, she stands up to authority. It's why we all love her. Mom now starts up in her rat tat tat way to Bosslady. Mom is mad at Bosslady and when Mom is mad she talks rat tat tat. No yelling, but firm, controlled. Humans refer to this behavior as professional.

I hear my name mentioned in all the sea of voices rising out of an area filled with disturbing scents, which makes me aware that I am the central cause of negative emotions. Everyone must now be disgusted with my behavior, even Bosslady—which I admit puts me in a rather lugubrious state of mind.

I do not stick around, not with an angry mob of humans, now with a "chosen" human, obviously here to arrest me, take me to dog jail. I head back to the underbrush, then off to the water.

As I trot away, I regard the fading rise and fall of voices. This causes me to ponder the all too familiar ebb and flow of humanity that tends to swallow the canine world with its occasional turbulence.

Chapter 14

Marcy
Hope surpasses guilt

DEBBIE SERENDON TROTTED down the road and driveway. Another car door opened and closed. Marcy could make out Lorene talking with someone who spoke in sharp, quick words, as if ordering Lorene to do something. Ellen.

"Look." Detective Serendon now stood in front of Marcy. She pointed her flashlight at the ground. "Do you really think you're going to trespass on other people's yards and find anything beyond a very annoyed police officer? And some people do have guns in their houses for protection. You could get accidentally shot. Plus, and let me be very clear about this, I know what I am talking about, Marcy. You will never find a dog by calling him."

The voices in the distance ceased. Lorene and Ellen slowly approached them.

"How do you know I called him?"

"Someone alerted us." Debbie assumed a stance of a police officer making an arrest. She waited for Marcy to reply. Marcy did not. "A call was put in to Ellen who contacted me. They said there was someone wandering around."

"If he is in the area? You may have ruined his capture," Ellen said, balancing on her high heeled sandals and holding her iPhone up to light the immediate area. "This is unacceptable, Marcy. I know you feel guilty but it does not good to make things worse. You're a dog walker. You're not even a dog trainer."

"I can train a dog. I've been to dog training school."

"She's really good with dogs," Lorene said. She reached inside her front pocket, pulled out a packet of cigarettes, shook one out, and placed it in her mouth. "Oh great, I don't have a match. And I'm sure you two don't have one."

"I know. I know," Marcy said, looking only at the detective. "He's feral. Sam is a feral dog now. So, OK. But here's the thing—Sam knows I get along with feral. He knows I can handle feral."

Lorene rolled her eyes and looked away.

"You can handle feral?" the detective said.

"Marcy has a problem anthropomorphizing," Lorene said quickly. "I'm her neighbor. I'm in her area team. We will of course work together. She's great with dogs. Great. I'll make sure she understands this."

"You will only succeed in scaring him. Have you ever dealt with a truly feral dog?"

"Not your kind of feral."

"You know, it's late and we have got to get going," Lorene said. "We just wanted to see the neighborhood where Sam was recently seen."

"Marcy, look," Ellen said as they all turned and walked down the drive back to the cars. "You may feel that because you lost the dog, it's important you find him, but this is not the way it works. Either follow the rules or don't get involved. Do you understand? You're a dog walker. You know the importance of rules right? You follow them all the time."

"Yes, she does," Lorene said, linking her arm with Marcy. "And we are going to follow all your rules right now. It was a momentary brain blip. A temporary loss of reason. Right, Marcy? Never to happen again."

After they were back in the car, Marcy opened her mouth to say something, but Lorene held up her hand. "Just drive. You heard the damn detective. The dog is not going to come to you. And do not go telling anyone about Henry being a stray. They may take him away. You didn't go through the proper channels on that dog. Knowing this detective, she'll take him to the nearest shelter. What a night." She cracked the window again. "Now, I'm going to smoke my cigarette and you're going to drive home and stop thinking about Sam. He's OK. Probably asleep right now, under some bush or shed far from here."

Chapter 15

Sam
Freedom can mean steak!

WHEN I WAKE up and trot down the first street in my peripheral vision, the sight fills me with immense relief, which, mind you, feels the same as a rub on the underbelly, a tickle under the chin, slight (very slight) kiss upon the nose. I am a rich dog! I no longer need to steal sandwiches near a bench, nibble upon the occasional cat dinner left out due to negligence of human cat owners and oblivious attitude of strange cat. I have something before me that guarantees my survival! Donation buckets! Lined up down the street, like blocks of gold. Precious donation buckets!

I pounce on the first one and it easily falls over, its top remaining closed. Opening it is not a problem. Pulling out the white bags, which are easy to penetrate, is not a problem. And what falls out of the white bag, you may ask? Steak! Yes, let me repeat. My first donation bucket contains remnants of steak! Jack pot, indeed!

I eat so much I have to find a log and sleep. I wake up and stare off into space, pondering my discovery. Then I ponder my observations the night before, the strange human behavior exhibited when my name was mentioned. Obviously, my departure and subsequent occasional pilfering from school children—OK, I stole sandwiches from children at school—has concerned everyone to such an extent they have brought in "chosen" humans who catch dogs. I suppose Bosslady is simply trying to survive in this free market world. She does not want to ruin her reputation, so she probably has agreed to capture me, toss me in jail. I fear she is also annoyed because I have become one more item to add to her long "to do" list—1. play with metal stick 2. sneak around human abodes looking at their square machines. 3. tap on big machines

4. walk down street with dogs—once in a while—and now 5. hunt down Sam for jail time. And Mom is quite the busy human as well. Her business was removed from me most of the day, so I could not observe and form opinions about her exact activity, but even at night she appeared distracted, preoccupied. She always had to find ways to feed me when she was preoccupied or away—which was quite often. So now she will have to add me to her list of to dos in a busy life. I assume, she also must ameliorate tensions that have obviously developed with the community over my theft of a few sandwiches (yes, a few, OK?) from the baby humans. (They were peanut butter! My favorite!).

I complete my pondering moment and conclude that avoidance of all humans is a necessary path for me at the moment. I also have to limit pondering moments, like this, and attempt to concentrate the ole mind, stay on the moment, because I am now in the free market world, too, if you will, and, unlike my previous socialist (again, I listened to Mom's debates) existence, this world has responsibilities.

Freedom is scary. Freedom is insecure. Freedom is work. But freedom is also the possibility of steak!

Chapter 16

Marcy
Perspective

FIND SAM! week 6

Facebook page: FIND SAM!
Total friends 6.8k

We have 6 traps set up. We also have a lot of raccoons. We think the dog needs to be a bit hungrier in order to make that vital decision to enter our trap. So, again, please no feeding the dog....Detective Serendon

New Comments:
Max (picture of Wheaten) *Ruff Ruff Ruff... Mommy says that means I miss you Sam. Come back ! Hey there is food in that trap. Go inside! Saw your picture on The View this week! So exciting!*

Saidie (picture of English bulldog sitting in wagon) *Sam, aren't you hungry? There is food in that cage. Your mommy was on the Today Show this week! She looked great. We love the detective looking for you. She was on the show too! Come back!*

Joe Raridon (picture of a gun): *You need a hunter to work on the team. I am an expert deer hunter. No real difference hunting game and hunting dog. We don't shoot the pooch with bullets. We dart the little guy. Poison darts. Put him right out. Call me. My information is on my page.*

Henry (picture of pit bull sitting on map of Russia) *We are all part of a dying planet controlled by humans. We do not know ourselves and we certainly do not know you. We need you. Please come back. (and the corner of Harrison and Leroy, has great garbage! Go there!)*

Mary Johnson (selfie of young brunette women in bathing suit, no sunglasses.) *So, seems the dog may be gone for good. How long has it been anyway? Are you, like, suing that dog walker? I would. I'd sue her.*

Twitter: @FindSam
Followers: 25.1k

#FindSam,#WeloveSam, #windhavenlovesSam #hugyourdogforSam #dogwalkersfromhell #corgipuppiesforsale #fireSamdogwalker #betterdogwalkersforwindhaven

Excerpt from CNN video clip:
—*Excuse me. Excuse me. Lorrie Tellmore, CNN? I know you're busy walking all your dogs but can I have a word with you?*
—*Ok. But just a minute.*
—*You certainly walk a lot of dogs. How many dogs do you walk*
—*I walk 4 -5 dogs*
—*I counted 8?*
—*5*
—*8?*
—*Are there any other questions?*
—*How do you feel about this dog you lost? How does it feel to walk dogs everyday knowing you are responsible for this owner's heart break. Do you feel guilty?*

MARCY TAPPED THE iPad on/off button with fury, its screen went black. She closed her eyes, breathed for a moment, but she could still see her face, hair dancing around her forehead, T-shirt torn slightly at the collar, dogs barking behind her, desperately trying to maintain control so she wouldn't knock out the reporter. She turned her ignition key and the car went silent, but she sat a while before stepping out.

She lightly knocked on the door. Nothing. Again. Nothing. She took out her key and very gently inserted it, turned the door knob, and stepped inside. Her mom's den was small but only two lived there, not counting the dog, so it was manageable. Or should have been manageable. The shelf contained a few hard cover books, memorabilia, and pictures—Marcy slumping in the back row of soccer team pictures; Marcy receiving her honors English award; Marcy graduating—a sardonic smile on her face. And then there was a shelf set aside for Edward—his gaming team, soccer team, a few team members in wheel chairs, his graduation—smiling, unruly hair, fists raised, as if to say, "free, free, free at last." But of course Edward would never be free.

Henry jumped up, wagging his tail, as if she were here just for him. She spent a moment massaging his neck, scratching behind his ears.

"Where's Edward, boy? Edward?" Marcy whispered. She could hear a fan in the back bedroom and nothing else but Henry's soft whining. "Edward, you up?"

She didn't want to wake her mother who worked as a receptionist at the library and a part-time aide for the disabled at the YMCA daycare program. She slept late on Saturdays.

Marcy walked carefully down the carpeted hall and stood before Edward's door, then placed her lips up next to the small crack where door met casing. "I am going to leave in five seconds, Edward. Did you forget our trap responsibilities? We have to set up a dog trap. Edward? You up?"

The door opened and Edward stood before her, unwashed, clothed in sloppy gym shorts and a T-Shirt—on backwards, its tag sticking up. He held old tennis shoes in his hands. "Early, sis. Too early. Not even dogs roam this early on Saturday. There is no garbage out on Saturday."

"Who cares when the garbage is taken out? We are checking a trap by the Sound today. It has to be done before seven for some reason. Put the shoes on in the car. Or, wait, just do it here."

"I have to get a donut. I need a donut before meds. Skipped them yesterday because we're low. And I forgot to refill my dispenser. I need another script. Fuck it all." His voice began to rise. "Fuck it all. I am not doing this anymore. No more."

"No more what? Look, just give it a rest. I'll look into everything. Don't wake Mom."

"I'll just take whatever is in the med cabinet. Just give me anything."

Marcy stepped into the kitchen, trying to ignore the pots in the sink, crumbs on the counters, cabinet doors open. It had always been this way. There had never been a clean kitchen in the morning during her childhood. Life growing up was chaotic and messy, but somehow she had managed to turn into a neat, clean person who liked dogs. Of course she had other issues unrelated to messiness. She opened the door and checked the pill dispenser, which was empty. The prescription bottles filled one shelf of the cabinet, most empty, all different dates, different RX numbers. Her mother had given up keeping track of all of it. Marcy had finally obtained a power of attorney and signed release forms allowing her to take care of Edward's meds. She gave up on social services. Technically, Edward qualified for mental health assistance, but the state budget was a mess and he was on some waiting list, which her mother said would exist forever. And if you said one thing to social security, they started asking if Edward had a job yet and then started in on lectures about making sure to report income, as if you were lying if you said no.

Deep in the back of the shelf, was a bottle of his anti-psychotic medication—the most important drug. It contained two pills. Two precious pills. And there seemed to be no refill.

"Edward, when is your next psychiatrist appointment."

"Last week. I missed it. Had to stay home. Special report, breaking news. Chemical weapons in Aleppo. Bad bad stuff happening in Aleppo."

"You skipped the doctor to watch CNN?"

"Breaking news."

"They always have breaking news. They never had normal news. Look, the doctor warned you he couldn't deal with this anymore. It took me six months to find this doctor, six months."

Edward had put the wrong shoes on each foot, which he noticed. He sat down again, now frustrated, which, when meds were low, created anxiety, which led to physical reactions, like throwing shoes at lamps. Which was what he did. Marcy ran to the lamp in time to grab it as it wobbled to the right. Henry ran into Edward's room. She heard him crawling under the bed.

Marcy opened the refrigerator, its food bins even messier than the counters, and grabbed a Dunkin Donut bag. The donuts were hard but still free of mold. Edward didn't seem to mind. He broke one in half, shoved the entire half into his mouth. There was one more pill on his med list, an anticonvulsant, but the bottle was nowhere to be found. There was a full bottle of Ativan, which was to be used only in emergencies, but Marcy figured this was a quasi emergency. She put an Ativan on the counter next to the anti-psychotic. Edward tossed both pills in his mouth and swallowed as he ate, then walked to the door, shoes still in his hands.

"Don't worry, sis. I don't need this stuff anymore, anyway," he said, opening the door quickly, causing a loud screech. Marcy's mother's voice rose behind the hallway wall, a muffled sound that indicated her presence was imminent. "And I never lost my shit on the job, you know. Benzos are not needed, but whatever."

Marcy didn't respond. Edward had held a job once. Costco. He was there one week. He couldn't find pickles for a customer, so he retrieved a ladder and proceeded to climb to the top of a large shelf filled with boxes and boxes of various condiments. But once on top of the ladder, he stopped looking for a pickle box. Instead, he looked out over the store and proceeded to lecture everyone, in a loud voice, about the sins of excess.

But, no, he had not really lost his shit. So he was right about that.

"Marcy!" Her mother was now opening her bedroom door.

"Gotta go, Mom." She closed the door, grabbed her brother's hand, and ran to the car.

PUTTING THE TRAP together took about thirty-five minutes. Ten of the minutes involved arguing with Edward about the psychology of dogs and why the trap was poorly constructed. Another five minutes involved undoing what Edward did, which was screw the door in upside down. It took another five minutes to find the screws Edward tossed after realizing he screwed the door in upside down. She placed the night camera on a tree opposite the trap. The camera was supposed to capture detailed pictures of the corgi sniffing around the area, then entering the trap, which had trails of hotdogs and fried chicken neatly placed, six inches apart, pointing nicely at a pile of hotdogs on a plate that was set to trigger the door collapse if depressed with a weight greater than twenty pounds. Of course, this would work if Sam kept his normal weight. If he lost weight, below twenty pounds, it would not work. A lower weight limit would unfortunately allow other animals to be entrapped, like raccoons. Once the camera was turned on, the team could watch from home. Marcy let Edward put the food in, because it made him feel important. He took the hotdog, smelled it, stared at the trap, then took ten, exactly ten, steps back. He got on all his hands and knees and circled the cage twice. He then closed his eyes for a long time. His body swayed. Marcy didn't ask why he did this, she simply stood and watched. Slowly he put the food near the door, then on the floor, spaced apart from each other by precisely the length of his index finger. He walked into the trap and placed the final plate of food on the trap plate at the far end. After he was finished, he slowly emerged from the trap and stood silently, shaking his head.

"So, this is OK. In that it calms the masses, sis. The trap calms everyone. It's like Syria. We need to look like we at least care, so we send in a few bombers, the Red Cross. But it's not effective. See . . ." He raised his palm knowing this would be the time Marcy would interrupt, move him forward. And he was right. "I've been thinking about that dog, like where it would end up? Would it go inside a crate? If I were a dog, and out of place, I would go back to my knowledge base. Like I have said before, Marcy, all lost animals study behavior of those around them.

"See, dogs, sister, have always been lost because they have been forced to live in a world that is not like them. I think dogs kind of drift without being lost, you know. Drift. So, I've been thinking, what would be the most important thing to study when you have to live in the world where everyone is not like you? And then what do you do with it? It becomes like gravity. It's like in the stars at night. Like if you think about the stars, look at them, there is gravitational pull, and this is the same pull with all animals. I don't know how it works exactly but we may use those stars. But that is not really the point. The point is that the dogs were already lost before they are actually lost. How they survive depends upon how well they studied us humans while they were in the lost state of living with us. I know you are thinking, how does Edward get this? How does he know what an animal, unlike animals he lives with, thinks? How do I know why this lonely animal wanders?"

Marcy touched his arm.

"And don't worry, sis," Edward continued, "about losing someone's dog. They think you're irresponsible, you couldn't keep your mind on things. They'll say you cannot work for us anymore, because you cannot get those thoughts reeled in, so they'll say we can't control you. But, sis, they don't know you. Just say to yourself. They don't know me."

"No, they don't. They don't know us, Edward."

"Same with dogs, sis. No one gets dogs . . ."

"Or you, Edward."

"Yes. I guess. And me. Yes. But, anyway, sis, videos are fun. We at least get to watch whatever these cameras capture. Wild animals are interesting."

Chapter 17

Sam
Human donations

TODAY IS A nice one, sunny, a slight zephyr, lots of robins out and about. I like to lie on my back on days like today, contemplate my existence, my place in the world. I am allowing myself the luxury of these pondering moments again. You see, I have done it. I am a rich dog. And when you are rich, pondering can begin again! Yes, it took time. Yes, it was an involved complicated process. But I have mapped out the donation schedule and am assured a steady stream of food. For Life! I'm set.

After I found one donation street, I roamed toward the large water on a hunch and sure enough, the next day, I stumbled across another street with buckets all lined up like sentinels. Easy to knock over, easy to open, all filled with lovely old food. I slept on the street and wandered the next day, and there was another street with donation buckets. I did this for a week and realized a pattern, trucks coming down different streets different days. In order to understand it, though, I had to use human day organization, which I developed back in my socialist days.

Here is how this human day organization works. Every five days, humans take time off—they sleep late, ignore the rising sun, refuse to emerge from their home and drive to where ever humans drive on the other days. I call these days human lethargy days. That has always centered me. I mark days in relation to these human lethargy days. So, the first day following the two day human lethargy period is called first day. The next day, second day, and so on.

So that is how I mapped out the donation schedule. I have noted certain homes as markers and studied their car patterns to determine lethargy days. And here is my schedule: The first day donation pickup is in a human living areas far away from the big water. Then, on second day, in an area a few miles closer to big water, buckets appear, all lined up down streets. The third day, buckets reappear in yet another area even closer to big water. And so on, until the last day, fifth day, which is today.

I believe the human donation transportation systems is quite cumbersome and rather odd. One would think the humans would simply pick up all donations on the same day. I pondered this for quite a while and came up with reasons they organized donations this way. This is what I think. I suspect humans have more donations than their limited supply of trucks can handle, so they have worked out this rather complicated system to more efficiently utilize limited vehicles. Of course, there are countless vehicles on roads every day. One would think the humans could borrow some of these vehicles to pick up donations at least one day—which would eliminate all these donation buckets in various areas at various times. But humans do not like to share. This is something quite apparent to all dogs who live with them. Sharing is a painful experience for humans. They do it, of course, as we can see, what with all the donation buckets. But it is painful for them and only done with items they no longer desire. They only donate what they do not want, rarely share items they desire.

So, that is what I have figured out during yet another pondering episode, here, under a tree, full of food. I am happy. I do of course miss my friends, particularly the homeless dog, Henry. He had great dog stories. Quite the storyteller, that ole chap. "Dude, I know what they do in dog jails," he said to me once. Homeless talk like this. Dude and such. It's their nature. "Fucking genocide. They take the bros down the hall and bring them back in bags. No shitting you."

The thought that out there are jails that engage in genocide terrifies me. Nellie suspected Henry told fiction for attention. Fiction, if properly delivered, does garner attention. But I trust Henry. The man has been around the block, understands the true nature of the universe, if you will. He also accepts the Bosslady, and accepting flawed humans says something good about a dog. I admit I do miss the ole Bosslady. Mom? Not so much. She was a decent sort, and I certainly enjoyed the comforts of her large home, and I do miss having a designated Mom (which, mind you, I know is simply a designation. She is not my real mom. I am *not* a golden, I am a corgi, I get reality.) But, Mom rarely tossed me treats. She seemed to appreciate emaciated dogs. I assumed she wanted her friends to think of her as a competent owner and competent owners starved dogs. They don't fully appreciate our different perspective. In our world, obesity is honored and indicates a special social status. The more weight on a dog, the higher up the social ladder the creature has climbed. Sadie, the bulldog, for example, was quite obese and always full of food, which was why we all assumed she rode in the dog limo the Bosslady pulled. We resented Sadie, but we honored her, for she had mastered the art of food consumption in the socialist world. I am hopeful my belly will expand into that honorable state.

Chapter 18

Marcy
Ah, the joy of being known!

MARCY PICKED UP her dogs for the morning walk. Sam had been replaced by a French bulldog, Sweetiepie, who didn't like most of the dogs, particularly the English bulldog. So, Marcy had to allocate more training time. This had always been her big selling point. The training was free. She guaranteed compliance with her walking routines. It had taken a week to sensitize Sweetiepie to the routine and other dogs. The owners, Ann and Tim Arden were investment bankers with two school-aged children, each at camp over the summer. So there would be an abundance of new dog walking hours, which meant more fees. They handed over keys to their house, but the house was boring, the owners smart and anal. Computers were locked. Everything had a place, nothing was disorganized or stuffed in drawers. She had no idea who these people were; the house could have belonged to anyone. She did find condoms, which didn't really indicate much of anything.

It took her twenty minutes to get Sweetiepie, because her owners lived on the northeastern side of town, off a very high-traffic throughway. Today Marcy planned a long walk since the sun was out and Sadie had lost a few pounds. She wanted to visit the park, secretly hoping Sam would see them all having fun and come join the fun. But of course that wouldn't happen. There had been no sightings for a few weeks now. In fact, the detective was now thinking Sam could have possibly left town. But Ellen hadn't given up, quite the opposite.

Find Sam was still all over social media. And while the first news segment on NBC had been quick and forgettable, Ellen managed, through connections, to obtain other publicity. The first three talk show mentions were short and quick, with only a picture of Ellen and the detective, because the discussion mainly centered on stray dogs in general. But now a major daytime talk shows had flown its host to Windhaven to interview all the volunteers. A cable news network also had aired a rather long segment on strays, highlighting Sam and the town's efforts to find him. *The Dog Whisperer* considered filming a show in Windhaven but no one wanted to volunteer their dog, as the dog had to have flaws and the flaws always reflected bad owners. Of course, there was always that one client that had a charming incompetence, loving the dog too much, treating the dog like a child, but not many wanted that on TV. What they wanted on TV was the community's charitable culture that led to a national dog hunting volunteer effort. So, he simply attended a meeting with the detective, all filmed by the local TV shows. A recording was also made for his show. He spoke with confidence, albeit with a touch of arrogance, highlighting how to approach a stray dog—with straight back, sharp noises and lots of pointing. The meeting was similar to the detective meetings, except hundreds of people from all over Connecticut showed up with their dogs.

This publicity, inspired everyone who was anyone in Connecticut to join Find Sam. The movement put the town on the national map. Windhaven's favorite lost dog and lost dog owner were staples on social media, twenty-four-hour cable news, state journals, and national magazines. Sam was heroically famous, Marcy ignominiously famous, and Ellen, a rock star.

The traffic today was particularly bad, so after Sweetiepie was settled inside the car, Marcy made a quick detour to Cup-O-Joe. The local coffee shop had too much wood and the piped NPR voices that sounded barely awake or stoned. The line was long, everyone staring at their phones. A woman ahead of her waved and winked, as if to say, I know you're famous, but you and I will keep it secret. Marcy always felt awkward in public; eyes seemed to move to her because she was notorious for losing a dog. She studied her phone, pretending preoccupation with texting and social media.

The radio talk show host was now asking her guest something. The voice was low and sleepy, a droning background annoyance. The voice that responded was not low and sleepy but professional and fast paced. It was also familiar.

"*. . . too many dogs. She was very busy when she walked . . .*"

Marcy stopped pretending to text.

Host: When you say she was busy, can you elaborate. What was her schedule?

Guest: Well, she told me she walked only five dogs, but I've heard she walked more.

Host: Is this normal for dog walkers. To walk with a lot of dogs?

Guest. I think so. But, with a storm , it can be difficult. It was hard on her.

Ellen! She was on NPR! The woman and man in front of Marcy suddenly fell silent. The woman looked over at Marcy. Marcy kept her head down.

"Isn't that the corgi's owner?" the man said.

Host: Do you think it's safe for all of these dogs to walk like this?

Guest: You know I don't really want to get into that. The point is no one blames her. We are focused right now on finding my Sam. That is all we are focused on.

Host: And the amount of time and money your community has spent on this one dog is quite remarkable. All of this time. And tell us about this detective you found. She is quite a national figure isn't she?

Guest: Oh, yes, Detective Serendon is amazing. We are so lucky to have her devoting so much time to this case. She does have to travel to other cases, but she leaves representatives of her detective service here to continue the tracking. It's an enormous responsibility.

The man in front of Marcy said, too loud, "If you ask me, someone has stolen the dog."

"Really?" another man ahead of them in line said. "You think someone stole the dog?"

The NPR voices continued in the background, now discussing all the national attention given to this one dog. Marcy raised her finger to get the attendee's attention. Maybe she could break in line, tell the barrister she had an emergency. All she wanted was coffee.

"Well, don't quote me," the man said. "My friend knows that officer who was out the night of the storm. Had a tree fall on him. Knocked him flat out. Lucky to be alive, if you ask me. No memory. He has none. For a month the guy could not tell you anything beyond some car chase he had been involved with. Chasing down someone who had run over barricade tape. But I am sure you read the last article about him?"

"No," the woman said.

"Well, and this is all public, mind you. I am not revealing anything not divulged to the media. This past week? Things started coming back. Amnesia is interesting. Sometimes a person gets the entire episode back in detail, more detail than the average person. Sometimes they get it half back, or only in pieces. My friend said the guy remembers a car filled with dogs. And one really mean, wolf-like dog in the front. The driver was some man. But it was all fuzzy. He didn't remember a corgi. Just this very large, wolf-like dog in the front seat that tried to attack him. He thinks the perp commanded the dog to attack. Who knows why someone has all these dogs in their car."

"And it was the same night the corgi disappeared?"

"Makes you wonder if that corgi was stolen," the man said. "Guy could be a dog thief, or maybe he saw the dog running and took him. Just my personal take on the situation."

Marcy stepped out of the line and went back to her car, where Sweetiepie was panting a bit too much for comfort. She started the car and turned on the air conditioner full blast. Wolf-like dog? He thought she was a guy? Of course she had been wearing a baseball hat, so maybe as he emerged from his dreamlike mental state, all he remembered was the Mets baseball hat. Or maybe he wasn't emerging from a dreamlike state. It didn't look too heroic chasing down a woman with a gun drawn. Maybe he was embarrassed and purposely lying. Oh please be a liar.

MARCY OBSESSED ABOUT the officer's memory as she walked the dogs, ending the day at the Nelsons, where her big screw-up had tilted her world. The housekeeper had left early today and no one was home. There were five plates wrapped in aluminum foil sitting at the front door. Marcy thought about taking them inside, but reconsidered, since bringing items inside would prove she didn't just let Nellie in the back door to the basement, but had actually entered the front of the house. She led the dogs to the back, let them all into the basement and wiped them down with paper towels she kept in her car. She then cleaned the place, as usual, so Elizabeth wouldn't notice anything. She figured Elizabeth was so unobservant, even a few traces of mud wouldn't matter.

After everyone had treats and were lounging on dog beds retrieved from the back closet,   Marcy collapsed on a sofa. She was feeling anxious, in need of meds actually and wondered if Elizabeth popped Xanax like some of the other clients. She rubbed her temples, going over all the constant monitoring of all her failures, and now this new revelation concerning the police officer's memory returning. She felt her head tighten, her back stiffen. The police officer could have been a liar, but, of course, who would know he was a liar, except Marcy?

She forced herself to stand. The housekeepers absence created an opportunity she could not ignore. She searched for the memory stick. Maybe Sam tucked it somewhere. She lifted pillows, checked behind and under chairs and sofas. She then went outside, wondering how to even begin to find a possibly buried memory stick. She gave up after kicking around the garden for a brief moment. Who cared about the memory stick anyway? It wasn't like whatever was on it was going to ruin her life, put her in jail. Of course, the police chase would put her in jail. But not copying someone's memoir. Or was it? Is that against the law?

Marcy walked back to the computer room before she left. One more check. And that is when she found the iPhone, on the desk, still turned on. Elizabeth's iPhone. Why would someone leave an iPhone at their house? And the iPhone was not locked. An unlocked iPhone? Middle-aged people never ceased to amaze her.

Marcy tapped it. The black screen was replaced by a page full of messages. Just sitting there for the world to see.

> Elizabeth, I cannot believe you're doing all of this for my Sam. What a wonderful person you are. We've hit a jackpot in L.A. My agent wants something, anything in her hand. Like yesterday.
>
> BTW, Have u noticed how nervous Marcy seems? I know she feels guilty but I keep thinking there is something we don't know? She's shifty. See u soon .... Ellen

Chapter 19

Marcy
Avoiding fame

FIND SAM week 10
Facebook page: Find Sam!
total friends 6.3k

"If anyone thinks by putting out water bowls and food you will be saving this corgi, you are wrong. And please know we do not harm the raccoons. No more mails about raccoons. We let all captured raccoons go. ....." Detective Serendon

New Comments:
Lolly Abner (picture of older woman in blue polyester suit): Maybe if you fed the poor raccoons they would stay away from the traps. Wish we could help!

Ben Carlson (picture of black cat) We are all praying for you. Our minister talked about Sam in his sermon. We plan to hunt for him in our town this weekend. We are however concerned about the raccoons.
Mary Walker (picture of teenager with pet possum) My best friend owns a raccoon. They are very smart.

Henry (picture of pit bull) Life is rich. It's all of us who are poor.

Mary Johnson (selfie of brunette in cocktail dress). The dog is probably in South Carolina. Does that dog walker still live in your town?

Twitter @FindSam
followers: 150.5k

#FindSam #WeloveSam #windhavenlovesSam #hugyourdogforSam #dogwalkersfromhell, #corgipuppiesforsale #fireSamsdogwalker #betterdogwalkersforwindhaven #saveraccoons, #raccoonshaveworthtoo #raccoonshatesamdogwalker

MARCY CLICKED OFF her iPhone and put it away, tried to concentrate on the video. The raccoons were cute and everyone got a kick out of watching them study the food, enter the trap, and dissolve into manic terror after the door closed. Tonight they had watched six nights of videos because everyone had been so busy they had to skip video viewing a few times. Marcy thought it was a worthless endeavor, and boring. After you've seen one video of trapped, squashed raccoons, you've seen them all. What everyone, or the detective and Ellen, seemed to not understand was how social raccoons were. They liked to eat together. So, while one raccoon would not set off the trigger plate, three would. And five plus babies would definitely set it off. It was amazing how many raccoons could fit inside a dog trap.

Marcy left the video review meeting early and arrived home, wanting to just lie on her couch a while. She had given up on the trapping, but no one else had, so she had to continue to wake up on her designated days, sometimes dragging her brother with her, other times, dragging Lorene, who had to smoke her cigarette first. She put out food, set the camera, and then picked up all the dogs for their walks. It was exhausting, but how could she stop? She had to look loyal and enthusiastic. And she desperately wanted to catch Sam. She missed him.

When the phone trilled, she didn't want to answer, but the caller ID said private caller, and she always answered private callers. Some of her dog walking clients were doctors. She wanted everyone she worked for to see her as the kind of person who answered her phone.

"Hello"

"Hello, can I speak with Marcy Thorpe?"

"That's me."

"This is officer Holt of the Windhaven Police Department. How are you today?"

Breathe, Marcy, breathe.

"Hello?"

"Yes, hey. I'm fine."

"Good, good. I'm the lead investigator on a case involving a hit and run."

"Someone hit someone and sped away?"

"No, not really. They left the scene, disobeyed direct orders. Anyway . . ."

"What is a direct order?"

"Ma'am, we will need for you to come down to headquarters as soon as possible. We have some questions to ask you concerning our investigation. I am sure this will all be clear once we meet."

"Is this about the missing dog? Sam?"

"Sam? No, ma'am. This is not about a missing dog. It's about one of our officers, officer Willard who was accosted during the storm? You may have read about it in the papers."

"Why does he want to talk with me?" Marcy felt a hot stream fall down her neck.

"He's still vague on the I.D. of this driver. All he knows is that the perpetrator was a man. But his memory is coming back and he now recalls a better image of this large dog the man owned. And apparently there were several other dogs. You're a dog walker in the area, so we thought it may be helpful to chat with you. Who knows, it could have been another dog walker in the area."

"I just walk my client dogs. I truly don't—"

"We'd like to talk with you as soon as possible. You may have seen someone. Sometimes questions jog the memory. You'd be surprised what we find out during questioning. This afternoon OK with you?"

Marcy hung up the phone, closed her eyes, and went over the lies she had created to cover herself to date. *Who knows, it could have been another dog walker in the area.*

MARCY CHANGED HER clothes four times, each change suggesting a different mien. She at first went for the black look—black pants, brown and black tank, black sandals—thinking black implied intelligence and responsibility. Of course, it could also indicate dark world view and depression. So, she moved to a loud, lavender sun dress, but the lavender could be viewed as flaky. From there she went shorts. Too much leg. So, she finally settled on jeans, a red sleeveless knit top, and tennis shoes. She went over her lie path, including all the time schedules. She had lost the dog after about eleven-thirty on Battle Street, a few blocks from the park. This distanced her from the police chase, which she figured occurred around eleven, or was it earlier? She reviewed her notes again.

The police parking lot was half empty. After parking, Marcy breathed slowly as she stared at the station. The Windhaven police station covered two blocks. It was one of the largest buildings in town, which had a population of 20,000 people who rarely experienced crimes more significant than petty theft and drug abuse. Most traffic violations involved cars passing through the town, the majority of which were driven by Hispanics. Occasionally, an African American would have an expired emissions sticker.

The oversized police station resulted from a large expansion initiated by the previous First Selectman who had been chairman of the Windhaven Police Commission prior to the selectman post. He just happened to own the construction company that built the police station. Marcy discovered this when she walked the first selectman's dog while he was on vacation. He didn't correspond on official town.gov email accounts, but instead used his own personal private email, which allowed for easy snooping. His dog was hit by a car a few weeks later, so Marcy's services were no longer needed. There were probably interesting emails she didn't have time to review.

An officer escorted Marcy to a small room with egg shell colored walls and a slightly scratched pine table. Two officers sat in aluminum chairs at the table, one looking vaguely familiar, the other bored. Two empty aluminum chairs sat on either side of the door.

When she entered, Officer Willard stood, introduced himself and shook her hand. He didn't look like someone a tree had fallen on. There was no scar on his forehead or face, and he appeared sturdy, well-built, healthy, alert. He also had a rather appealing, shy smile, as if he didn't take all of this seriously, or not as seriously as the Windhaven Police Department took it. The other officer, Ned Holt, lean, middle-aged and not worth attention, also shook her hand and introduced himself.

"This will not take too much of your time," Officer Willard said, smiling at Marcy. "I know you need to get back to your dog walking. And dog hunting."

He laughed. Officer Holt did not. Marcy tried to smile but didn't feel her lips move in the proper formation for a smile. They seemed stuck in a permanent pinch. Why did he laugh about a lost dog?

"Just joking. Hey, we're all on the lookout for the pooch, too. Got that poster out in the lobby, and all police officers keep an eye out for strays."

Marcy thanked them and sat.

"So, let's get going here."

"I will be glad to answer your questions, Officer Willard," Marcy said.

"Just call me Don."

"OK." Marcy's lips were more relaxed, so her smile felt as if it were a real smile. She looked right at Don when she smiled so it would appear almost flirtatious. "Don it is then."

"Let's see now, you've been at this dog walking for three years right?" the other officer, Ned, said. "I assume the dogs are primarily Windhaven dogs. Is this right?"

"Yes, every dog is from this town. I've thought about other towns but it's just too much to drive to all the locations, pick up the dogs, then walk, then drop them off."

Don was looking at her a bit funny now. His head was cocked. "Pick them up? You pick up the dogs in your car? How many dogs do you walk?"

"Not a lot. But of course if you haven't walked a dog, five is a lot. You know." She waited, hoping they would think she had answered five, when she really hadn't.

Ned wrote something on his pad. Don continued to look at her. She smiled. He smiled. She wished she had worn the sun dress. She could cross her legs or something.

"So, do you know any other dog walkers in the area, any who may pick up dogs in a car too. Do you go to the parks?"

"I really don't know other dog walkers. Well, I knew a few at one time when I first started out because I went to this training school and met other walkers, but they were from other towns and I never stayed in touch." They stared at her. "I don't know why I didn't stay in touch, just didn't."

Ned wrote on his pad again. Don looked over her shoulder at the wall which had no pictures or clocks, just plain white paint.

"I remember dogs better than people anyway. When I am out with the dogs, at the park or whatever, I introduce myself to the dogs first and humans second. I rarely remember the human names."

"Is that so?" Don said. "Do you remember meeting any pit bulls? The guy driving the car had a pit bull. At first I remembered something else large, like a mastiff, but actually no. It was a pit bull."

"No. Well, yes, I have run across pit bulls of course. I've walked some, a few. But I really don't recall owners."

"He was also wearing a baseball hat. I do remember that. Slim guy. Lots of dogs. Lots of them. I didn't look at the dogs, but I remember lots of dogs. Do you recall anyone at the parks, or walking, with a lot of dogs. I am talking this guy must have had twelve dogs."

Marcy felt her face start to drain, but smiled quickly, hoping the smile would force the blood back into her face. She tried to recall where her Mets cap was now and who had seen it. Lorene of course knew of her Mets baseball hat. Had any client ever seen her wearing the Mets hat?

"Do you remember what kind of baseball cap he was wearing?" Marcy asked slowly.

"I want to say Mets, but I'm not really sure."

"Don had a pretty bad concussion. But we think details will be clearer over time. We've been asking around the neighborhood about that day. This guy could be dangerous. Not just because of his pit pull, but Don thinks he could have had a gun. At one point he remembers chasing him on foot. Willard had to pull his gun out."

"I was at the intersection of Stephenson and Langley. You know that area?" Don said.

"Sure. That's near Armory, the Nelson's street. I walk Nellie, their dog." Had Elizabeth ever seen her in the Mets hat?

"If you walk the dogs in that area, then, when did you pick up the Nelson dog?" Don said.

"Oh, I was over near the park. I had picked up the Nelson dog earlier, much earlier. We hung out at the park. That is how I got stuck in the storm."

Ned scribbled.

Don leaned back in his chair. "Wish I could remember more."

"Well, you remember a gun and the pit bull. That's a pretty good recall." Marcy winked. "Of course a gun is a big deal. I suppose pulling a gun out would stick in that memory."

"He had help with that," Officer Holt said. "We jogged that memory a bit. We found the gun by him and then there was that bullet lodged in a fallen white pine. Traced it right back to Don's Smith and Wesson. Sure enough, there were some rounds fired off in his gun."

"You fired at the guy with the pit bull?" He fired at her? He fired his gun at her because Henry was a pit bull. This was outrageous. She had probably assumed it was thunder. "And the reason? The pit bull growled at you?"

"No, no. Had nothing to do with the dog," Officer Willard said quickly. "The guy put his gun out the window and fired."

"I think we're getting a bit off topic here," Ned said. "All we are trying to do is determine if anyone in the immediate vicinity had also seen this guy."

"Wow, all you remember is a baseball hat on the guy but amazing details about his gun aimed at you? Will this be in the paper? The shooting, I mean?"

"We've already informed the paper about developments in our investigation."

Don clasped his hands on the table and stared at his fingers for a moment. "He was a strong guy, I think. But skinny. Hard to tell how tall he was because he was behind the wheel."

He looked at Marcy and said nothing for a while. Marcy didn't smile. She could barely breathe.

"When you say big, I assume you are saying muscular? A muscular man with a gun and pit bull dog. Wow. Dangerous stuff," Marcy blurted out, wondering if they jailed people for sass, because if she stayed any longer she would need to call her mother for bail money. She winked quickly. Sometimes winking eliminated sarcasm.

"We're not saying anything right now," Ned said. "We're simply saying this was a small man, maybe muscular, maybe a bit sinewy. Possibly with a Mets baseball hat. And a pit bull. Have you or have you not seen anyone like that in that neighborhood? He could have been canvassing the place, got caught in the storm, and maybe became nervous."

"Nope. I think I would remember anyone fitting that description. I definitely would remember anyone with a gun." Marcy looked at Don, who was now studying his pen. "Too bad you didn't knock out one of his tires with one of your bullets. I can't believe this strong guy and his pit bull shot at you then got away."

"He may not have shot. I only remember the gun trained on me," Don said quickly. "But sometimes, when everything is confusing, we see something shiny and think it's a gun." He laughed. Marcy did not. Ned did not. "It may not have been a gun."

"Are there any other questions?" Marcy said.

On the drive home, Marcy felt legal relief because the officer had fired his gun and now had to have a reason for firing it, which necessitated a contrived story involving a strong man with a pit bull. At least the pit bull part was correct. She felt certain that even if he ever remembered her, he would choose to stick by the story about a man with the gun. However, the Mets hat and pit bull would hit the papers, and now everyone was reading the papers, particularly Ellen Maher. *I know she feels guilty but I keep thinking there is something we don't know? She's shifty.*

When Marcy returned to her apartment, she retrieved her Mets cap from the coat closet shelf, then ran to the kitchen to find scissors.

Chapter 20

Marcy
Empathy is the answer

MARCY TAPED SEVERAL small magnets to the edges of the baseball cap's blue rim then pushed it on her refrigerator door, hoping it resembled a blue smile, but it didn't. It looked like trash. She left it, grabbed her broom but before she could begin sweeping away remnants of her favorite Mets baseball cap, Grateful Dead started screaming their lyrics out of her cell phone.

"Sis. I am now ready. I've finished my analysis and am now ready for the reveal."

"Edward, that's great, but your reveal will have to wait. I'm kind of busy."

"This will only take a moment. I'm waiting."

"At Mom's?"

"No. Here. I am here."

Marcy looked out the window. Edward was sitting on the sidewalk, legs crossed, a leash in his hands. His t-shirt was on backward, again, so the collar was tight against his throat and the tag was out, tickling his chin like a dog's tongue. His jeans were loose because he had stopped taking his mood-stabilizers—anti-convulsion meds which had puffed his body with fat and water retention. So, now most of his clothes hung on him and since his brain had not yet adjusted to this abrupt change in medication, he was a bit tricky to deal with. His appearance was even more disheveled than usual. Of course, no one really cared about his appearance anymore. Marcy's only priority was safety, not appearance. The whiskers on his chin, backward shirt, tag flipped up lapping his face, were inconsequential to his survival.

Marcy looked around the parking lot. It was empty, no neighbors standing around to witness any slight hiccup in their exchange. Two years ago, Lorene had almost called the police when Edward had come to the apartment looking for Marcy. He had roamed around the parking lot talking loudly, insisting there had been a kidnapping. Once Marcy claimed him as her brother, Lorene's face transformed quickly from terror to pity. Since then, the pity seemed to bind her to Marcy in some slightly maternal way.

"I still have to walk a few dogs again later today, so I'm not home for long. I was at a meeting. What is this about?"

"Garbage." He crossed his arms over his chest. "This, sister, is about garbage. And the Ukraine. The Russians are going to attack, then demolish. Their vehicles are now in Donetsk Oblast."

"That's interesting. I see your interest has moved away from the Middle East."

"The media is controlled by the military who tell us what they think we need to know. I stick with breaking news."

"Does the garbage have something to do with all of this?"

"No. It's separate. I'm updating you on where we are in the world conflict, then I will help you on this local conflict."

She stood, considering her options. She could simply tell him she would discuss his garbage another time and deal with the constant phone calls, text messages, and emails about garbage along updates on world conflicts.

"OK, follow me inside. I will give you, about ten minutes to discuss garbage."

"No. I am not here to tell you about garbage. I am going to take you to garbage."

"I assume this has to do with Sam? You think he's around someone's garbage? I'm sure he is, but there's no way to tell whose garbage he's around."

"This is not a correct assumption. Marcy, let me tell you how I would think if I were lost and could not find anyone. I would have backup plans. You may not know this, but I actually do have backup plans." Marcy felt her face go warm. "I think about the world without a house and I think about what is very important to my existence. So, if I lost my mother and my sister how would I get these vital items? You see? I think about this. I am prepared."

"That would be food, right? You think about how you would obtain and store food, and shelter. Right, Edward? Look, you don't have to worry about this, I've got a plan . . ."

"No, Marcy. No. That is not what I worry about at all." He stood now, looked off into space as if imagining himself lost and in need of sleep. "I will sleep somewhere. And there are food banks. What I worry about is TV. Cable news. Breaking news. How would I watch CNN breaking news if you and Mom were gone? Twenty-four hour news, mind you, is vital. How would I keep an eye on Russia? So, I have taken it upon myself to figure out how someone without a home can watch the news? One place would be appliance stores. Another bars. Churches have dens with TVs, and you can always log onto computers at the library to live stream CNN."

"And this has what to do with garbage?"

"Dogs need us. They also have a desire to escape us, so probably consider plans if the dependent style of living fails them. For a dog, plans would be for food. See, sis, dogs don't just like food, they obsess over it. It is beyond vital. A dog thinks about food all day. Do you notice this? I have noticed this about Henry. I watch him all day. I think he considers life without a human food source. He has a backup plan. All dogs have a backup plan. In order to have one, a dog must always study human behavior around food."

A door slammed in the distance. Marcy held her palm up and looked around Edward's shoulder. It was a neighbor, now starting his Honda. She waited for him to back out of the lot and turn down the street, then dropped her hand.

"Today, is Mom's garbage day, and as you know, everyone wheels garbage to the road. Not all neighborhoods have garbage days the same day. For example, your neighborhood has garbage day Friday. We are a Tuesday garbage day. And do you know how I know this? I am responsible for taking our garbage out. I used to forget or take it out late, and the garbage men would miss us. Then I would have to drive our garbage down the street, chasing the garbage men. Sometimes I would have to drive a while before I detected the garbage truck. Sometimes I would forget the route. And you know what I discovered? I discovered that certain people had overflow garbage cans. Bags coming out of the tops, ripped open, food scattered everywhere. Once I saw a fox running away from these garbage cans. That is how I know. I observed this. I didn't think anything of it, because food is not my big priority. But a dog would notice the garbage. A dog would see us toss food away, take this food in a large can to the street. Just as I know how cable news comes into the world and where else that cable news is presented to the public."

"This sounds great. It really does, but I doubt the dogs are aware enough, even Sam, to understand garbage routes."

"But you see, I drove around the routes for days. I have collected addresses of overstuffed garbage cans. I've got them right here." He held up index cards with scribble on them. One fell on the ground, and before he could grab it, the wind took it. His scream was loud and high-pitched like a toddler and his facial expression changed quickly. His cheeks turned red, his mouth hung open. The tag on his backward shirt bent under the weight of his chin. "Why oh why!" he shouted as he jogged after the index card. "All my addresses for key garbage targets!"

It was no use trying to calm Edward. Once he became hysterical, the only way to end the hysteria was to put an end to whatever triggered the hysteria. So, Marcy took off after the index card. It skipped over a Ford Escort and landed on the grass. After she stepped on it, she heard Edward behind her, his keening now soft and low, similar to a whimpering of a puppy. He bent over, grabbed the index card covered in addresses and descriptions, and pulled it from under her shoe.

"This! This will get your dog!" He held the card to his chest and rocked slowly back and forth. "I know all the garbage routes. We will find the dog on the garbage routes."

"You may be right, but, truly, if we find Sam, it will probably be in another state. And he will be hungry. I assure you." But his keening grew louder. He grabbed his hair right when Lorene pulled into the parking lot.

"OK. Let's see what they say at the meeting tonight. I will back you up," Marcy said, quickly. A Taurus pulled into the parking lot. He let go of his hair. "I will back you up on this. I promise, OK?" She looked over at Lorene, now stepping out of her car. "So, thanks, it's brilliant."

"Well then." He stood, shoved the index card into his front pocket. "I am glad I can help you with this, sis. I think this may be what I am meant to do." He brushed off his pants as if nothing had happened, a momentary blip of the brain. "I can get into the mind of dogs. I can do this one thing."

Chapter 21

Sam
A dog must manage perception

SATIATED. I AM a satiated dog. I learned this word from Mom. She always said "No" when I begged for food after supper, then she would say, "Sam, you just ate. You are now a satiated dog." And I assure you at those times I would think, I am not sure I am feeling this satiation from precisely one cup of dried corn and protein grizzle. Satiation from dry dog food is not the same thing as satiation from roasted chicken. My mom ate roasted chicken with garlic herbs dressing and small potatoes broiled in olive oil with a touch of salt. Oh and she also had broiled salmon with creamy dill sauce. I remember her salmon nights. Always salmon on the night before fourth day, one day before she came home for lethargy period. Chicken on first day. Pasta on second day. The midweek meal was something she picked up elsewhere at human cooking establishments. But salmon was always on fourth day. I knew this because I am not a cretin. I managed to puncture donation bags in the house, retrieve a few morsels of donations without leaving any evidence of my pilfering.

Anyway, my meal today included smelly leftover hamburgers, old bread, and cookies. Oh, and bless the soul who tossed half a can of tuna fish in the large donation can.

I need water, though, because these streets are removed from my creek. So, I am making my way around the back yards, looking for a bowl of water left out for a dog or cat. They sometimes leave out water, even cat food, which is not half bad, not as good as hamburgers or stale cookies, but sufficient enough for my taste.

I am now wandering about in a rather claustrophobic yard, much smaller than my mom's yard. The houses around here all look the same, too. I finally find a little water bowl sitting on a wooden patio, so I lap it all up because I am thirsty, I have worked arduously all morning pushing down donation buckets.

That is when I see her. And there is no question that she sees me.

She looks nice, actually, and she smells nice, like Mom when she used to lie prostrate on the sofa. This one looks like she's been satiated on many occasions. She is round, like the breeders, but she doesn't look like she is breeding. This could mean she enjoys food and thus will enjoy feeding me. I do admit, I miss the humans, the way they massage you, comfort you, wash you when needed. I miss them. I miss socialism.

She is merely ten feet from me and approaches furtively. I stand still, thinking, well, Sam, just let her do it, let her pick you up and take you. This woman smells OK. She'll be my new mom.

But the woman does not pick me up. She suddenly steps back, pulls out her metal box, places it on her face and taps. I hear a click. She then puts it to her ear and starts talking. You'd think she'd at least say something. Most humans say something. But, no, she goes back inside the house, then looks out the window. Before she heads into the house, I get a whiff of her. It has turned sour, salty. Anxiety. Bad sign.

I am thinking this stranger is not quite right, so I regroup. Sam, ole boy, I say to myself, don't deviate from your original assumptions. These humans now cannot be trusted, stick with your free market world. You have succeeded in it! You are rich for God's sakes! So, off I go, back to the street, around another house—this one home to a large Lab with a big mouth. The asshat starts his yelling, "get your fucking ass out of my yard or I'll kick it good." And so forth and so on. I say, "Look, ole boy, take it easy, I am simply passing through, no harm, no foul." But he yells at me, then yells at his neighbor—some beagle and the beagle starts up his "fuck you, fuck you, fuck you, fuck youuuuuuuuu." Beagles have limited vocabularies.

I stop and yell back. "What the hell? Fuck you, too."

But they all keep yelling, then one of them, some poodle-like dog, yells at his mom who runs out into her yard, stops then puts a metal box up to her face. I am rather baffled by this human behavior, but I do not pause to study it. I am gone, under some bushes around the shed, through another yard. All I see is grass and tree bark and edges of houses. I am running so fast, I barely know where I am, which is dangerous because I need to keep track of this area, due to the weekly donations.

I squeeze under a fence, around another yard, this time with some asshat cat, who chases me while speaking in that language no one on earth understands.

I finally make it to a street that feels safe. The houses are a bit larger, so I decide to hang around here a while, check out their schedule. I may be able to add another weekly meal to my calendar.

I find a shed and squirm underneath it. I'd like a little water but I am not desperate enough to risk it. I'll take a quick nap, then go looking for water, maybe one of these houses that sprays water on the grass like Mom. I've noticed a few with running faucets. I can smell salt in the air again, which means I may be near the ocean, a good thing, of course. I can always follow the shore and try to find that place where I have seen and smelled Bosslady

I stay put a while, and, well, what can I say? I ponder. I ponder human behavior, which seems quite strange and disturbing, indeed. Did they always behave this way and I was simply not paying attention? Or, is the behavior related to the fact that I am no longer the dog I was before? In the world of humans, who you are, what your scent offers to the world, what your expressions indicates, make no difference. The human behavior is directly correlated only with perception. I have done a poor job managing this perception, I admit. So, what can I say, my friends—I am a corgi, yes, but I am also a dog.

And that is when I see it. The small, metal raccoon prison.

Chapter 22

Marcy
Dissemination of information

THE VOICE ROSE, strident and slightly pedantic, from the detective's face, which completely covered the iPad screen. The iPad was tilted upon a stand in the middle of the splintered picnic table in Bradley Park. About twenty women sat around the iPad. Today the park was covered with blue sky, and the New England aviary denizens screamed their presence. The picnic table was near a large field that turned into three separate baseball diamonds. A few pedestrians walked dogs near one diamond, an unattended boy, about eight years old or so, kicked a soccer ball by himself in another, which bothered Marcy. She kept her eye on the lonely boy, ignoring the iPad face. No one else cared about anything except the talking face on the iPad.

The Find Sam meetings were now held two to three times a week. Sam had been missing since May. It was now August. There had been five traps placed at various sighting locations. But, no Sam, so the atmosphere was generally despondent.

After the detective's quick summary of their progress, Edward, sitting across from Marcy, put his hand into the air forcefully.

"You need to put out water. A water bowl. No food. Just water. The dog is eating. He eats because we are messy. Human beings are messy and careless. Dogs take advantage of our messiness. They watch us during the day, see what wasteful creatures we are." Marcy reached across the table and touched his hand. "Garbage. I have the routes. I know which streets smell."

Ellen's eyes moved around the table, then stayed on Marcy. They were the usual eyes everyone had around her brother. The looks all said, I am tolerant, and he is sad, but there is a limit to my tolerance.

Marcy smiled at her and squeezed Edward's hand. "Edward, I think we understand your theory. They are going to try this trap thing for a while, OK?"

"So, thanks, Edward. Anyway, guys, thanks so much for showing up. And thanks to our leader, Detective Serendon, who takes time out from her other job to Facetime with us." Everyone applauded. "So, today we are setting up cameras at two traps located in the most recent sighting area."

"The area we'll be going to today is Patrick street, not too far from here," Edward said, as if Ellen had not talked. "Slobs. They're slobs on that street. This slobby-ness is related to a lower class of humans. You got working class citizens on this street and they eat hamburgers, hotdogs, processed food. They drag it to the end of the driveway and do not secure the tops. The way I see things, humans in this class can barely make budget. When you are simply getting by, aesthetics are of no concern. If it's all you can do to roll out of bed? Well, just slip on whatever clothes are on the floor." He held his hands behind his head the way a confident athlete does when discussing a recent baseball game. His collared sports shirt was a size too small and crept up over his small belly, revealing his large belly button. A deep black line of hair extended from the belly button to the end of his gym pants. "That street is a Monday pick up area. The dog may or may not know this. I suspect the dog brain is more advanced than we know. The dog brain is bored. The dog brain spends its entire day with empty time. All it can do is try to figure out our strange world. By now he has obsessed over us. Obsession occurs when you are fearful and dependent. Anyway, I'll take charge of this neighborhood. Not today, though."

Marcy poked Edward. "Please," she whispered. "Just listen."

"Forget cameras. I'll sleep in one of the bushes, disguise myself. I'll ask them if it's OK. Working class don't care. They don't care. I know these people. I don't work, but when I do, that's who I work with. People like the ones on Patrick Street, who live on stinky streets and wear bad shoes. That's where you find your lost dog."

They sat for a moment. No one said anything.

"I'm sorry, it's hard for me to hear. Who is talking?" Detective Serendon said. Her talking face on the screen reminded Marcy of the

Wizard of Oz. Ellen leaned into the screen, as if the voice was inside her iPad needed closer attention.

"It's a volunteer," Ellen said. "Edward. About the garbage routes?"

"Oh, yes. Edward? That is actually a good idea, and garbage is certainly where many strays find sustenance, but a hopeless strategy. I mean chasing garbage routes is hopeless. It is impossible to find a dog that way. Too many routes. And even if the dog attacks a garbage route one day, he will wonder and perhaps never return. But we always like you guys to think about new ideas. This is good. Keep it up. Ideas are good."

"The routes are"—Edward dribbled on, as if no one had talked to him—"Darlington's pickups are Tuesday, Windhaven's on Wednesday. Thursday is Scramford, and Greenstown on Friday. And recyclables on Friday, too, but dogs don't care about those. The dog will know plastics are worthless."

He leaned back, looked around, avoiding Marcy's eyes, waiting for everyone to clap or say wow. But no one said anything. Marcy wished Lorene had attended. Lorene sometimes had a calming effect on Edward and kept him quiet at these meetings. Also, the third person made it less likely someone would ask for a ride

Today, the person who asked for a ride, unfortunately, was Mindy Wilton, an enthusiastic friend of Ellen Maher.

On the way home, Edward unfortunately allowed Mindy to sit in the front seat so she could chat with Marcy. Mindy told them she had to miss most meetings and usually contributed other ways—benefits, distribution of posters and letters to various local newspapers. She was very excited to be part of Find Sam, particularly excited about its national attention. Marcy didn't speak, only listened. Edward talked about every three minutes. Last week the Russians had bombed Aleppo, and Edward had written two letters to his congressmen, informing them that Russia had to be stopped. Marcy dreaded the inevitable spillage of thoughts on Russian and the Middle East. Luckily, Mindy did not seem like the type who would pursue this conversation, so Edward, who was learning slowly to avoid certain topics with certain people, stuck to dog talk, which was also rather strange and obsessive, but it least it was dogs, not Russia.

"This is just getting so upsetting," Mindy said to Marcy, after Edward finished his theory on garbage routes again, to no avail. "The longer he goes missing, the greater the chance he will simply be stolen, or leave the entire area."

"Well, the last sighting was five days ago, so he is here. And we are determined," Marcy said.

"Yes we are. And all the national attention. Can you believe it? Ellen said *Twenty-Twenty* is coming out next week. It's amazing. Did you see the *New York Times Magazine* article? I think we're bringing lost dogs to everyone's attention. At least everyone will know how dogs are lost, why it's never a good idea to be out with them in a storm."

Marcy said nothing.

"Of course it was not your fault," Mindy added. "You know. You're a dog walker, and you got caught. It's not like you were in a house then left in a storm, or left when you saw the storm."

"Marcy is a good dog walker. She was where she was supposed to be," Edward said.

Marcy assumed this Mindy was one of those women who never paused before releasing words.

"Ellen told me a literary agent approached her about writing a book about Sam. They thought a movie was marketable, too. Stray dogs are a big thing ever since *The Dog Whisperer*."

"And immigrants," Edward said.

"Immigrants?"

"Refugees are the big thing now. Refugees are a bit different from immigrants. But given what Russia is doing, there may be mass immigration from that area of our world, too, not just Syria."

Mindy smiled and looked straight ahead.

"Actually, Sam would not be a refugee," Mindy said.

"I think you are right there," Edward said. "As far as we know he had a good, safe life. He would be more like an immigrant. So, metaphorically, that would work. That would be the literary device an author would use."

"That's interesting, Edward," Mindy said. "Elizabeth Nelson is working hard on all of this again. Not just because of Ellen, but to keep her mind off her problems. Anyway, she told Ellen she wrote seriously, I guess. She said she could write the book. Or screenplay."

Oh, dear God, Marcy thought. This beats all.

"So, what if we never find Sam?" Marcy said, trying not to reveal her disgust with Elizabeth trying to author a book.

"I think if we never find Sam, the book, the movie, would not work. The world just cannot deal with dead animals, as you probably know. Who wants to watch a movie, or whatever it turns into, about a dog running away and dying? You only want to read about a dog running away if the dog is found."

Marcy said nothing, thinking about the pressure now hanging over this search.

"Elizabeth said she was writing a memoir but hasn't paid much attention to it for a while. Other than that, I'm not sure she's written anything. Ellen said it was better to get a ghost writer. Or someone who knew about writing, but I don't know where it's going."

"Of course, refugee is a good metaphor for Sam now because he is hanging out on garbage routes," Edward said. "He's eating well, better than before, probably. He also thinks the world misunderstands him. Sometimes good metaphors work with internal dialogue. Which is not literal."

"So, anyway," Mindy continued. Edward rolled down his window and the air whipped into the car, tossing his hair around. "You were an editor weren't you, Marcy?"

"I got laid off. They went through a huge restructuring. So."

"Maybe you'd think about working with them on the book or screenplay?"

"They're actually going to do this? Don't you think we need to see if Sam is actually found?"

"Oh, of course. It's just that Ellen has so many contacts in the movie industry. Out in Hollywood." Mindy sighed, pulled her hair up, and clipped it. "Just thinking out loud. I think Sam is bound to enter a trap one of these days."

"You need to put the trap on garbage routes that are messy. Sloppy neighborhoods," Edward said.

They were now at the address, thank God.

"Time to get to work," Mindy said as she opened the door. "They can always write the story first, or screenplay first, then make sure the story comes true." She laughed.

Marcy didn't laugh.

"Dog movies don't really move me," Edward said as he opened the door and stepped out. He walked to the front and got in the passenger seat by Marcy. "We would need to film all the sloppy garbage bags in messy neighborhoods." He closed the car door and reached for his seat belt. "People don't like admitting they're messy. It's a privacy issue."

Marcy took a longer route home, to give her time to talk with Edward without interruptions from her mother, who tended to edit Edward and drift off topic with irrelevant observations. At the next stoplight, Marcy looked over at her brother. His whiskers dotted his chin and upper lip. Some were longer than others, which gave him a canine appearance. He held both hands in his lap and looked straight ahead, as if unaware of her stare.

"So, thanks for all this help. You're doing a great job."

"No one really listens to me. But they will. I think the pressure to find the dog will make everyone realize that all thoughts are important." He turned to look at her as she drove on. "Do you think they're going to catch the dog?"

"No. No, I don't. Sam's not going to come to any of these people, and by now he probably doesn't trust me either, although, I keep thinking if I saw him once, just once, he would pause before running, give me a chance to cajole him or pull out some treats. I know he's scared, though."

"The world, sis, is a scary place. There is no end to the breaking news. No end. Just so much out there that can terrify you."

They drove in silence a while. Marcy opened her mouth to speak but closed it when she looked over at Edward, his expression reminding her of the terror he had been through at such a young age. She would never get the image of Edward out of her mind, the day he was surrounded by police at the park. Running around, waving his hands, hysterical, his weak, puffy body shaking as he ran. A pedestrian had called the police. What else were they to do?

This was back when he was twenty years old and on five meds, which he finally threw out, frustrated with his weight gain and memory loss. He tossed them in the garbage one afternoon. Three days later he roamed neighborhoods, wandered down roads, ending up at a park in a contiguous town, which was a good thing, as no one knew her there.

After her mother had called, Marcy had left her job and raced to the scene.

Edward screamed at her to get down, get down. "The fox is here to recruit me. He is here to take me to his burrow. The fox talks."

One cop became anxious and pulled a gun. Marcy ran in front of him, figuring this was it, this was the end of her life because she was going to take a bullet for her crazy brother. But she was tackled, then Edward was tackled. He stayed in the psychiatric hospital one month.

"Edward. Look, you don't have to worry. You don't have to research places that provide free cable news. I will make sure that if anything happens to Mom, you get cable news."

"It's not the cable news I need. It's breaking news."

"I just want you to know that I am here. OK? So, if anything happened, you'd just come live with me. No problem. No need to roam around trying to figure out how to find a TV. I've got one."

"You'll always have breaking news?"

"Yes, Edward. I'll always have breaking news."

Chapter 23

Marcy
Fame and shame

FIND SAM week 17

Facebook page: Find Sam!
total friends: 9.5k

"*Thank you Elda Jeneris for talking about our FindSam movement. In case you guys out there have missed it, Elda showed one of our videos on her show, then invited us to be guests! We look forward to talking with you, Elda! The entire nation is with us now! This fame should help boost awareness of missing dogs...*"... Detective Serendon

New Comments:
Sally Hampton (picture of maple tree): *I loved the video you guys sent into the Elda show. Great publicity for our town too!*

Harriet Whelchel (picture of lab): *ruff ruff, My Mom's been following FindSam for weeks. Wish he was lost up here in Minnesota, then I could help We always watch TV when you guys are on.*

Jaynie Spector (picture of camera): *I run a photography store. We do dog pictures. Boy has the demand for corgi pictures gone up!*

Henry (picture of pit bull) *Our discarded waste is someone's found treasure. Life always recycles. Except in Russia. There, life vanishes.*

Mary Johnson: *(selfie of young woman on sofa, cat in lap).* I think, folks, the dog is long gone. I was wondering....you guys think the dog walker stole it?

Twitter: @FindSam!
Followers 325k

#FindSam #WeloveSam #windhavenlovesSam
#hugyourdogforSam #dogwalkersfromhell
#corgipuppiesforsale #fireSamsdogwalker
#betterdogwalkersforwindhaven #saveraccoons
#raccoonshaveworthtoo #samisfamous #dogwalkerthief

MARCY, TAPPED OFF her phone, shoved it in her back pocket, and continued to clip around the park, her dogs on leash, obedient and playful. Even Sweetiepie was obedient and playful now. Henry trotted by her side, off leash but still attached to the group. The dogs had played in the mud today, so Marcy decided to give them a quick rinse at the Nelson's before returning them home. Elizabeth was in New York today and the housekeeper had taken the day off. No need to have owners complain about muddy paw prints in kitchens and basements. Besides, she hadn't watched TV in a while and a TV show would help take her mind off of what now was an obvious tragedy.

It was reaching the point where most people would give up. The weather was beginning to change and it had been over four months since Sam escaped. But, no, no one was giving up. Even with no dog. Ellen still managed to keep her dog's name in the news or social media. A YouTube of Sam had gone viral. Several national news journalists continued to interview Ellen. And after Marcy's disastrous CNN interview—Marcy looking all defensive, messy and of course guilty— all journalists wanted to talk with Marcy. She assumed since Sam was now desperately missing, her guilt was even more newsworthy. *"Do you still have hope Sam will be found? What do you think when you see all these people working so hard to find a dog that you lost on the job. Can you share how this makes you feel?"* But the persistent media attention probably kept clients from dropping Marcy, because they didn't want national journalists to paint the community as unforgiving. So, they stuck by Marcy's side, complimented the way she had helped their hunt, which was now a national movement of sorts barreling toward a tragic outcome.

Marcy still reluctantly helped with traps and tried to keep her mouth closed as they pondered the failures. All her ideas were dismissed at the meetings with the detective.

"The dog we are after has been missing for quite a while now," the detective said to her once when she tried to suggest they let her at least call his name. "Sam is slightly above the level of a wolf—feral. He has learned how to survive. He could possibly be eating live rodents. Corgis and terriers are very good at catching mice. If he smells something even slightly familiar, he will abandon the area. OK? We are dealing with a feral animal."

Lorene had shaken her head in agreement. She was a better team player than Marcy. She followed orders, worshiped the detective, and had been placed in charge of all trap monitoring. In fact, Lorene was officially Vice President of the Find Sam Movement. So, all of this had been great for her—a new social group, one connected to a more elite crowd.

Marcy, meanwhile, was turning into a social recluse. She used to have smart friends—consultants, editors, product managers. They used to all have dinner together at least once every two weeks to discuss boyfriends, jobs, social media. Marcy had been the eccentric—the dog walker with a college degree and editing experience. But now Marcy had no desire to congregate with successful women with real jobs. A dog walker hanging with smart, career friends was one thing, a failed dog walker was quite another. Her only current social outlet was the Find Sam movement. And Lorene.

Marcy opened the door of her Toyota van. All the dogs jumped in, a few leaping into the back, Henry up front. She lifted the bulldog out of the wagon, shooed the dogs away then placed her gently in the back seat.

She trusted all of them to refrain from fighting, but today the car was stuffed and anything could trigger a growl. She could barely see out the back window—always a risk since police notice visibility issues, but she knew routes rarely traveled by police. However today, before she made it to the low traffic streets, Eric started up his barking, which, due to the crowded conditions, inspired group barking. Marcy tapped a blues station on the radio screen and an old southern man's voice rose from the speakers singing about despair. Soon, the van filled with panting, barking, farting and loud southern, sad music, until soon the barking turned into growling. Marcy pulled over.

"Stop growling! We're singing blues here." Silence.

A mild growl rose from the far back, where Max, the Wheaten, sat, his head drooping. She had to settle him down or he'd get them all started again, so she turned off the engine and opened the door.

She saw it after her foot left the car, so there was no time to pretend she didn't see it. Red and blue flashing lights. She closed the door, closed her eyes, and waited. After the light knock on her window, she opened her eyes, forced a smile, and rolled down the window.

"Hey," Marcy said, after a pause to take in the shock of the familiar face. "Nice to see you again. What's the problem?"

"Hey there." Officer Willard leaned over and looked at Henry and Ed. Oh, please don't growl, Marcy thought. Please don't bark. Don't do anything. She shifted her eyes to Henry. He looked at her, as if he knew why she was scared. He didn't growl or bark. But the Wheaten did. Then the Lab. Then, the herder, who had by far the most obnoxious bark of any dog she walked.

"Would all of you shut up. I mean it. Shut up!" Marcy yelled.

The dogs quieted down, but it was a transient quiet, one filled with panting and snorting, pending the outcome with the encounter with the man they all seemed to hate.

"Well, I see you have your hands full here. All these dogs your clients?" Officer Willard looked at Henry.

"Yep. Are you concerned about all the dogs, like, maybe, the distractions? Because, officer, I am dropping them off right now."

"That dog looks familiar." He nodded his head toward Henry.

"He's a pit bull."

"But that particular pit bull looks very familiar. The black spot over the eye, you know. I thought you didn't know anyone with a pit bull? Remember our discussion?"

She said nothing, just looked at Henry.

"This one's new," she said, slowly. "Just got him to replace the corgi I lost."

"Who owns that dog?" Officer Willard said. "And why doesn't he have tags. Even walking, the dog should have tags on. You know that, right?"

"It belongs to the Roses, in Darlington. Quite a drive from here, I know, but I got to eat. The tags were on his collar. His collar has been missing. They don't know where it went. Probably playing around at the park and another dog yanked it off. Or something. I told them, I said, look I can't walk your dogs without tags. But they, like all my clients, are very busy. Working parents." Marcy shrugged and smiled.

Officer Willard didn't.

"Does anyone else walk their dogs?"

Marcy paused a moment. "You know, that's a good question. I think I'm the only walker."

"Let me get that name from you. You got a phone number, too?"

Marcy wondered if she could she be arrested for lying to a police officer. Was that against the law? Or was that only when there was an investigation?

"I only have the cell for the Ms. Rose. It's 203-565-9876."

After he wrote this down, he asked how the dog hunting was going, then stood, cocked his head, and stared at her again. She smiled. He stared. Eventually he walked back to his car, shaking his head. She immediately started the car and took off carefully. She wondered if he would call that number. If he did call it, when would he call it? Would he call it today? Or would he wait? Of course, she would have to let Lorene know she gave the police officer her cell number.

Marcy was so distracted by this incident that she didn't see Elizabeth's BMW in the driveway when she reached the Nelson house. She was going over an internal dialogue in her head as she opened the door, let the dogs out and walked around the house to the back door that led to the basement. Elizabeth stood in the garden outside the door. Marcy stopped. Elizabeth looked at Henry then Nellie.

"Hey, Nellie. You have a good walk today?"

Nellie leaped up, licked her face, her tail wagging furiously. She turned in circles twice then ran around the back yard, which resulting in Henry following her, barking. Marcy had the other dogs on the leash, except for Sadie, now sprawled out on the grass, her belly spread out like a fat lady's thighs. Elizabeth put her hands on her hips as she watched the dogs play, squinting, as if trying to recognize Henry.

"I've never seen all the dogs like this. I thought you only walked four others? They look dirty. And who owns a pit bull?" "Pit bull" came out as if the name had been caught in her throat for a long time and she had to push it out. "Is it a rescue?"

"Henry's from Darlington." Marcy felt slightly faint. She tried to will the blood back into her head. "I think he was purchased as a puppy, so, I don't know. He could have been a rescued puppy of course."

Elizabeth stared at the dogs and said, without looking at Marcy, "I suppose you're wondering why I'm home today. I had told you I would be in New York." She turned to look at Marcy.

"Did you? I guess you did. I suppose your plans were cancelled right?"

"Were you planning on bringing all those dogs into my house to wash them off?"

"They were all barking and anxious, so I was going to walk them around, then stuff them back in. We were pulled over by the police who was worried about all the dogs in the car. And of course they all started barking and jumping around, which made the police officer even more concerned. It was a bit stressful. So I decided once we got here to let Nellie off, I would let them out just a second."

"I see. Makes sense then. I've wondered, though, because all those dog beds we have were misplaced once. Not misplaced, but placed into the closet differently than I remember arranging them. I noticed they were a bit soiled. Not too much but just enough to get me wondering. You know. I notice when things are misplaced."

Nellie was back. She leaped up and licked Elizabeth again. Henry sat by her, panting. The other dogs were now seated. Marcy leaned over and petted the herder who was staring at her intently.

"Of course, I am that way with everything," Elizabeth continued. "I notice things. The only thing I am bad about is my computer. I don't notice things about the computer. Larry does. He's always on it, always noticing the slightest malfunction, you know. But not me. But this is the thing, Marcy. I notice my surroundings. For example, out here? In the garden? Most people would not notice a small hole dug near my azalea bush. Squirrels are burying their nuts constantly. But I notice because I garden. I am in this soil every day. I just love the feel of soil. Do you garden?"

The herder licked Marcy's hand. She leaned down to pet him. Henry lay down by the bulldog, now snoring.

"If you gardened you would know that the best way to garden is with gloves off. Gloves off. Feel everything in the soil that way. You never know what you are going to find, sometimes a worm. Why don't you follow me. I want to show you something."

Marcy regarded her dogs, now all sitting or lying. She dropped the leash and followed Elizabeth to the garden, a horseshoe shaped collection of slowly fading color—azaleas, day lilies, Siberian iris, lavender. The entire edge of the garden was highlighted by New Guinea impatiens, now thick bushes of reds, oranges, and whites, throwing off their last bit of color before fall destroyed them.

Elizabeth stopped by the azalea bush, kneeled, and put her hand in the soil. That one movement toward the soil, the one slight look back at Marcy said it all. Marcy would always remember the small oblong leaf touching Elizabeth's hand, the smell of the soil, the slight hint of perfume—a sweet melon odor.

"Here," Elizabeth said. "Right here is where I found your memory stick."

Chapter 24

Marcy
Using shame to obtain fame

ELIZABETH CROSSED HER feet on the wooden coffee table, appearing relatively relaxed for someone who was aware her computer had been turned on and perused while she was away. The dogs were on their beds, except for the herder, who at least was not barking due to the Nylabone in his mouth. The basement carpet was a bit soiled now that the dogs had sniffed around, but the coffee table had been polished, side tables organized, windows wiped, as if Elizabeth had cleaned up to make some sort of metaphorical statement.

"Can I get you anything?" Elizabeth asked. "I forgot to ask before we settled in down here. That's the way it is with dogs, right? You're so busy taking care of them, cleaning everything for them, you forget about yourself?"

"Look," Marcy said, tucking one leg underneath her as if getting comfortable for a long chat. She sat opposite of Elizabeth, in a small club chair. "Thanks for finding my memory stick. I must have dropped it one day a long time ago. I've noticed it went missing. I think I lost it when you guys were out on vacation."

Elizabeth said nothing.

"I suppose you knew it was mine because you looked on it, right?

"Yes, I did but, but I would never go into your personal folders. I didn't click on anything. I only checked to see if it was mine or my husband's." She stared at Marcy, then looked over at Nellie splayed out on the largest dog bed. "I figured it was for work, right? There was a work folder."

"I'm really sorry I did that. I sometimes bring work with me. I do consulting jobs to make ends meet. I had a deadline. So." So, did she wonder about the noneofmybusiness folder? Was she even curious?

"All you had to do was ask to use my computer. I do feel a bit uncomfortable about someone on my personal computer you know. "

"Again, I'm really sorry. I just worked on my memory stick. I guess, then, you'll fire me for using your computer without your permission."

"Well, no. Not really. Nellie likes you and I have to have a dog walker. We're out of town so much. Visiting kids. New York. And, while I'm confused as to why you would lie, I think it was a stressful time. The computer use will not happen again, unless you have my permission. From now on it will be password protected. Plus, we need you in Find Sam. It's become a national sensation and we have some possible developments in the PR category. Would be nice to have an editor, someone with those important New York contacts. Has Ellen talked with you yet about Hollywood's interest in her dog?"

"Ellen? No. She doesn't really chat with me often. I see her at the Find Sam meetings and she's nice to me."

"Well, you know Ellen is very well connected. And she has done a tremendous job publicizing her lost dog. That is her job as you know."

"Oh, yes, I know," Marcy said. "Ellen's friend told me. Windy, or Cindy? Something like that. Anyway, she told me Hollywood is charmed by all this national attention, and were encouraging a story, or movie, or something along those lines. I was not a surprised."

"Ellen and her friends know I like to write, so they approached me. But I'm an amateur. I couldn't write something like that, and I'm too busy. But, truly, they are adamant about this. And I don't know. Maybe it would be something good to do. Fun. We could certainly use a good editor. Someone with the kind of connections you have would be nice, too."

"I'm not sure I am qualified. Is this a screenplay?" Marcy didn't mention Elizabeth's reference to contacts, because Marcy's contacts would not add to interest, only subtract from it.

"Or novel, or both. We don't know yet. Ellen's agent said to simply put something down and she would try to market the idea. She has connections in L.A. but not New York. It would help to have an editor who had that line back to a big publishing house. You have to know we have a national interest right now. Social media. Talk shows. They're still talking about our Find Sam movement. Everywhere. We have to capitalize upon this fast."

"Well, I hope we find Sam, so that can move forward."

"But, see, we have to work on all of it now, right now, Marcy. For the good of all lost dogs out there. We work on this, so it's all ready once Sam's found."

"What if you don't find him?"

"We'll write it. Then Sam will appear!" She laughed.

"I think it's best to find the dog." Marcy stood. "And I've got to get these dogs back."

Elizabeth followed her to door, then out to the car, all the dogs surrounding her. After the dogs were settled inside the car, Elizabeth rested her elbows on the open car door window. The engine was humming, the dogs panting, and Marcy shifted the gear into reverse, but Elizabeth leaned on the open window preventing retreat.

"Marcy, let me ask you a few questions. I have done a bit of research. Just a bit, on your story about this dog? I'm sure you lost the dog. Don't get me wrong. It's just that the details surrounding how you lost the dog are a bit confusing. I called you, see, around, what, eleven-fifteen or so. Remember? You told me you were walking the dogs. Is that correct?"

Marcy nodded.

"Walking the dogs back to the car, I talked to Ellen about this and she told me, yes, you said you lost the corgi near the park. Am I right?"

Marcy nodded.

"But, well, when I looked on the memory stick? I couldn't help but notice the time you logged off? I did check time and date, OK? I didn't read your work or your personal folders."

"OK. I trust you."

"Anyway, you logged off at eleven-fifteen. Here is the thing. How could you have logged off, gone to the park, lost the dog, all by eleven twenty-five? And I thought you had been at the park for a short while when I talked with you."

Marcy looked right into Elizabeth's eyes. "I saved my work on my computer."

"Well, yes. See, I clicked on your editing folder, real quick, just to see when you last modified it and lo and behold, there it was 11:15, May 16."

"I left, then walked to the park, then you called." Marcy was falling into the potholes of her lie path. She focused her eyes only on Elizabeth. She read in a blog that liars always shift their eyes around.

"Was someone else walking the dogs for you? Is that why the times were different?"

The bulldog took a long inhale then blew out a breath loud, which sounded like a rumble of flapping flesh. The herder jumped up, rested his paws on the back of Henry's seat.

"I'm guilty. It was just that once." Once a lie is discovered, find another lie to reconnect to existing lie path. Marcy didn't read that on a blog, she made it up.

"I believe you." Elizabeth didn't smile. "I'd make a good detective wouldn't I? Don't worry, your secret is safe with me. We're a team, or will be anyway."

Elizabeth took a quick breath and paused a moment, waiting for Marcy to respond. She didn't.

"I know your brother's disabled, so you have a lot going on in your life. I'm Chairman of the Board of Education, you know, I understand the difficulty of special needs. They certainly burn a hole in our budget each year."

A hot flash fell down Marcy's neck. She tried to concentrate on Elizabeth's eyes. She breathed deep to prevent the bitter sass gurgling up her throat from escaping.

"Anyway, I think this project will help all of us focus our energies on all dogs. And, you know, if this sells, we could get a TV show."

"Well, who knows, I may like writing or at least editing something about Sam. We'll need to find him, though."

"Dogs can be found." Elizabeth was still.

"Yes, they can." Marcy said. *Dogs?*

"I think we'll make a great team." Elizabeth pushed away from the car and watched Marcy back out of the driveway.

Two firsts, Marcy thought as she drove away. Someone actually wanted Marcy on their team. And a new, fresh lie popped up to save her, one she wasn't even responsible for.

Chapter 25

Marcy
Famous and shameless!

"WHAT DO YOU mean, someone's going to call me about a pit bull? Is this Henry?" Lorene had just poured herself a glass of wine. An unlit cigarette hung from her lips.

"Just in case he calls, your name is Martha Rose, you live in Darlington, and, yes, you own a pit- bull, and, yes, you have tags. But say they fell off."

"I'm thinking this is police, right?"

"Yes."

"Name of officer." She sat on the sofa and took a long sip of wine.

"I don't know. Willard?"

"Officer Willard? The one who was chased by some maniac during the storm? Wait, didn't the maniac have a pit bull?" She put down her wine and put both hands over her eyes. "Oh God no, Marcy. I am not doing this. He's calling to see if I'm any relation to the guy with the pit bull. You want me to risk my reputation just to save your stray dog? I am sorry. This is too much. You've got to do something, like adopt the dogs, get them licenses. You can't keep this up."

Marcy hated Lorene's memory. "He probably won't call. If he does, all I'm saying is say you are Martha Rose and, yes, I walk your pit bull."

She stopped talking, hoping this would pass quickly and they would finish their wines, drive to the Find Sam meeting. Tonight was another video show. Apparently, a video had captured another animal with corgi-like ears. Marcy figured it was a fox. However, there were three sightings this week, each in different towns. There was a map posted online with all the sightings so that the detective could study the wanderings, make sense of the dog's mindset. Edward had studied the map and recommended the traps be moved to new locations near certain the garbage routes he had studied. His suggestion was ignored.

That had been last week, and after the meeting, Ellen had approached Marcy to request she reconsider bringing Edward as he tended to disrupt too often. "We love Edward, of course, and appreciate his help. You know this, right? We just think he would be better off helping with the search in other ways."

Tonight she told him she wasn't going and he had shrugged and mumbled OK. She felt awful lying to him. Everyone seemed to lie to Edward because they were too cowardly to confront him.

"Marcy?" Lorene stared at her cigarette she was rolling between her thumb and forefinger. Marcy didn't look up or answer because the tone was maternal and soft. Lorene always used this tone before unleashing advice.

Marcy already had a mother, and while Lorene was a very cool woman, she was un-cool when she wanted to become Marcy's second mother.

"Where's your Mets cap?"

"I don't have a Mets cap."

"Yes, you do, sweetie. Or you did. I remember distinctly coming over here and seeing you in your Mets cap. I remember because it was the first time I had encountered Henry."

Marcy said nothing.

"You had lied back then. You had said something about the dog belonging to someone else? I believed you. After a while, it became obvious the dog was a stray you were keeping. But I remember the Mets cap, because, as you know, I'm a Yankees fan."

"Oh yeah. I tossed it. One of the dogs chewed it up. You know."

"When did you toss it?"

"Can't remember."

"Because, I remember the stories about the officer, that officer Willard? The only identifiable feature the officer recalled was a dark baseball cap, maybe he said, a Mets cap. It was in the paper in one of the follow-up articles. That and the pit bull. Seems, you have, or had, both a Mets cap and a pit bull."

"But I don't own a gun. You know that. And if I did, I would not shoot an officer. So."

"So."

"OK. He was an asshole and I needed to get around the cordoned area. It was the only way out of the street, and so, yes, Lorene, yes, I sassed the jerk, but he started asking about Henry, because, as we all know, a pit bull equals violence. He wanted me to step out of the car so he could question me about my pit bull. And Henry was barking, not like I'm going to bite you barking, but barking. But any bark from a pit bull is threatening. Lab, OK. Golden, OK. Pit bull? One peep, and everyone assumes violence. It's called profiling. The asshole was profiling Henry. So I took off. I did. I took off and he came after me, then trees fell and I looked in the rear view mirror and there he was out of the car with his damn gun drawn. I was, like, he's drawing a gun on me because I have a pit bull? And here is the thing, Lorene."

Lorene's mouth was open, arms crossed.

"Here is the thing. That bullet they found in the tree? Did you know this? Was this in the paper? They found his bullet in a tree. He shot at me, so he had to say, well, the perpetrator shot at me first, which is a lie. So he'll never I.D. me, because then he has to actually admit he shot at a woman with a pit bull who does not own a gun. He shot because he profiled a pit bull."

"So you want me to say this pit bull that this officer profiled is mine? Wow. What friend?"

"He'll never identify me. Too embarrassing. And who will believe that I own a gun?"

"You don't own one do you?"

"I told you I didn't."

Lorene chugged the wine, put the cigarette in her mouth, the pulled out a lighter. "I get to smoke on this one. Sorry, you can open a window later." She lit her cigarette, placed it in her mouth. Its end brightened. "You also told me, and the whole world, that you walked the dogs and lost Sam near the park, and you returned without incident to your apartment." As she talked smoke escaped and drifted around her face. Marcy got up to avoid inhaling it. "You told me the stray were owned by another family. You told the police your pit bull stray was a client's dog. Now you say you don't have a gun, didn't shoot an officer."

"Let's go to the meeting. It's really not worth talking about. Look, you don't have to say anything to the officer. Just don't answer the phone when the police department calls. Or any strange number. Just think it over."

Lorene pulled on her cigarette again and slowly stood then walked quietly to the kitchen, where she methodically poured out her wine, put the wine glass in the dishwasher, turned on the water, and put her cigarette under its flow. She walked to the front door.

"Let's go. I'm sick of thinking about all of this. Whatever happened, happened. And I am attending the meetings and helping with the posters and traps for a while longer, but there will reach a point when we all may have to admit the dog may be long gone. People are still seeing him, but one day, the sightings will go away and we all have to admit that the dog is gone or dead."

ELLEN'S HOME WAS 6,000 square feet with a living room as big as some houses, but the den was still crowded, people flowing into the foyer and kitchen. There were cameras set up at either end and a few journalists roving around asking questions. Everyone was dressed elegantly casual, with makeup and freshly blown hair. Sam had been sighted several times this week, and the news media were here waiting for the inevitable discovery and reaction. There was evidence that Sam had actually traveled near a trap because some food that had been placed out had been eaten, and in fact the video set up near the trap had caught the tail end of the corgi.

This time, Marcy agreed that the image was indeed the rear end of Sam. The heart shaped bottom, missing tail, sturdy thighs. That was Sam alright. The problem seemed to be Sam's total lack of interest in the trap. So, the meeting went over various food options, everyone emphasizing that no one should feed the dog in any town. The detective had actually found a water bowl in the woods behind a sighting area. She had written a letter to editor admonishing anyone responsible for trying to feed or hydrate the dog. "You have to understand, the dog has to be hungry and thirsty enough to enter the trap."

Not only journalists were filming the Find Sam meetings and tracking expeditions, but also popular talk show hosts were arriving with cameras, all fascinated by Sam's story. Ellen's appearance on the *Elda Jeneris Show* was a huge success. They put up pictures of Sam and all the community volunteers, including Elizabeth Nelson and about twenty of her closest friends. The town First Selectman was interviewed as well as Detective Serendon.

Lights had been set up around Ellen's living room and two large men holding cameras stood on either side of the projection screen. One man with a camera, that resembled a weapon, resting on his shoulder stepped in as Detective Serendon began to speak. The lens was so close, the detective paused and smiled into it self-consciously, as if she wanted to acknowledge someone at home watching.

"This week we are going to concentrate on the southeastern sightings. Seems our friend likes to wander around the Sound." She stopped talking as the cameraman moved his camera around the crowd. A few women brushed the hair from their eyes. The woman to Marcy's right smiled and waved.

"I'm not going to go through the map again, the one we discussed on our conference call, but I do think we all need to keep checking my website for additional information on sightings. Monitor these videos nightly. Every night. We are in the fall season, folks, not too long before the weather turns frigid. And we do not want that, we do not want to be looking for a dog in the cold."

A journalist holding a microphone raised her hand. "If we go into the winter, what will you do? Do you think dogs migrate south when this happens? Will it be time to put this to rest?"

Ellen stepped forward before the detective could speak. "I will not give up on Sam. We will find him. And, no, Sam will stay in the area. I know my dog."

The journalist shook her head. The detective continued while the journalist stepped into the back in front of a large lighted screen. "And there it is—the words of a determined owner who has the support of her entire community. They have been looking for the pooch for four months now, but there is no sign this community will give up. No one is giving up on this dog. This is a community dedicated not only to its human citizens but it's canine ones as well. If you want to help, you can join the Find Sam Facebook page or follow Find Sam on twitter, or go to their go fund me account . . ."

After the presentation was over and the journalists left, Lorene held a small meeting of volunteers for the silent auction. The proceeds wouldn't just assist the Find Sam movement, but also a rescue organization that had joined in the effort to find Sam. Marcy sat quietly in the back, keeping an eye on Elizabeth, who had roamed the room talking to volunteers, eventually huddling with Ellen in the corner. Marcy got up, stepped over to the bar, poured herself a bit more wine to anesthetize her mind, help her forget the bad week that included new lies, which required an alert mind. She took a long sip.

"Ellen and I would like to have a quick chat with you." Elizabeth's voice hit the air behind her, startling Marcy into spilling wine over her hand and onto the hardwood floor. She turned to find not only Elizabeth, but also Ellen smiling at her. In her peripheral vision, she could make out Lorene walking toward them.

"If you don't mind, we're stealing Marcy for a moment," Elizabeth said when Lorene arrived by Marcy's side and opened her mouth to talk. She closed it quickly. "Good job with the auction, by the way."

"I'd love to talk but I'm the designated driver tonight," Marcy said. "Lorene has to get back. Why don't you call me?"

"No, no. You go ahead." Lorene gave Ellen the requisite pitying smile and concerned look. She probably assumed this was about the dog. "I'm fine, and Marcy can talk with you as long as it takes. I'm in no hurry."

"This will take a second. Really," Ellen said.

THE SMALL STUDY felt dark and foreboding with its brown leather upholstery, maroon-colored walls, mahogany desk. Ellen sat quickly and studied her computer a moment before turning to talk. She smiled brightly at Marcy then chatted with Elizabeth briefly about the Find Sam progress, both agreeing Sam would be found in the next few weeks. Elizabeth nodded as Ellen went into a few details about publicity, suggesting how important it was to keep Sam in the news. There was another interview on a national morning news show.

"And speaking of keeping things in the news. Elizabeth told you, I hear, about Hollywood's interest our little dog hunt. Human interest stories are very popular. Dogs are popular, too. If you were to go to YouTube, dog videos are more popular than cats. And the most popular, trending subject when it comes to dogs are rescue dogs." Ellen paused as if to consider Sam, who was of course not a rescue, but now a stray, which was related to rescue. Not one dog Marcy walked was a rescue. "The community has been amazing. Our country's concern for my dog is amazing. And that is the key selling point. It says just how wonderful our country is. Our love of dogs, that is."

Marcy glanced at Elizabeth who met her eyes and held onto them.

"And, as Elizabeth told you, it has captured an agent's attention. She's a friend. Well, a friend of a friend. It's not like I need publicity or money, it's that, well, Marcy, I think, it's my obligation as Sam's mom to tell his story. It's our obligation as dog lovers to reveal to the world the struggles families go through when they lose their dogs. A movie, or documentary, or book, TV show, would do wonders for the rescue community."

"Well," Marcy said slowly. "Elizabeth told me some of your contacts informed you the story wouldn't be marketable if Sam was never found. If you work on something and Sam isn't found, it will be a waste of time. I'm not saying he won't be found. This is hypothetical. I'm amateur. There are ghost writers out there. I can help find them."

"I thought about that," Ellen said. "My agent doesn't want to bother paying someone, if all she needs is a story, an outline. This could turn into a movie, a show. If it sells, then we do a serious write. I was hoping that you, with that experience you have working with a publishing house could help us, or maybe you could help our agent with some of your contacts. We may need those New York contacts."

"I've been giving this thought," Marcy said. "Not too much because I haven't really had a lot of time to think about it, but I have given it thought, and I just don't think I'm your person. I don't think I would be good at it. Like I said, it's best to go with a ghost writer."

"This is the plan, actually," Elizabeth said, as if Marcy had not spoken. She pulled up a chair and leaned into Marcy, all business, as if Marcy had never turned on her computer and done work without her permission. "We go over the story of Sam, maybe some funny scenes with you and Sam. We make this your story maybe. You, the dog walker, because guilt is something that is so universal. Guilt is understood. And guilt, your guilt, has been selling. Have you noticed the journalists' interest in you?"

"Guilt sells," Ellen said.

"I don't think I write guilt well," Marcy said.

"Then we can have some sort of sub-conflict going on," Elizabeth continued. "Like, for example, what if the dog walker, you, didn't check the weather, but went out walking and the storm took you by surprise. Maybe there is a reason she lost the dog, one she is hiding."

Was she blackmailing Marcy? With the secret about another dog walker, which was a lie?

"That is important to these stories—subplots. We stretch the truth a bit, because it is creative nonfiction."

Marcy felt both nauseous and dizzy, yet in a strange way relieved, although she didn't know why she was relieved.

"Creative nonfiction?" Marcy said.

"Yes," Elizabeth continued. "Creative nonfiction. Tweaking nonfiction. And a story like this will make you look great. Flawed, but forgivable. We will take care of finding Sam. We *will* find Sam."

"And how long will this all take? And when you say story? Is this a screenplay? Publishing houses do novels but, I don't think . . ."

"Screenplay, yes, then if that works, a book. I just don't know. Just write, OK? My contact," Ellen said as she stood, "said we have to get this out as soon as we find Sam. Like dog found, manuscript sent in within two weeks. That fast. I'd say, give it a month. If they accept it in Hollywood, I think a publisher will also accept a book. That's how it all works, according to my agent. Movie, then book."

"Write a movie, or documentary, or book?" Marcy said. "What exactly are we writing?"

"Something that will put us on the map," Ellen said. "Maybe turn into a movie, or a TV show. Not like the ones they have now, but a special one, one with a niche. My agent is exploring everything right now and just wants a script, for the basic idea. It will put all lost dogs, all rescue dogs, on the map. This will be dedicated to the stray dogs of the world. And who knows maybe it will turn into something else, something that could employ you."

"You don't want to be a dog walker forever do you?" Elizabeth said.

"No, I guess not. I just hope Sam is found."

"We have seven traps. And our detective is contemplating another. Sam is going to walk into a trap. No problem. We will have the dog."

Chapter 26

Sam
Thank you for donating,
but please stop with the raccoon prisons

I'M GOING TO take it easy today because it's nice here by water. I have already taken a bit of a swim. Swimming, however, is getting more difficult to manage, due to my weighted, anchored existence. I suppose I am now heavier due to this hard life, if you will. I seem to move, even swim, more slowly. I'm still in shape, mind you. When you have to run to five different donation areas to eat, you stay in shape.

What may have contributed to my weighted condition is second day food. Second day has streets populated by very unorganized, messy humans. These humans have rather capacious donation buckets, with torn bags, not exactly messy, like Bosslady's car, but out of order in appearance, I will say, because of their intermittent rips, donated food peeking out of edges, dropping onto streets. They also had a splendid effect upon the ole olfactory senses. One house always donates untouched hamburger. Every second day, this one house has a lovely hamburger in its donation bucket. And I am not suggesting a hamburger with missing bread, bits of meat nipped, small pieces of cheese or bacon. No, this is not half eaten, it is a hamburger in its entirety, as if the humans place a hamburger in front of another human every week, and this human refused to touch the hamburger in question; nevertheless, the humans persist! The unsatisfied human is forced to sit before said hamburger then donate it. To me! I get that hamburger!

At times I am forced to compete with some of the raccoons—the ones who do not walk into the human mobile raccoon prisons—more on this later. I gorge myself before raccoons arrive. I make my way to all the routes from there, but, truly, no route is as nice as second day.

The worst is fifth day, by the water, where the skinny humans live. They simply do not donate the food that satisfies a homeless dog's palate.

So, I'm doing fine! After a full week of eating, I lay on a bank and take in the water, the delicate temperate air, although lately it has the intermittent chill that portends the dark death march of winter. I put the future aside today and stay here, with the sun overhead and the blue jays squawking in trees. I look toward the squawking trees and notice another mobile raccoon prison in the dead center of a footpath. I see only its edge. A while ago, I had encountered another one of these raccoon prisons, full of the flustered and fearful rodents. It was surely a sad sight, but they are the ones to blame, as clearly the path of food leads into a prison. It does not take much study to recognize a prison. Humans used to put us into these systems when we were young and could not control bodily functions. Humans despise any fecal matter elimination in their homes.

There is this rather strange pattern I have detected that indicates a disturbing possibility. Once, a while back, I had encountered a human who engaged in the regular routine—see me, put box to face, then disappear. This happens quite regularly, by the way. Anyway, I returned to this familiar ground a few days later only to discover another mobile raccoon prison had been placed in the precise location the human had stood with box to face. I am a bit worried that the mobile prison was not meant for the raccoons but for me. This would explain the predictable pattern—I lap up water, pee in yard, snack on cat food or bird seed, human witnesses my scofflaws, human behaves strangely, next day mobile raccoon prison appears. I now wonder if—and indeed this is quite disturbing as it alerts me to the dangerous nature of humans I have never witnessed before—these humans congregate, share stories about me—the now wayward corgi who is stealing cat food—then contact "chosen" humans who bring mobile prison. The humans intend to catch me!

Let me emphasize that I am not certain the humans intend to harm me. I do believe humans will only incarcerate me. Humans are very intent on consequences for rule breaking. I suspect they would scold me, then call my mom, who will scold me.

I find it quite disconcerting that humans consider me so unintelligent that I would walk into the mobile prison. I've seen several raccoons, one possum, and one fox become entrapped. There is always food on the outside periphery, then little morsels dribbled in a straight line leading the poor cretins to a large board at its end, which, once depressed, pulls upon wiring that releases some latch that results in the door slamming shut. I've witnessed it. I always yell and yell, but they either do not care or simply have no clue how to translate dog language. I never stay around to see what the humans do to the dumb rodents. It has been my experience that humans truly detest raccoons.

It has not been my experience, however, that humans torture, although I have heard about many sociopathic humans from the Bosslady's homeless dog. Based upon his stories, one simply cannot tell which human will turn out to be a sociopath. Their smells are predictable, yes, but they seem very adept at hiding their insanity from one another. And, according to Henry, humans do not avoid sociopaths like us canines do. Many actually enjoy the company of sociopaths, and some communities of humans select them to be "leader" humans. I have no idea how Henry knew this. The homeless always have reasons for their homelessness, and these reasons create a knowledge base. The reasons also scare me.

The whisper of wind across my fur eases my concerns. It is as if the sun and breeze capture the anxious thoughts and thrust them away, allowing me to exist in the now. And the now is free of the mom, the structure, the security. However, security can never be overrated. I do miss that security.

I used to love my days with Bosslady. She allowed me itty bitty bits of lovely food that tasted like liver. She gave me choices, conversed with me about her life challenges. Her internal monologue was rather confusing for the other dogs, but not for someone like me, who can easily translate the English language. Besides, all humans who ramble like Bosslady are simply in need of listeners, and, unfortunately, there are not many human listeners. I miss that, I suppose, more than I miss security. I really miss listening to humans complain.

Chapter 27

Marcy
Fame with no dog equals fame with no money

THE MEETING TODAY required tight black pants. Marcy never liked how she looked in tight black pants. When she was an editor, she tried to keep up with the fashions, but her fashion statements always began with tight pants. She didn't have long legs and slip hips. Her legs were too short, hips too high. She looked good in baggy jeans and boat neck sweaters, which she figured was one of the reasons for her being selected for the first round of lay-offs at the publishing house. That and her tendency to piss off writers. Then there was that computer hacking incident.

Ellen told Marcy to look like a "hip former editor." The woman they were meeting, Margaret Cunningham, was apparently one of the hottest agents in L.A. She had optioned five novels over the past two years to good producers. Cunningham had agreed to at least talk about what had evolved from novel, to screenplay, to reality TV show, which had of course been done, but reality TV shows can be done again and again. For now, everyone simply referred to their efforts as "the project." Marcy had purchased a screenplay writing guide—which recommended the number of scenes, pages, and characters—but she had no idea how this now translated into a reality TV show, or if the show even needed a writer/editor. She had contacted a friend who had successfully marketed a screenplay for guidance. One friend told her to simply write a story first, then kind of "squish it into a screenplay framework." There had been a rough outline, about seventy-five pages of writing, some of which had been reviewed by Ellen and Elizabeth, some reviewed by Marcy's editor friends. The basic story she tried to write had very nice characters, charming, bucolic New England scenes, and lots of dogs. The dog walker had innocently gone on a walk in the storm near a park (far away from where the police officer had been chased by some "man" with a pit bull—which was not at all mentioned in the story). She didn't write the subplot they had all suggested.

Besides tight black knit pants, Marcy wore a flowing lavender silk shirt that fluttered over her hips and landed mid-thigh. Her shoes had heels, which caused her to trip and fall to her knees at the front door. This did not leave rips in her pants, only two dark spots and dirty hands. When Ellen answered the door, Marcy lifted her hands, palms out, and asked for the powder room. Ellen escorted her to the small bathroom off the foyer hall where Marcy cleaned her hands, brushed her legs, and made her face presentable.

The woman seated in the den was covered in a tight Chanel pants suit. She had barely any hair but what was on her head was very blond. Her lips were bright red, which matched the small red balls that hung from her ear lobes. Marcy felt the usual disassociation that always washed over her when dealing with overdressed and underfed women of the agent world.

"I've heard a lot of about you," Margaret Cunningham said as she shook Marcy's hand then sat, clasping her hands and waiting for Marcy to get comfortable.

She leaned into Marcy as if the entire meeting was about her. In fact, Margaret talked as if Marcy were the only person in the room, even though Elizabeth and Ellen sat on the sofa staring pleasantly into space and Detective Serendon sat in another chair to the side of the sofa.

This was not the detective Serendon Marcy was familiar with—the Detective Serendon who spoke about feral dogs and GPS map systems. This was another Detective Serendon. She still looked like an ex-police detective, except this ex-police detective cared about her looks. She wore makeup, tight business pants suit, and heels. Of course in the room full of expensive upholstery and tight black pants, she still looked a little dumpy, uncomfortable, and out of place.

"Marcy, can I offer you coffee? Pastries?" Ellen said.

There was coffee dispenser on the side table, a few china tea cups, a small pitcher of milk and pastries displayed on a Wedgewood serving platter. Marcy said no. She had gulped about three cups of coffee before she headed off this morning.

"And I checked on your reputation with one of my writers who knew some Ransom House people," the agent continued. "Some of whom were very disappointed to see you leave. Rough around the edges they said, but brilliant editor." She paused, looked over at Ellen.

Marcy felt a kind of rage building. Who in the hell said she was rough around the edges?

"Ellen has been filling me in on this amazing story," Margaret continued. "And her lovely friend, Elizabeth, have also discussed the progress with your writing. I've even taken a peek at what has been written to date, and, importantly, at the outline and plot summary. That's actually more important than the writing at this point. We have plenty of writers who can help us massage the message."

"Well, actually what I have brought with me is revised and better. I don't think the original actually reflects the editing I've done."

"No. Don't worry. We'll take a look at it. This is such a huge story, the writing will be easy. It's not as important when the story's gone viral. Find Sam Twitter feed is exploding. There are even Find Sam posters out in California. Did you know this? In California. Let's hope poor Sam didn't travel that far!"

She laughed. Marcy smiled. Detective Serendon laughed too hard.

"But, well, as we know, rescues are a very popular cause out there and we all want to help. Truly, if you don't own a rescue, you have some explaining to do out in L.A."

She laughed again, so Ellen and Elizabeth laughed again. Marcy smiled, thinking about all the purebreds she walked in town.

"Well, at least look at this version," Marcy said. "You may find it more readable."

"Oh, of course, of course. I will add it to my reading list. You would not believe how large that has gotten. Whew! It's all I do nowadays." Margaret took the manuscript, stuffed it in her oversized handbag without looking at it. "We had been thinking about alternative possibilities on this, Marcy, as others may have told you. A little movie, a story would be nice, of course, and it really fit nicely into that niche. But HBO has defined the TV movie market, and this is a bit too sweet for HBO. Unless you're going for a documentary. That may work. A story as a documentary type thing. Yes. It has to be not only about this lost dog, but all lost dogs. We need to follow the lost dog trajectory. How it impacts the owner, the community.

"And I will tell you this, OK?" Margaret looked at Detective Serendon. "We absolutely love this detective. Everyone at our place just loves Debbie. The detective is our hero."

"The flawed dog walker is loved, too," Elizabeth said. "We all love flawed heroes!"

"Oh yes," Margaret said. "The dog walker is key. The story is great because of that guilt, the guilt of the dog walker who lost a dog. Everyone just loves guilt, Marcy. It sells. Guilt sells."

Everyone stared at Marcy. She held up her hand and waved with only her fingers.

"Our team is amazing," Ellen said.

"We have an amazing town," Elizabeth added. "All of the Find Sam movement."

"Well, I have to say this is the most amazing group of people I have worked with, particularly this woman," Detective Serendon said, looking at Ellen. "Ellen is a dedicated dog owner. A truly dedicated woman."

"Oh thank you Debbie. But you are the best, and you know it." Ellen's quick glance at Marcy indicated it was her turn for flummery.

"She certainly deserves credit," Elizabeth said, then stared at Marcy, waiting.

Detective Serendon sat like everyone, waiting for Marcy.

Marcy managed to force a noise out of her throat to indicate agreement with the group, even though she was starting to question what in the world was going on and why no one had mentioned the dog.

The Find Sam movement appeared to be failing as of late. Sam was avoiding the traps, now numbering eight in three different towns. And there had been no sightings in two weeks, so the detective managed to keep everyone's hope up by suggesting her track dogs had picked up Sam's scent. But the detective's dogs had picked up the scent of Sam just this week over near one trap in Norfalk, which Edward had questioned since there was no garbage pickup on that day. According to Edward's calculations—which were based upon a study of ripped bags on garbage routes—Sam had increased his circle of wanderings to include Ridgetown, a town at least twenty miles away. "We, Marcy, are now looking for a fat dog," Edward had told her in the last phone call.

And it was beginning to get cold. A reality that everyone tried to avoid mentioning.

"So, here is what I've been thinking," Margaret said, clapping her hands two times quickly. "This story, if it ends nicely of course, which I am sure it will, could be a kind of documentary pilot, produced like a story. It would serve as a kind springboard into a detective dog whisperer-like reality TV show. There are others, but none with these stories that have town support. I think we have a more unique take on finding a dog. We start with this story, then produce other real stories, with the same type of characters. You know, flawed."

She smiled at Marcy.

"So, the story will have the detective at the center of it," Ellen said.

"I assumed it was from the point of view of the dog walker," Marcy said, thinking it was obvious the entire script had to be rewritten and her month had been wasted. "That's why I was asked to write. I guess I'm confused. "

" The story depends upon your participation, of course, and your point of view is important," Ellen said. "Guilt. Remember the marketability of guilt. You will not be the hero, you will be the flawed character we all forgive. It's what will set us apart from the others out there."

"And who knows. I may be able to use a dog walker," Detective Serendon said.

"Oh yes. The detective hires the flawed dog walker," Margaret said. "That says so much about our country. That is good reality TV."

Marcy said nothing, only imagined working with the detective, tracking dogs, setting up traps. Never finding dogs.

Ellen, Debbie, and Elizabeth were all in agreement about the story segueing into a reality TV show that emphasized flawed dog walkers or owners, or something like that. Ellen emphasized she had the capital to invest and would therefore take on the role of one of the producers.

No one seemed to consider the possibility of never finding Sam. In fact, the lack of progress with the Find Sam movement wasn't even an elephant in the room. An elephant in the room implied that the unmentioned issue was a huge problem. But Marcy didn't feel as if there was any concern at all about possibly not finding Sam, which made the elephant in the room belong only to Marcy. Marcy didn't know if it was appropriate to mention Sam. She didn't even know if mentioning him would even upset Ellen, but she felt his name, the possibility of his lost-ness being permanent, rise up like bile, forcing her to suppress its release with mind control techniques.

The meeting went on for an hour, until Margaret stood to announce she had another appointment. She shook hands, handed out her business card, admonishing them against calling her unless it was an emergency of sorts.

"Besides," she said. "There's no need for any further discussions until I pass around teasers, see if there's interest."

Everyone walked to the foyer.

Before they opened the door, Margaret turned to Ellen and Detective Serendon and said, quickly, in one breath, "OK, if there's interest, and I'm sure there will be, we're going to need a dog. Reality TV has to be real, but it cannot be sad. Three weeks. A dog."

"Don't worry. We have eight traps out," Detective Serendon said.

"I think we have to consider the possibility—" Marcy said.

Everyone fell silent.

"The possibility, albeit small. OK? Small."

Silence.

"That, well, that Sam won't be caught. OK. There is that possibility."

"Margaret, I can assure you there will be a dog," Ellen said. She looked over at Elizabeth Nelson then back at Margaret, ignoring Marcy. "Sam will be here on time."

Chapter 28

Marcy
Delusions can be solutions

IT WAS SEVEN-TEN a.m., and Edward and Marcy were in Norfalk, Connecticut, in front of a small ranch house, waiting for Lorene, who wanted to see what Edward had discovered, too. Marcy had to bring four of her dogs, all were leashed and eagerly sniffing Edward. Edward always had interesting smells. He now held a half-eaten chocolate donut, which he proceeded to split four ways for the dogs.

Edward had finally convinced Marcy to at least try to understand his garbage route analysis. He had explored the town, travelled down many major streets early mornings, studied the cans on each street, the types of food in the cans, the types of neighborhoods. He had a poster of the town that covered one wall in his bedroom—pins dotting all the streets, a number above the street name, indicating total ripped bags. He had scribbled the number twenty by Anderson Avenue, the highest of any street in Norfalk. He had also concluded this street was in one of the sloppiest neighborhoods, which had, according to his research, the most slovenly denizens, and thus the smelliest, greasiest garbage.

"Why not look into this?" Lorene had told her after listening to Marcy's description of his research poster.

Sightings were now nonexistent. The traps didn't even catch raccoons anymore. And now Margaret Cunningham had found a deal for Ellen and the crew. The network had agreed to a pilot, and if that was popular, a reality TV series could follow. This was no longer just about Sam anymore.

Marcy pulled her sweater together. The fall air was not quite cold yet, but the wind created a certain cool discomfort. The change in weather reminded her that winter was on its way, and Sam would be a cold lost dog.

"OK, today we begin the journey to Sam. It starts here," Edward said, after inspecting one garbage can.

A ripped bag hung over its side. Marcy noticed Edward had not shaved in a week. She made a mental note to talk with him about shaving. She was usually good at monitoring any deterioration in Edward's hygiene, or at least before he went anywhere in public with her, but she was distracted. The pressure was on, and she thought of nothing but finding Sam.

The herder started barking, which set all the dogs off. Marcy shushed them and managed to treat them into sitting. The object of the barking was soon apparent. Lorene's Taurus pulled to the side of the street. She hopped out, coffee in one hand, cigarette in mouth, hanging limply. Since she was only wearing a shirt and light button down cardigan sweater, she crossed her arms tightly and hopped from one leg to the other.

"Hello, Edward, Marcy. Look, I've got to be at work by nine-thirty, and as you know Marcy, we have to check a few traps today. I don't know why we're still setting them out but I don't want to not do my duty. Our luck, the one time we miss a trap, we'll miss something very important, maybe even Sam. Although, how long has it been since we've had a sighting?"

"There will be no sightings," Edward said. "I will have more ghost sightings than we will have dog sightings."

Lorene looked at Marcy. "You seeing ghosts, Ed?"

"That is an area of interest, yes. Not quite as intense as, say, Russia."

Once again the dogs started barking, indicating a need to move forward. The dogs Marcy had today were working dogs and they had to move.

"OK, Edward, I don't think Lorene is here to listen to your rants about Putin, or Syria, or ghosts. We are here because you have a plan."

"And we need to do this fast," Lorene said. "We're supposed to be checking on the trap for the group."

" I know this. You just said it. If you would rather go do that, then fine. You can certainly leave anytime."

"No, no. I said I wanted to see it. I just don't want to spend too much time in this town, when we have traps in another town to check before I got to work. And, just so you know, I got yet another call from that officer. I traced the number to Willard. Don't ask me how. Anyway, you think the memory is returning?"

"Are you sure? You didn't answer it, did you?"

"Of course not. I also got some strange cell phone number calling, too, but who knows, that could be a man I met at the party last weekend. I could be missing out on a date, and when you're my age, missing out on a date is a big deal. This is beginning to interrupt my life. But I am not answering the phone and getting stuck lying. He'll ask to come see my dog at my house. It's too much. Have you heard anything? Any updates about his memory?"

"What memory?" Edward said. "How do you know this officer calling you has a returning memory? You would have to actually answer the phone to ascertain memory function."

"Edward, this is personal," Marcy said. "Why don't you start the inspection of garbage cans. Lorene, it'll work out. I truly believe it will pass."

Edward walked over to a nearby garbage can and began inspecting its contents.

"Also," Marcy continued, her voice lowered to almost a whisper. "I think if his memory does return, it's a positive. Who wants to admit they tried to shoot some woman whose only crime was owning a pit bull? An unarmed woman. And unarmed pit bull. His memory will never come back. He's calling you because he's curious. Don't answer that phone, though."

"I hope you're right." Lorene lit her cigarette, took a long drag, and blew out jet stream as she followed Marcy, now moving forward with the dogs. One dog lunged, another on her flexi ran ahead of them. The other dogs trotted quietly by Marcy's side.

Edward stopped his inspection and followed them down the street. The houses that lined the street were square and brick, most with small porches lined with trimmed hedges, a few with remnants of summer gardens. One man emerged from a house near them and rolled his large gray container to the street. Since all the towns were required now to divide trash into food and recyclables, the days for garbage in neighborhoods where no one thought to compost were smelly days.

"Hello there," Edward said as they walked past the man now moving his garbage can next to his mail box. "May we have a word with you?"

"Edward!" Marcy's whisper sounded like a threat. She told him not to bother anyone on the streets he studied. He never listened. When he was in public, he forgot all admonishments. "Don't bother this man."

Eric, the herder, stopped to smell the garbage can. The Lab raised his leg and peed. The setter sat and panted, waiting for the man to pay some sort of attention to the more important visitors—dogs. He did, petting the setter first then calling the Lab over, which led to Nellie, the golden, engaging in her usual crotch ram. Nellie demanded attention and usually got it. It was something Marcy had noticed irritated Sam— Nellie's insistence on attracting the most human attention.

"Have you guys put up signs around here?" Lorene asked.

"No, I ask people," Edward said. "We don't tell Putin or the Syrians where we are bombing do we?"

"Signs about what? Putin?" The man stopped rubbing Nellie's ears.

"Sir, I hate to bother you," Marcy said quickly. She pulled quickly at the herder's leash. "Sit." He sat. "We're looking for a small dog, a corgi. He's golden colored, but maybe very dirty by now, so a brownish golden corgi."

"I've seen small dogs around here occasionally. And foxes. They run so fast it's hard to tell sometimes. Fox and dogs look alike, you know. But, no. I usually get out here by seven-thirty. So. You think that may be what is scattering our garbage around the street, huh?'

"That is precisely what I think," Edward said. "I'm sorry to bring up something way off topic. Putin obviously has nothing to do with the dogs we're after." The man stared at Edward who now directed his attention to Lorene. "But, Lorene, Putin is not an irrelevant topic. Not at all."

"Do you notice any of your garbage bags torn?" Marcy said quickly. "And if so, when do you think it's done? The night before or early in the morning?"

"Morning, I suppose. Some of us roll out the garbage the night before, but that's risky 'cause of all the coons in the area. You put out the garbage the night before you better duct tape it shut. And some do that. But those of us who bring it out in the morning, usually don't tape it shut. And some of us bring it out a bit late, like me, right before work."

"Which means, if our corgi is around these streets, he's out in the morning," Lorene said. "You probably know about the dog we're talking about. He's a national sensation. Find Sam? Been all over the news and talk shows for months now."

"I don't do news. Got sick of it after the last mass tragedy. Shootings eat up news time. I will occasionally turn on Fox. That kind of thing. No newspapers, either. Too expensive when it's all on internet. I hate the internet. Got sick of it after the last election a few years back. Don't read, don't watch, don't care. It's the way to be now."

"Sorry to hear that," Lorene said. "Well, our dog is quite famous."

"And I am thinking he may be out on this street," Edward said as he pulled out several sheets of paper from an unzipped backpack at his feet.

The pages were worn and wrinkled, covered in writing that looked tossed from a high place and allowed to splatter on the page. There were sentences that marched horizontally across the page, others diagonal. As Edward shuffled through what looked to be at least fifty pages of notes, he finally found a page that had a table of sorts. He pulled that out, then folded the other papers and stuffed them back in his backpack.

The man patiently watched all of this. Lorene took a long drag on her cigarette and leaned over to view the table.

"This street has by far the highest number of overstuffed garbage bags per house. It is the only street with separate garbage bags sitting outside the containers. And my observations, weekly observations, indicate there has been intrusive investigations of the garbage by an animal. Some animal is eating this garbage."

"You may be right," the man said. "Only a crate will catch a dog. I've caught one before. You got to really camouflage it, though. You have to do it the right way, or the dog will figure it out. Dogs figure shit out. Good dogs, that is."

"Well, we have a real pro working for us. She has traps everywhere," Lorene said.

"That's great. Well, look, I wish you guys luck. I'm going to be late for work. You got a number I can call in case I see the dog?"

"We have posters actually," Lorene said.

"No we don't. We don't have posters. Here's my number." Marcy searched her handbag for paper, finding a free deposit slip, which she used to write her cell number. Before she handed it him, she added Edward's cell phone number, too. "You call if you see any small dog. OK?"

Edward was busy writing something on his table and didn't appear to pay attention to what had transpired. They walked on after the man went back to his house. The dogs were eager to trot a while and Marcy wanted to think about what the man had said, what Edward had put together.

"You aren't handing out posters? You don't want them to call the detective?" Lorene said.

"They have not done a great job finding the dog so far."

Edward stopped to inspect a garbage can, then wrote something down and moved to the next can.

"But she keeps a record of sightings. She's mapping out this entire affair. We can't not follow her instructions. She's an expert."

"Yes, I guess she is. An expert and soon to be a TV star. But she is under pressure and she'll just put another trap out and tell everyone on this street not to feed the dog. We'll lose him."

"What do you mean star?" Lorene said.

"Here, right here. Look!" Edward held a plastic garbage bag in his hand. Its top was ripped and food dribbled over the side. "Hamburgers! This one has hamburgers! Bingo. We are talking dog heaven here. This street is dog heaven!"

"OK. I've had enough. I'm going to check on the traps," Lorene said. "This is not going anywhere. But you stay. I'll check the traps by myself. Stay with him." She touched Marcy's shoulder lightly. " You're a good sister. A good person."

"No. I'm not. Really, I'm not."

Chapter 29

Marcy
Fame plus dog!

FIND SAM 22 weeks

Faebook page: Find Sam!
Total friends 40.5k

"It's now a bit chilly, so we need to up the traps. We now are under time constraints. Winter. We will have seven groups out this weekend checking traps, knocking on doors. Focus. We need focus!" Detective Serendon

New Comments:
Max (picture of Wheaten) *Mom and I are coming out this weekend. I know we can find him. Just a matter of time.*

Hui Yan (picture of sleeping shar-pei) *We so excited but also nervous. Been a long time without dog. But everyone over here in China is hoping!*

Sally Hampton (picture of pond) *I've met so many people on twitter, thanks to Sam. Can we all stay in touch after we close up. I'd love to start another group.*

Mary Johnson (selfie of brunette female, eyes loaded down with make-up): *I was googling and found this article about a police officer who was chased by a man with lots of dogs the same night this corgi went missing? Has anyone asked the*

*dog walker about that? Just wondering. I mean, no one seems to
be asking the dog walker tough questions.*

Twitter @FindSam!
Followers: 500k

#windhavenlovesSam #hugyourdogforSam
#dogwalkersfromhell #corgipuppiesforsale
#fireSamsdogwalker #betterdogwalkersforwindhaven
#saveraccoons #raccoonshaveworthtoo #samisfamous,
#findsammovie #baddogwalkermovie #coldlostcorgi
#hopelesslylostcorgi #criminaldogwalker

MARCY PUT HER iPhone away. She had dropped the dogs off at
their homes, and left Elizabeth's dog, Nellie, for last. She didn't really
know Elizabeth's schedule, but the housekeeper had taken the day
off, and there was no car in the driveway, and a walk around the back
revealed no car in the garage. The backyard was starting to show signs
of winter. The perennials were drooping, and the garden boxes that had
been overflowing with herbs and tomatoes all summer was now covered
with canvas.

Marcy sat in a patio chair and let Nellie sniff around the back yard
for a moment. She pondered Edward's work on the garbage routes,
how alive the dog hunt had made him feel. He had something to live
for. It was almost OK not to find Sam if the hunt was breathing life
into her brother. Of course, she did fantasize that suddenly Sam would
appear, maybe near the garbage route, maybe in a trap. She had stopped
obsessing over her guilt long ago, but there was still an image that
loomed in the back of her mind—Sam, dirty, hungry, and struggling.
Now this image was changing with the weather. Soon, Sam would be
cold and shivering. She recalled his sassy way of being in the world, his
strutting, his immediate attention to her commands, his tolerance of old
Sadie. It all stressed her. And then there was now all this pressure from
Hollywood.

The agent had no problem landing the deal. There had been
immediate interest due to the national attention and social media

explosion. Everyone liked the screenplay, there were other investors lined up, not only for the pilot, but also for the potential reality TV follow-up show. But they had no dog. And without dog, nothing would happen.

Marcy let Nellie into to the basement, made sure there was fresh water, then pulled out the dog bed. She stared at the hall leading to the computer room. No, she wouldn't go there. She had turned a new corner in her life, learned her lesson. No more snooping. She turned to leave, but then stopped. She turned back, walked to the door. Then stopped. She turned and ran to the computer room, flipped the light switch. The computer was on. Why in the world would Elizabeth leave the computer on knowing Marcy had used it at least once without her permission? Maybe Elizabeth was out running a quick errand and forgot to lock the computer. Marcy stepped in front of the screen. Before Marcy could tap the keys, her cell phone rang. The caller ID revealed a picture of a glass of red wine. Lorene.

"Hi. I know I told you'd I'd meet you at the trap, but I got distracted," Marcy said, not bothering to say hello.

"Guess what I am holding onto right now?"

"A cigarette?"

"A lot bigger than a cigarette."

"A bottle of red wine?"

"Give you a hint. It's muddy, skinny, with a bright red tongue."

THE WINDHAVEN VETERINARY was not very busy, as most appointments were scheduled either before eight or after four, making mid-morning their slowest time. The lobby had only one patient—a well-behaved golden Lab. The slow business was a good thing because it left room for ten Find Sam volunteers, two police officers, and several reporters. The low din of mumbled voices filled the room, and several flashes of cameras put an end to the Lab's good behavior.

Marcy managed to ignore the barking and cameras, squeeze through the phalanx of reporters, and sneak through the hospital side door. She knew how to slip into vet offices, because on occasion she had to surreptitiously bring Henry in for a de-worming. She had contacts in the business. She winked at a technician and jogged down the hall, where Lorene stood with Elizabeth and Ellen. Elizabeth saw her and clapped her hands. Ellen was engaged in what looked like an intense conversation with the head Vet, Dr. Milner.

"Can you believe this? How perfect!" Elizabeth said. "Lorene is our hero."

"Lorene! You've done it!" Marcy said, barely able to contain herself. She wanted to pick Sam up, swing him around, take him out to the park, feed him treats. She figured he was probably starving for good food.

"I'm a hero," Lorene said. "And I may be fired, because I missed an important meeting this morning at my job."

"I will put in a phone call. I know the district manager for Calder Insurance Group," Elizabeth said. "Besides, you will be on TV, in the paper, and maybe, just maybe, in our pilot."

"Your pilot?" Lorene's arched her brows and looked at Marcy. "Is this something you know about?"

"Well, yes, but we were keeping it secret. That is for later. Can I please see Sam? Where is he?"

"Being checked on," Lorene said. "He's muddy, but otherwise in great shape. They've given him some shots. He just needs a lot of love. But, here, follow me. He's back in this room. I'm sure they won't mind if the dog-walker peaks in."

Lorene took Marcy's hand and they stepped to the next room where two vet technicians were preparing the corgi for a bath.

Lorene cracked the door, poked her head in. "Can the dog walker come say hey to cutiepie?"

Marcy heard a voice say no, then another voice said, "Oh, is that Marcy? I know she must be relieved." It was Janie, the tech who had checked on Henry. "Sure, she can come in for just a moment."

Sam was so soiled, he was unrecognizable. His body was not really as dangerously thin as one would expect. In fact he looked normal, just dirty. But his eyes were not the ones that used to talk with Marcy. She could always tell exactly what was on his mind. But right now, she tried to imagine his mind, what he was thinking, and she couldn't. Of course that was to be expected.

"Sam? The corgi man!" Marcy leaned over cautiously. Sam's tail wagged, and he looked right at her, with that familiar corgi grin. "It's me. Marcy. Your dog walker? Hey boy!" She gently tickled his chin. He jumped up and licked her face. "God, this is so great to have him back. What a dog you are Sam. Look at you."

Marcy picked him up before anyone could stop her and hugged him.

"It's amazing how dogs just jump back into the swing of things, but we need to be cautious for a while. He's had a pretty traumatizing few months, right little guy?" Janie, the vet tech, gently took Sam from Marcy and put him back on the table.

"Sam, boy you scared all of us." Marcy walked to the table and stroked his back. This time more cautiously.

Sam panted, moved his eyes around the room. Another technician gave him a biscuit and he ignored Marcy and chewed. Marcy had an idea. She pulled out her treat box from her coat. She had emptied it so there was no real smell to it. She took it out, held it in front of him. There was no reaction. He chewed and looked over at Janie for another biscuit.

"And so what have we here!" Detective Serendon stood at the door. "Look at him. Perfect! He looks perfect." She stepped into the room without asking permission. "Well, good thing I didn't take off this morning like I was supposed to. I would have missed the greatest day of our lives. Right?"

"It's all you, Detective Serendon. This happened because of you!" Ellen held out her arms and gave the detective a big hug. "The reporters are out there waiting."

Marcy ignored them, only looked at Sam. She bent over. "Sam? I'm so sorry, buddy. It was me, all me. I owe you big time." He laid back down then looked over at Janie, waiting for another treat.

After the vet dispersed everyone, and each took a turn with the local reporters, Marcy waited in the parking lot for Ellen, who lingered by the door, talking with volunteers. When she walked to the car, Marcy trotted up to her.

"So, when do you think we can get Sam back with the gang. I know he probably wants to trot around the park, hang out with his friends. Should we wait a few days or what?"

Ellen seemed distracted and looked at Marcy at first as if she didn't really understand what she was saying.

"Maybe we wait. Right?" Marcy said. "But I'm sure Sam will want to walk with his friends again."

Ellen looked at Marcy intently. But said nothing.

Chapter 30

Marcy
We got dog, we got story

FIND SAM week 25 weeks

Facebook Page: Find Sam!
Total friends: 122k

"*As you can see from the picture we put up, Sam is happy to be home. Our strategy worked, although it certainly took a while to capture this smart dog! We want to thank everyone for your support and help, couldn't have done it without you! Remember the Elda Jeneris Show, Thursday November 25! Don't miss it. We'll all be there. We are keeping this page but changing the title to Find Dogs! Stay tuned for our exciting documentary on our efforts, which will be appearing on Nat Geo in the near future!*" Detective Serendon

New Comments:
Harriet Whelchel (picture of lab) *We are so excited for Sam. Will be watching the show. We are starting a detective group here in our town, just in case anyone loses a dog.*

Jaynie Spector (picture of camera). *We're sold out of all corgi pictures. I am thrilled for Sam. We are having a party to watch the show. Can we have a picture to sell?*

Max (picture of Wheaten). *We can't wait to walk with you again big guy!*

Henry (picture of pit bull) *Sometime we wonder away from the discarded waste and end up trapped. They got you, but don't worry, we have your back.*

Mary Johnson (seflie of woman in hoodie) *"So, is the dog walker going to be on this show too? I suppose she redeemed herself.*

Twitter: @FindSam!
followers: 550k

#FindSam #WeloveSam, #windhavenlovesSam
#hugyourdogforSam #dogwalkersfromhell
#corgipuppiesforsale #fireSamsdogwalker
#betterdogwalkersforwindhaven #saveraccoons
#raccoonshaveworthtoo #samisfamous #findsammovie
#baddogwalkermovie #foundSam! #Samdoestalkshow
#dogwalkerredemption

EDWARD STOOD AT Marcy's front door, for once nicely attired in a clean sweater, corduroys, and new tennis shoes—clothes which had taken almost an entire social security disability check to purchase. He wanted to help Marcy with her dog walking.

"Just one dog," he had insisted on the phone. She told him no. Her walks were a bit more difficult because the pack had expanded and Sam, now behaving strangely, had to be acclimated into the group.

But Edward still showed up at the apartment ready for the walk. For some reason he felt new clothes were necessary to walk dogs. He had nothing to do now that Sam had been captured, except of course wait for CNN breaking news, but so far the breaking news had only covered a shooting spree in a mall and an actor who overdosed. News of Russian interference in the Middle East had died down, replaced by their interference in the US elections. He didn't follow politics.

"Look, the owner doesn't really want me walking Sam," she said when she opened the door. "Sam's not acclimating well to the world.

Trauma and all that. She's not really comfortable with me taking him on a walk with the gang so soon."

He stepped inside and went into the kitchen.

"I've got to be extra careful." Marcy followed him and watched as he opened the refrigerator, moved a few items around, as if searching for something in particular.

"The media will not allow her to fire you, sis. The media is on your side. I can tell by the reporting."

She leashed Henry, told Edward she'd be back and they would discuss it later, but he followed her to the door.

"OK, I give up, let's do this," Marcy said. She always did this when Edward persisted, because it was so exhausting telling him no. "I will let you take the herder today since I need to cut my pack down. I'm meeting with a client, I can't take all dogs. You know, they're kind of not aware of exactly how many dogs I walk."

"No problem, sis. I got this."

"The dog's name is Eric and he loves the park. You take Eric to the park stay there until I get there. How's that?"

"I can do this and I will be good at it, sis, as good as I was at dog hunting, although that didn't turn out well, I admit. Not properly equipped. As I said before, sis, it was very strange Sam was in an area far away from garbage pick up. I've been thinking that maybe he saw me, understood I had caught on to his survival plan. Or there is a possibility he chased a rabbit and forgot his plan. That can happen with a lost dog. Distraction. You got a plan, then some thought pulls you away. I get this. But walking also requires mind control. You gotta get into the mind of the dog." He bit into a hunk of cheddar cheese he had taken from her refrigerator. "So, a dog named Eric."

"The Rigardos are huge Eric Clapton fans."

"Oh yes. That Eric. Eric Balfour had come to mind. Buffy and the Vampire Slayer? But, OK, guitars are important too." He walked to the door as he shoved the last bit of cheese into his mouth. "Vampires are interesting."

MARCY DROPPED EDWARD and Eric at an intersection two blocks from Bradley Park and watched them slowly cross the street.

Eric looked to be leading Edward, which was fine. She trusted Eric would make sure Edward made it to the park, where he could sit on the bench and wait for her. She picked up her dogs then parked at the Nelsons. Ellen was there with Sam. She thought it was best for Sam to get reacquainted with one dog before entering the pack again. Marcy considered this introduction unnecessary because dogs remember friends' scents, but whatever calmed Ellen's nerves was fine with her. They will do the sniff and dance around him. Ellen would see that her fear was unfounded.

But that is not what happened, no sniff and dance. Sam seemed overwhelmed by the four dogs Marcy brought to meet him. The dogs reacted as if they had to start all over again. Not only did Sam shy away at first, he stood disoriented and anxious. When she leashed him and cajoled him to at least sniff a few dogs, he jerked his body around. But today Elizabeth was full of energy and didn't appear concerned, or as concerned as Ellen.

"I think the fresh air will be good for him. In fact, it's best to acclimate him into our world fast. Get him used to stimulating situations. He will have to be ready because the publicity is not slowing down, you know. We have the show to promote now."

Marcy looked down at Sam, now panting and more at ease, ready to walk. She had not really forgotten about the show; it was in the back of her mind, somewhere, lost in all her other concerns and anxieties. No one had discussed her role with the show that was now definitely moving forward fast, but everyone had insisted she would be involved. It was a turn in her luck—an opportunity for some semblance of financial security. But she still felt a bit off about it, as if it were too easy.

"What kind of promo are we doing with Sam?" Marcy said. Ed sniffed Sam again then backed away. Sam sat on Marcy's foot.

"Well, to start," Ellen said, staring down at Sam. " *The Elda Jeneris Show.*"

Sadie waddled up to Sam. Sam stopped panting, a low rumble rose from his chest. Marcy pulled on his leash. Sadie ran back to the wagon.

"You mean Sam? On TV?"

"Isn't that exciting?" Elizabeth said, ignoring the impending dog conflict. Ellen pulled Sam back to the door. "Our little documentary is moving along, and now the Jeneris show wants another Find Sam day.

This time with Sam. It's unbelievable. I will be hosting a community party to watch our famous Sam."

Sam went back into Elizabeth's house and peeked around Ellen's legs.

"Well, maybe he needs to go more slowly," Ellen said. "Baby steps. Keep him nice and calm for his big TV debut! Why don't you take a quick break, bring the dogs around back. Elizabeth and I need to show you something, real quick."

Marcy thought about Edward at the park with Eric waiting for her. She told Ellen OK and texted Edward.

Running late. Everything OK?

Hey sis, Eric good, but lonely. Where u?

Leash Eric and walk him around.

OK. I'll find him.

What do you mean find him?

No worry. He's here somewhere. Dogs need space.

"I can't stay long, can you simply email me?"

But Ellen and Elizabeth were already leading Sam and dogs around the back. Marcy followed them around and into the basement. The dogs trotted inside their familiar resting place and quickly sniffed for any new smells since they were last there. Soon there was heavy panting, a few growls, portending chaos until Elizabeth brought out balls and toys. Marcy texted Edward again.

Did you get Eric?

I see him now.

What do you mean see him?

"Marcy?" Ellen stood before her with a plastic file box in her hand. It had a large label with TV SHOW in bold font taped on its front.

The dogs picked up on her kinetic energy, and nipped at each other, two humped in the corner. Elizabeth retrieved several Nylabones, tossed them around. Ellen ignored the dogs, sat on the sofa, and opened her file box. She retrieved a manila folder marked "lost dogs" which she handed to Marcy.

"We have a lot of work to do," Ellen said. "A director's working on the pilot, looking at actresses for various roles, cleaning up the writing, scouting for locations. He did not feel Detective Serendon's home would work. Too small and middle class looking. We're going for a more Dog Whisperer type set up. Ranch, with a rescue atmosphere. What we need,

Marcy, and you will be well compensated, I assure you . . ." She paused to let this sink in. Money. " . . . is research. You need to reach out, find more lost dogs for us. And we of course need a website, which can easily be set up for this purpose, right? I am assuming you can you put together a website?"

"Oh, that's easy, but what exactly am I doing, again? What kind of research?"

Jimi, the setter, like all the dogs, kept trying to sniff Sam's ass, causing Sam to nip, then bark. Nellie trotted to Elizabeth's side and a few other dogs walked over to get a better view of an impending fight.

Sam was unusually agitated and didn't want anyone messing with his butt, as if any dog nose in his space was too difficult to handle. He also seemed hyper vigilant, the way dogs usually get when taken to the dog park for the first time.

Marcy jumped up and leashed Jimi, walked him to the sofa, shooed the other dogs away, then reached in her pocket for a treat and stuffed it in Jimi's mouth. She waited for Ellen to call Sam but Ellen didn't even look up, only kept pulling files out of the file box.

"Detective Serendon of course had clients who are eager to put their pets on the show," Ellen said as she opened a file and withdrew a form. "But perhaps you can coordinate all of this for us. And, we need some releases signed that allows the company to use bits of your life, your story for the starting pilot, which will be creative nonfiction, as we discussed. Standard practice." She placed a form in front of her.

"I thought the show would air only if the pilot worked?"

"Oh, but it will air. No question," Elizabeth said. She sat on the sofa by Ellen. "This is such a success story. There are other reality shows that try to do this, but none with this kind of fame and support. We will beat them on ratings. No question. Our effort has also succeeded in putting our detective on the map. Her business has boomed. Like I said, she has clients now. We can always mine that for story. But she has to find the dog."

"What is her success rate?" Marcy said. Sam was now growling at Max , the Wheaten. "Max, come."

Max hung his head and slowly loped toward her, leaving Sam alone in the corner, panting, as he looked around the room, as if searching for his next victim. Acclimating him back into the group was going to take time.

"What do you mean success rate?" Elizabeth asked.

"How many dogs has she caught in those traps?"

"Well, she has certainly found dogs, or dogs have been found, but I think Sam is the first one we actually caught by trap. Others, I believe, were found by shelters, neighbors and such. I am sure she'll catch another in that trap. The show would certainly have to have the dog captured by the detective. In the trap. The show will find them in the trap. It's creative nonfiction. We may have to be creative."

"Creative?"

"Marcy." Elizabeth stood and clapped her hands. "I think the dogs have to get going We can't just sit here with them. We just wanted to give you this release form and papers. And, well, tell you, Welcome to the show!"

Ellen held out her hand. Marcy's handshake was weak, distracted. She was still confused about her actual role outside of managing the dog detective website. And what did they mean by creative?

"Have a great walk. I think for now, we'll keep Sam here, let him calm down before journeying out again. He just needs time. And, Marcy, get excited! This is wonderful time for all of us. A lot of work, but it will be worth it. And don't forget the show."

"The show?"

"Elda Jeneris," Elizabeth said. "Remember? Sam's going to be on *The Elda Jeneris Show*. He'll need a lot of exercise in the next few weeks. We need him nice and calm. Sam's our best advertisement. Proof of our detective's talent, our community's strength, Ellen Maher's incredible devotion."

IT TOOK EFFORT to calm the dogs down, all of whom seemed unusually worked up after seeing Sam. Every so often she texted Edward but he never returned the text. Oh please let him be OK, she pleaded to whoever ran the world and fucked up her life. She could not stop thinking of another dog lost. When she texted Ed one final time before returning to the park, she finally received a reply: *"Small hiccup. No worry, sis. Dogs need breathing time. They need to realize the world is out there and it receives them. He will return. The key is to allow it to happen.*

He was without the dog.

Chapter 31

Marcy
And the stories begin. Or do they?

EVENTUALLY HER PACK resumed a steady gait and within about six minutes, Marcy was at the park. In the distance she could make out Edward waddling around the old closed pool, a leash dangling from his left hand, a bag of treats from the other. She let the dogs off leash and walked slowly toward her brother. When she reached him, she said nothing, only looked down at his bag of treats.

"He likes me, sis."

"Why wouldn't he? You let him go. It's me who is in the not like phase. You are aware that I have already lost one dog. And the entire nation knows me now as the dog walker who lost this one dog."

"And, my sis, the dog was captured, proving to the world that one gets lost and one gets found. He decided to go back into the human trap set up to capture him. The traps were so obvious, any dog that walked into one has had enough. The dog is saying, OK, take my freedom, I don't care."

Marcy turned around. "Eric!" She ran away from Edward to the far end of the park. "Eric!" She ran around the periphery, the other dogs panting behind. "Fuck you, Eric. You cannot do this to me!"

She jogged through the woods contiguous to the open field screaming, all five dogs behind her barking, then back out into the open. The field was hard, the grass browned and ready for snow in a month or so. A few evergreens dotted the surrounding woods, but for the most part, trees were now naked, stripped of foliage. If she simply stood still, she could view movement, life around the park. She turned slowly, studied the land, the edges, and beyond that, neighborhoods peeking through the spaces between trees. The dogs fell quiet, Edward lay down on the ground quietly, arms out. Marcy could only hear her breath.

Then, in the distance, far distance, a bark. A distinct, obnoxious herder bark. Then another bark, one slightly deeper and more insistent. It could have been a neighborhood dog. Another bark. Another return bark in return. The two barks faded deeper in the neighborhood beyond the woods, then nothing. Gone.

"I never call him," Edward yelled to the air above him.

Marcy walked over to his prostrate body and looked down at his face.

"Someone calls you, they always want something," he said up to her. "Has anyone ever called you to give you anything? They call you and there is something you didn't do, something they want you to do, or something you have to stop doing right away. And if you're happy in that one moment and you get a call? Then, that happy moment vanishes. So, I don't call dogs."

"You don't call dogs. Great. But this is not your dog, it's a client's dog. Get this through your head. If Eric is gone then I am, like, in big trouble." She started walking away. "It's the Rigardos' dog," she yelled back at him. "They both work, usually late. So we have till six."

She figured this was why they wanted her on the show. They knew she'd keep losing dogs. They would have a new story line each episode based upon another dog Marcy lost. She walked then ran in intermittent spurts, as her mind raced with thoughts, all different issues that would develop from yet another lost dog.

Edward held up a bag of treats over his body, into the air, as if offering them to the Gods. He shook the bag. Nothing happened. He shook it again. Nothing.

Marcy had to get the dogs she brought with her home, particularly the setter because his owner would be home soon and expected a dog in her house. She would just have to wait on retrieving Eric. Or maybe not. Maybe she should start the process right away. If she waited and never found him, she would have to lie again, create another fictional lie line, but this time Edward would be on it, unless she convinced him to stay away and lie about it. Edward was great making up stories or explaining stories with bizarre observations and summaries, but he could not lie.

"OK, Edward," she yelled back. "I've got to get the other dogs back. Eric really doesn't have to be back until six, so, I'll come back."

Edward put his hand behind one ear indicating he didn't quite understand her.

She leashed the Lab and approached his body, looked down at his face. "I said, I'll come back and help look, if he's still gone. Then, I don't know. I guess we have to report it. I guess they will add this story to Sam's, and both will be on the Elda show, and of course our new TV show. Or they will all fire me and that will be that."

"No. They will keep you for the TV show you told me about. I don't know, I'm not sure about dogs and TV. TV is for humans. A few dog stories are OK. But for the most part, dogs shouldn't be on TV. They are not breaking news items."

Edward extended his arms again so that he looked like a crucifix, a sacrificial offering to the universe. Marcy quickly looked around the park to make sure no one was staring. When Edward behaved strangely there was always a risk of misinterpretation. She spotted a lone figure near a baseball diamond walking a small dog, but he was not looking their way.

"It's OK, Edward. I'll find Eric. And if not. I'll think of something to tell the Rigardos."

"It's best not to talk."

"What do you want me to do? Are you going to stay like this? I'll come back, walk the contiguous neighborhoods. We'll find this dog. Don't worry."

"I will stay like this until I am herded away."

Edward didn't seem guilty, anxious, but at peace. He hadn't even mentioned the news. He was in a new world, the world of losing dogs, and Marcy supposed this was how he was handling it. She had not handled her lost dog world well either.

"I think, I can do this."

"Yes, bro, you can."

Her smart phone vibrated. A happy Irish setter face flashed on her screen. Marcy ignored the call, gathered the dogs, and headed toward her van. After they were all in, she turned for one last look at her prostrate brother. He had not moved. In the distance, beyond her brother, at the edge of the park where brown grass met the naked twigs of woods, stood a small Australian herder. He crouched down low, put his head down, as if he spotted a stranded sheep, then he trotted slowly toward Edward.

Chapter 32

Marcy
Dog, this is fame, fame, this is dog

ELDA JENERIS SAT neatly in her club chair, one leg underneath her, hands folded in her lap. She had finished her dance up and down the aisle, then spent some time on selected home videos that had been submitted to her website. Today was pet appreciation day, so everyone had sent in videos of family dogs. A dog who jumped in the bathtub to rescue a bathing child. A dog who climbed up a ladder and slid down a sliding board with the toddler. Dogs who slept with owners. Dogs who played on trampolines and of course all the skateboarding and surfing English bulldogs, none of whom reminded Marcy of Sadie. At all.

After the last video, Elda looked into the camera. "That was fun. Good stuff. Good stuff. Well, as most of you who watch my show know, I love my pets. Lila and I own dogs and cats and they are the center of our family. I can't sit down to eat dinner until my cats are fed. I think my greatest fear is losing my pet. I cannot imagine anything worse than that feeling. Knowing your pet is out there somewhere, lost, maybe injured, hungry, scared. It has to be the most hopeless feeling in the world. Am I right? So, just how far would you go to find your dog? When we come back, we will be talking, again, about the Find Sam movement. Ellen Maher, Sam's owner will be on our show. This is her second appearance, I had her on a while ago, after she had lost her dog and started what became a national sensation, the Find Sam movement. This woman simply would not give up. And her story is amazing."

Elda's warm face on the TV screen was now replaced by a gorgeous brunette model holding a mascara stick. Marcy picked up an apple slice and took a nibble. Elizabeth Nelson's room began to come to life with a low din of voices, occasional laughter. Lorene excused herself and stepped out the front door, a cigarette in her left hand. The other Find Sam volunteers—about twenty women—kept talking and eating, a few leaning over and saying something to Elizabeth who was strangely subdued.

The past three weeks had been filled with news about the upcoming pilot documenting his rescue, and Sam's continued popularity with national media. NPR had completed a long segment on the entire story—how the dog was lost, how Ellen, a well-known public relations manager, had single-handedly turned a tragedy viral on social media outlets, successfully raising awareness not only of her lost dog but all lost dogs. The Jeneris show, which had followed the saga after Ellen Maher had made a brief appearance months earlier, were devoting the entire show to dog rescues. Ellen Maher's agent, or Sam's agent, had hired a dog trainer to prepare Sam for the audience's potential screams of delight. Marcy had managed to acclimate Sam into the gang again, although he was not quite comfortable and tended to follow, not lead. Trauma had scarred him. She only hoped it wouldn't last.

The four minute commercial break was concluding and once again, calm and cool Elda Jeneris appeared on the screen. The camera came in close then focused on Elda's face, her smiling blue eyes. "I can't tell you how excited I am about the next guest. She's my hero. When most owners lose a dog, they panic and do all the wrong things, things we all do because when we lose a pet we love dearly, we will do anything to get him back. Right? We drive around in our car, yelling his name. We go to the nearest park and leave food, water, toys. Then we put up posters, put the dog on lost and found dog sites, put the dog's poster up at every vet. But what happens when none of that works? Well, a lot of people give up. But this owner didn't give up. She used her public relations skills to advertise her lost dog on social media. She contacted news outlets. She hired an amazing—and I'm talking amazing—dog detective."

The audience laughed.

"No, I'm not talking about dogs who are detectives."

More laughter.

"Not saying a dog would not be a good detective, just that cats may be better. But, this detective is not a dog catcher either. That is not someone you want to call. She is a real detective who specializes in catching dogs. I had her and the detective on this show two months ago when their site was beginning to generate a lot of national interest. Well, as you certainly are aware of by now, they found Sam."

The large overhead screen now flashed a picture of a happy, panting corgi sitting alert and ready. He looked like someone enticed him with a ball in order to focus his eyes above the camera lens. His fur was clean, bright gold, with touch of white on his chest. His tongue was pink and healthy. The audience's "awww" was followed by applause.

"Please join me in welcoming my first guest, owner of Sam, Ellen Maher."

Ellen Maher wore a tight beige dress that stopped a few inches above the knee. Her makeup was subtle, giving her overall appearance of sophisticated but simple. She hugged as an acquaintance would. Because she was an acquaintance. One of Ellen Maher's clients was good friends with Elda Jeneris. They had met a few years earlier, one of the reasons the show took a special interest in Find Sam.

After she was seated and the audience became quiet, the women joked a bit about how they knew each other. Then Elda went through a series of catch-up question for those who were unfamiliar with the lost dog, the Find Sam group, the detective and the national interest in the rescue.

"So, tell us what happened three weeks ago. Where were you when they called you?"

"I was home, taking a day off to get some errands run, and one of our fantastic volunteers called. She was screaming so loud, I could barely understand her. He's here. Right here. In the trap!"

"And so how did you feel when you drove out and saw him."

"Well, mixed. I was so excited to see him, but he had been through quite an ordeal, so it was tough seeing him that way. Dirty, hungry. He didn't even recognize me. But, of course, he is back to normal now."

A picture of a dirty corgi appeared on the screen. Marcy thought Sam didn't look that bad, just dirty. He wasn't even that thin, not really. Ellen had always kept Sam in very good shape. He had always been lean. Marcy used to call him the lean mean corgi machine. The only difference was his personality, which was less aware, or maybe it was just less alert. Sam was a very alert dog. Now, he seemed dazed, which was of course expected.

The interview progressed as all interviews of Find Sam progressed. How the warm and giving community banded together to help a citizen. How Detective Serendon helped raise awareness of just how difficult it is to find and capture a lost dog.

Detective Serendon was introduced, and she appeared in tight black pants and a silk pale blue blouse. Her appearance was surprisingly feminine and, although her talk bordered on pedantic at times, she maintained a warm mien. She even discussed charming anecdotes of other successful recapture stories.

Marcy could tell she had been coached by the agent as well as the director of the new show about the type of personality that was important for ratings. Warm, but tough. Pedantic, but open and empathetic. They then discussed the upcoming show, or movie. This was the most important moment, the gathering of an audience for their show. Everyone in the room became quiet as the movie was discussed. The reality TV show was not mentioned as it would only progress if the movie was popular.

The grand finale of course was Sam, who trotted out and sat by his owner who petted him lightly on the head. Elda Jeneris stood and bent down to rub his chin, which he accepted without complaint. The audience clapped and there were several oohs and awws. Sam stood during all of the applause and appeared a bit difficult to handle, but he eventually calmed down.

Elda then distributed presents to her special guests. A free trip to the dog-lover spa, a spa for both human and dog. While the dog enjoys doggy fun, including dog friends, balls, treats, and a dog swimming pool, the adult has yoga class, sauna and massages by the pool.

After she awarded Sam a full year supply of dog treats, Elda pulled out a liver dog bone and held it up for Sam. He looked at it then shifted his eyes away.

"Wow, I've never had a dog resist a liver treat. Maybe it's me he's resisting?" Elda bent down and let Sam smell it. He sniffed and turned his head.

"It sometimes takes a while for dog food to be appealing again once they've been in the wild," Detective Serendon said.

Everyone in Elizabeth's den erupted in conversation after the show ended. Excited talk about Sam putting Windhaven on the map.

A friend of Elizabeth Nelson's came up to Marcy and congratulated her on the upcoming movie, but Marcy had a hard time paying attention. Her mind kept going back to the scene with Sam. It bothered her.

"Well," the lady said, trying to catch Marcy's wandering eyes. "I think it's going to be a big hit. I'm sure of it! Ellen will make sure of it. When she sets her mind to something, she does it. And Elizabeth is co-producing the show. Right? That reality TV show you guys will do after this movie is a hit?"

"Elizabeth Nelson is going to help produce it?" Marcy had no idea Elizabeth was still that involved.

"Oh, yes. Elizabeth has so much energy. I don't know how she does it."

"They're still doing a TV show? I thought it was a movie." Lorene looked at the woman. "I can't keep up."

"Yes, movie. I helped with the initial show, a kind of documentary, which I guess sucked because they hired another writer. But they want me to do the website and research for the reality TV show that the movie will segue into. I feel a bit funny about the research. I don't know why, I just do. But who cares. I get royalty, a bit of royalty. At least they said I will."

"Why was this not discussed on *The Elda Jeneris Show* if it's out?"

"They probably don't want to go talking about a show on national television until all the ends are tied up. To be safe. The documentary is a go, the show is not."

"I thought it was definite?"

"Ellen told us everything is fluid in Hollywood, but it is definite in a fluid way."

LORENE ASKED ONE question after another all the way home. Marcy answered quietly, her mind still not quite in the conversation. She kept replaying the last scene on *The Elda Jeneris Show*. The scene of Sam. It wasn't right.

"So, are you quiet because you think I'm asking too many questions? Or are you quiet because you're thinking about the show? Something about the show bothered me. Did it bother you?"

"Yes. I mean no. Maybe yes. What bothered you about the show, Lorene?"

"Ellen. How she treated Sam. Something was off about it."

Marcy made the final turn into the apartment parking lot and parked. She turned off the engine and sat for a moment.

"You look worried. What're you worried about? Or is that a secret? You still have secrets?" Lorene had a cigarette in her mouth now but was not searching for her lighter.

"Sam has always been a real pig," Marcy said slowly. "A pig. He was obsessed with my treat box. And he loves liver flavored treats. Loves them. I always brought them on walks because Ellen starved him."

"It's sad how they change after something like this. He'll be back to normal soon."

Marcy's cell phone vibrated. Edward.

"Hey, sis. Watched the show. Boring and sad. Sad, because I got a call this morning by that resident of Norfalk. Remember the street with ripped bags? Well, apparently, he couldn't stop thinking about our dog. He called and said I better get over there, he had something to show me. I said, I will, but I got distracted. I was going out there tonight, but I had to watch the show about the dog. He said what show? I mean this guy does not watch the news. I cannot understand how he exists in the world. He is the reason for our madness. We are oblivious."

"Edward, I'm kind of busy. Is this going somewhere?"

"Yeah, give me a second. The guy is all excited, wants me to come out right away. He had set up some trap. I have to say, I had gone back out there to visit him, because it had really bothered me, his lack of interest in news. He promised to turn on CNN. Anyway, I'm here now."

"So, you helped him join the CNN audience, and he built a trap. Is that the story?"

Lorene lit her cigarette and cracked her window. She took a long drag and exhaled slowly.

"No. Hold on, OK? So, I told him we found the dog and Find Sam is over, but that I was now using my talent to walk dogs, not just my dog, or our dog, but other dogs. I was a dog walker in training. I hope that is OK for me to say."

The image of the herder, Eric, trotting toward Edward supine upon the green earth came to Marcy. There then gone. "Yes, Edward, you are in training."

Lorene laughed. Hearing only one side of the conversation must have been amusing.

"I emphasized, again, how important it was that he pick up a newspaper. I said if you had just read the newspapers you would know this and you wouldn't have spent time building this trap. I said, this is the problem with our country and why we waste our efforts and money when Russia is the real problem."

"I am now home and sitting in the parking lot. Is this the end?"

"This trap is much better than the ones the fancy detective lady set up. He put branches, grass, all over it. Camouflaged it."

"Well, I'm very sorry he went to that trouble. And you're right, if he just read the news, he would have saved time and effort. So, you're right. Once again."

"He caught a dog."

Chapter 33

Marcy
So many dogs, so few shows

THE MAN WAS standing with Edward in about the same place he had been standing back when Marcy and Lorene had originally followed Edward to the neighborhood to investigate garbage. He was a different person now. He moved his hands wildly as he talked, his face slightly pink and animated. Edward, arms limp by his side, wasn't looking at the man but toward the side of the house where a large mound of limbs and leaves appeared to have burst through the soil. This was a garbage day so plastic garbage containers lined the street, some toppled over, lids open, a few torn plastic bags by their side.

"Hi. Marcy, and this is Lorene. We met you about a month ago." Marcy shook the man's hand.

Lorene moved her cigarette to her left hand and shook his hand.

"Well, I didn't know you found the dog. Your brother here's been telling me all about the importance of news again. I missed the big show, I guess."

"I also updated him on Putin's corrupt offshore laundering."

"You found a dog, though, right?" Lorene said through her smoke. "I guess you need help with what to do with him? How'd you catch it?"

"I put water in there, so the dog is OK. But he's been there a while. I don't want to get bitten, so I waited for you guys. It's the trap. As I told your brother, here, you got to have a better trap, or crate. Did he tell you I've trapped animals before back when I lived in Pennsylvania? That's where I'm from. Anyways, I did watch the local channel once after Edward visited and they showed the trap. Bad, bad trap. You gotta camouflage it, leaves, limbs, even garbage. Just can't put some crate out in the middle of nowhere. So, I took an old dog crate, made it look like a pile of trash. I spread garbage everywhere inside and out, put out a trail of food leading to it. Leftover hamburgers. I kept the door up with a thread which I snaked around a tree, along my fence, around the hedge, where I waited this morning. I wasn't looking, missed the dog entering, but I could hear him in chowing down. It makes sense it wasn't your dog, obviously, now that I think of it, because of course your dog wouldn't bark, or maybe he would. I figure your dog would be skinny, feral and quiet. This one's different."

They followed him to the mound, which smelled like rotting food and death. When Marcy bent over the dog barked. She couldn't tell what the dog looked like because it was so far back. She and Lorene removed the branches and leaves and pulled an old blanket off the top. The dog was now barking hysterically.

"Hey there, cutie pie. Calm down," Lorene said.

Marcy didn't speak, just stared into the eyes looking back at her. It's fur was black with dirt. It was also wet and terribly matted. The face under this matted hair looked like a small collie, its nose long and slender, its forehead large. It appeared to be laying down in scattered garbage. Several French fries littered the ground near it. The dog barked again.

"It was following the hamburger trail. I guess he liked hamburger. Our daughter never eats hamburger, but we keep trying. Looks like he ate the entire thing, bun and all. Maybe we'll just put a picture of him in the newspaper. Or, I guess we take him to the vet. Do you know a vet for rescues around here?"

"We can use the same one we took Sam to, right?" Lorene said. "Hey boy, don't be so nervous. You need a bath. That's for sure."

No, the dog wasn't lying down. Marcy realized the dog was standing.

"I've tried to get him to come to the crate door, but he just stays back there and barks. I don't want to go sticking my hand in there. He'd probably get around me and take off."

"I can throw a net over him," Edward said.

"No, no net," Lorene said. "We don't throw anything over his body. That would make him panic. Let's get a leash first then try to coax him out. That's what we did with Sam."

Marcy studied the crate door, then slowly unlatched it. She crawled inside, which at first agitated the dog and instigated another barking frenzy. She held out her hand so he could take a sniff, which he did. His tail wagged. His eyes brightened. He started panting.

"Sam? Where in the world have you been and what the hell have you been eating?"

Chapter 34

Marcy
Will the real Sam stand up. Or sit down

TWO TECH ASSISTANTS—the same team that had greeted the first lost Sam—were waiting at the door when Marcy and Sam 2 arrived.

"Look how fat this dog is. Who fed him?" The attendant bent down and petted Sam who was still wagging his tail furiously.

"Sam's always been a pig," Marcy said. "I knew the minute he was released from a tightly controlled diet, his waistline would expand."

They walked into the lobby, now occupied by an older man waiting for his dog. Edward shoved his hands in his pockets and started walking around the small waiting area, as if looking for something.

"Hey, boy, you are a dirty fat thing," Janie said. She came through the door, rushed to Sam, and picked him up.

"So, I guess the other dog belonged to someone else?" Marcy said. "Wow, two lost corgis caught. This must be a first."

"I don't know, though." Janie handed Sam 2 to another technician who took him through a door.

Sam started barking, loud at first, then soft and intermittent. The sound of panting and barking soon faded, until it was replaced by a male voice saying, "Hey boy," then the soft click of a door closing.

"This may be another dog," Janie continued. "We have no microchip, and Ms. Maher swore the other dog was hers. Coloring . . . everything. But this is surely an amazing coincidence. I checked online and there are a few corgis around the tri-state region that have gone missing. Four to be exact. One went missing only a month back. We'll check this one for a microchip. That would solve everything."

"You won't find one," Marcy said.

"Don't jump to too many conclusions." Janie smiled and left the room.

"She'll come around once she sees him," Lorene said as she sat heavily on the sofa. "If it's him. She should have put in a microchip. There would be no confusion if there was a microchip."

"She thinks they're carcinogenic." Marcy plopped down by Lorene. Edward was now studying the bulletin board where several pictures of lost dogs were posted. "She's also anti-vac. Good thing she has no children. She fed Sam exactly three quarters of a cup of organic dog food once a day. She asked me not to treat him. I ignored her. She'll be one of those mothers who doesn't let her children eat anything but organic food. They'll have fruit at their birthday parties. I never trust people like that."

"If this dog is the real Sam, we may be on to something," Edward said, now standing before his sister as if he just woke up. "We may be dealing with a conspiracy."

"Edward, I have to say, you are amazing," Lorene said before Marcy, who had rolled her eyes, could say anything. "No, really, he is. He captured a dog. Even if this isn't Sam, you got a dog. You're talented. He's talented, Marcy."

Edward straightened his back, his face, covered with patches of long whiskers missed when shaving, now belonged to someone who accomplished something other than memorizing TV news items and internet blogs. He was a man who studied garbage cans for weeks, mapping the routes and pick-up schedules, analyzing the most likely streets a dog could find attractive for dining. And he found the dog, well, a dog. He had done something. If this dog was Sam, and Edward was responsible for his recovery, it would be beyond amazing. It would be the first time Edward had succeeded at anything significant in his entire life. Would they put this in the papers, on social media? The wrong dog had been caught, and Edward found the right one. Would Elda Jeneris call again? For Edward?

Marcy stood and grabbed Edward's hand with both of hers. "Edward? You may have done something incredible here. I've been so busy freaking out about us possibly finding the wrong dog, I didn't realize the significance of you finding the right dog."

Edward said nothing. He left his moist, fat hand in Marcy's for a moment longer, then looked down at it.

"I just got another man motivated. He's watching CNN, too!"

"Edward's a hero. The *real* hero," Lorene said. "Not this detective. Not Ellen. Not Elizabeth. The hero here is Edward! Of course, Marcy, this may impact your project, but there could be a different story, a different show, right?"

"What project?"

"The pilot? Reality TV?"

"What reality TV?" Edward said, his hand still inside both of Marcy's hands. "TV is always real. I don't watch unreal TV."

ELLEN ANSWERED HER front door and smiled. It was a smile that was too broad and too fast. Sam 1 was by her side. He didn't even bother to sniff Marcy, only gazed at her briefly before trotting away. "Come in. I've been expecting you. What a week, right?"

"Yes. It's been quite a week." Marcy stepped inside and looked around. Not only was Elizabeth Nelson seated in the den, coffee in hand, but also, the agent, Margaret Cunningham, this time dressed more casually—khakis, appropriately tight, and red sweater. Ellen had spent time at the Veterinarian office and had concluded that Sam 2 was not hers. She then put out a statement to that effect. All the papers were now covering the amazing story of the new corgi found due to the efforts of "a volunteer." No one mentioned that the volunteer had gone rogue and had caught the dog with no help from the detective. Marcy called the papers to inform them of her brother's efforts. No one returned her calls.

"Come in. Can you believe two corgis have been lost around the same neighborhood? What a wild thing, right?" Ellen said. "And of course I've been using my channels of social media to help out all I can."

"I've put in some phone calls. I just feel so badly for the owners of that dog," Margaret said. "All these lost dogs. It's just taken my heart."

"Yes, I feel for all of them," Ellen said.

"Which dogs?" Marcy said. She eyed the coffee dispenser and started in that direction.

"The dog your brother found," Ellen said. "And, you know, just all the dogs out there."

"Sam?"

"Sam's right here."

The corgi lay prostrate on his dog bed in the corner. He didn't pick up his head.

"This is Sam," Ellen said. "We've been through this. I know my dog, Marcy."

Marcy walked over to Sam 1, bent down and petted him, pulling the fur back from the collar, searching, for something, what she didn't quite know.

Ellen quickly touched Marcy's shoulder. "Come have a seat so we can chat. Sam needs a break from all the attention."

"So, where's the other dog, the one I wrongly accused of being Sam?" Marcy stood and fixed herself a coffee. "Still with Elizabeth?"

"Well, Elizabeth called a few owners who'd lost corgis, not in this state but in New Jersey and Pennsylvania. But they all had their corgi microchipped."

"And probably riddled with cancer by now, right?" Marcy said. Ellen did not smile. "Well, this works out for the show. Boy, that would've been hard to explain to everyone. We found the wrong dog. All the publicity and excitement in the papers and on TV, particularly on *The Elda Jeneris Show*, would somehow have to have been reversed, or transferred to the new dog, which was found not by our detective, but by my brother, a disabled mentally ill man who said crazy stuff at all the Find Sam meetings. Not good for a reality TV show."

"I think this is a bit personal for you. Maybe you should consider withdrawing from the show," Ellen said. "We'll, of course, pay you for the work you've done to date."

"What's Elizabeth going to do with the stray we caught?"

"I'm hunting down a corgi rescue group."

"Corgi rescue?"

"They do exist. But not in our state."

"I've got contacts and am helping Elizabeth with this," Detective Serendon said. "We'll take the dog to the rescue in a few weeks, after he has been thoroughly de-wormed. It's a great group. They'll find the dog a home. We will, of course, continue our search for the owners, but he's not microchipped, so that's hard."

"That dog Edward's contact found was Sam. I know it. I know Sam. He's smart, alert, and it makes sense he's fat. Sam would find food. Don't you want your real dog, Ellen? Is this show that important?"

"The meeting is about the show," Elizabeth said. "It's not about Sam, who is doing fine. Are you still in the show with us?" She looked over at the dog, then back at Marcy. Ellen looked down at her hands.

"You know, that dog's owners are probably worried sick," Marcy said, staring at Ellen who hadn't moved her eyes from her hands. "Where did you guys find him?"

"I think I've heard about enough," Elizabeth said, standing up. "We'll pay you for the work you've done so far, but Ellen knows her dog. I have no idea what you're implying but this kind of talk is stopping now. Right now. I'll walk you to your car."

ELIZABETH HAD ENERGY to her walk. Marcy had seen this before—the quick bursts of speech, jerky movements of hands, fast walk—back when she had found her memory stick. She also understood Elizabeth's controlled, distracted state, because when one lies, the mind morphs into a kinetic existence, one ready for chain reaction lying. She understood this stress of dealing with constant alterations of information, quick stories created on the spot, molded to fit into the fictional universe—a mental activity that resulted in a mind that was constantly alert and worried.

"And I want that corgi," Marcy finally said when they reached the car. "I'll call him whatever you want me to call him. But I want that corgi."

"You can't have the corgi. It belongs to another owner. Somewhere out there. We're transferring him to a rescue group and they may be able to find the owner. If not, they will certainly find him a new home."

Marcy couldn't help but wonder what Sam was thinking. He saw her, then was taken away from her, not to his owner but back to Nellie's house. He was probably confused and scared. Or maybe not scared. Sam was probably teaching Nellie how to raid the garbage.

"Well, at least let me walk him with Nellie and friends. Can I walk him?"

Elizabeth crossed her arms and took a big breath, as if she were dealing with a recalcitrant teenager. "Here is the deal," Elizabeth finally said, looking off into space, not at her. "You have to drop this business about Sam. OK?"

"That dog in there is not Sam. And you want me to agree to go along with this cruelty to the real Sam. Oh, and God knows where you guys got that dog. He looks well bred. Did you steal him?"

"Let me say something here that may encourage you to shut up," Elizabeth finally said. "I know why you lied to me about where you were the day of the storm. You lied because you had another man walk the dogs, one who was chased by that police officer. I am assuming this was your boyfriend? I have no idea why he chased him. But I know this. OK?" She held up her hand, palm out, to stop Marcy who was about to interrupt. "I know you are a liar. I have not revealed this, but I know it. You were in my house on my computer and another man lost the dog. Wow, will that not look good. You lied to the entire world!"

"OK, so you got me, I guess. This is why you wanted me involved with this stupid show. You knew I would know the dog was not Sam. You figured, well, if she is in on the show, if we can get her some money, real money, she'd just shut her mouth. What you didn't know is that we would eventually catch the real Sam. You guys just assumed Sam was stolen or dead."

"So, here is what you do. Drop this dog stuff. OK? You have to drop it. Or I spill everything. Is that what you want?"

Marcy opened the door, stepped in and started the car, thinking the motor movement would keep her quiet. She read in a blog that if you want to talk and shouldn't, then start moving around right way. Marcy lifted her leg and pointed her toe, then bent her torso over in a yoga move she learned a year ago after one class. She had only taken one yoga class. Perhaps if she had at least taken a year full of yoga she would not be in this situation. She rolled down the window.

"Can I at least walk him with Nellie and friends?" Elizabeth shook her head no. "Just let me do that before you send him off. Just once more. Please."

"Will you shut up?"

"I'll shut up," Marcy said, sensing, once again, she was heading down the lie path.

Chapter 35

Sam
I'm here. I'm gone. I'm here. I'm gone.

SO, IT DOES appear my path is not a linear one, but a circular formation of sorts, which makes sense to me, as I am influenced more by eastern theology than western. I am in the same place I was before my journey away from humanity—or my journey away from inside intimate dwellings of humanity—although, I have always remained on the far edges of humanity. I suppose if I had simply not moved back when I was left with Nellie, I would never have ended up running around hunting down food in donation buckets. I would not have been in too bad shape here, mind you. Nellie's room is quite comfortable. Her mom is adequately accommodating, in a superficial "baby-talk" way, yes, but still civilized and generous with food. Of course, the food sucks. Pardon the language.

Here is what I have learned to date—my enlightenment, if you will. I was not trapped in that disguised cage as punishment for eating hamburgers. That was my original supposition, of course, as I sat there all day, full of hamburger and fries, satiated to the extreme. I had said to myself, I said, Sam, ole boy, they are going to get you now. Now you've done it. It is only natural that hamburger owners would be particularly piqued at pilfering. I had anticipated the arrival of one of those mobile raccoon prisons, placed carefully near the stolen hamburgers. I was on alert. But these humans were smart, they fooled me, they were creative. The cage resembled a rubble hole, or ground hog abode. It took me off guard, and I crawled inside. I had assumed that was it, and I would be off to jail. Then, there she was, Bosslady! Not angry. No! She pulled me right out of my other world, into the human world again!

All it takes is one welcoming human to force you from one world of great food and fear, into anther of bad food, structured human life, and security. I had to survive the dreaded place where they take you every once in a while for obligatory poking and cleaning. But I was exonerated for my past sins. For a brief moment I saw Mom, but it lasted only a quick second. She was there, she was gone. That fast. Bosslady hung out with me a long time. She talked to the other humans who were doing their poking, then left. Then, the next day, I was placed in a car, and when the car door opened, I was at Nellie's house.

So, I now belong to Nellie's Mom, which makes me think there will be competition for affection. I do not like competition for affection. And Nellie is a competent competitor. Since this has been Nellie's home a while—her territory, if you will—I have to tolerate her bossiness. "Don't go there, Sam, Mom doesn't like us doing that." Or, "Sam, stop yelling. Mom says to only yell at night when I suspect a stranger is entering the house." Or, "Sam, you can't get on the living room sofa. Like ever. Bad, bad. Off, Sam." And another annoying aspect of her personality—which, as I have mentioned before is a trait of goldens—is her obedience to a point of disregard for her own (and my) well-being. For example, Nellie does not know a thing about donated food. She has never noticed her mom placing donations in a bag, putting bag in donation bucket, then taking bucket to the street. She is oblivious to this human routine. Observation of one's surroundings is a trait I have always been proud of, but not one I expect all dogs to have. Occasionally, I try to open the cabinet where donations are kept, like I used to do at home (until Mom had to lock the cabinets, which was quite disappointing at the time), but Nellie becomes quite agitated, screaming and yelling for me to stop. She is truly a bore.

And I'm feeling a bit lighter, which makes trotting around a bit easier, but takes away that status symbol I had achieved. I appreciated Nellie's envious stare, in awe of my belly when I arrived. "Wow, you have a gut now," she had said, after we greeted each other, nipped paws, sniffed butts then ran around for a while to please the humans. "It comes with freedom," I told her. "Once in the free world, you are subject to the dynamics of free market, which means, if your skill level is high, you can find food and devour it, any time. Of course, lower skill levels mean you cannot find food, and you of course have a problem. But if you succeed at survival skills, well, you move to a higher level of existence in the free world." She looked at me with respect. I felt extraordinarily proud of myself. "But, Nellie, I missed the human contact. I have to admit, I like our socialist world. It provides that necessary comfort that allows for lounging and deep sleep."

I was quite eager to show off my belly, tell the gang stories, but so far I have not been allowed to walk with the gang. When Bosslady comes, Nellie leaves me, and I am alone in the den. I play with some of the toys, lounge on the sofa, trot back to the room where Bosslady used to play in the past. But there is really nothing to do. I don't understand why Bosslady doesn't want to see me. I understand my mom's anger, but not Bosslady's. Bosslady certainly never seemed mad, quite the opposite. She seemed rather glad to see me, which makes the entire ordeal disconcerting to say the least.

It's time for Nellie's walk today, so I settle down upon the sofa. Nellie's mom arrives to lead her outside. But, then, something extraordinary happens. The mom puts a leash collar on me, too! Nellie is quite happy for me, which touches my heart, I must say, and of course, I am joyful, too, because I realize I am going on the gang walk! I cannot help myself, I am dancing, dancing, dancing. I run around the place, up the stairs, down the stairs. I even yell, but of course I try not to break house rules. So I yell only once. I hear wheels, smell her. Yes, I smell her. She is at the door! Bosslady!

There she is! There is Bosslady! She has everyone with her, not at the door, only a few at the door, but I smell all of them on her. Even fat ole Sadie. I am beside myself! I am not merely Sam the corgi anymore. No, I am Sam the adventurer! I am Sam the survivor! I am a world-weary dog! I yell at Bosslady, wag my butt. I want to see Henry so I can tell him, yes, I've been homeless, too, I have stories, I have scars, I've seen the world!

Bosslady is a bit strange at first. She doesn't say my name. I say, hey, it's me. "I am Sam, I am Sam. Hey Bosslady! I am Sam!" But remarkably she averts her eyes, only once shifting her glance from Nellie's mom to me, as if I am not behaving, but of course I am what I have always been, nothing different, except a bit toughened by the world.

Once outside, she says my name, like nothing has changed. She doesn't say, "Oh poor baby." She doesn't tighten the leash. Once again,

I am in charge. She takes off my leash, lets me hop in the car and off we go.

"Hi, I am Sam! I am Sam! I am Sam!"

"Hey, Sam. We know. We know," all my friends say.

"I am Sam! I am Sam!"

"We know. We know."

"Sam, calm down, big guy," Bosslady says. "Enough barking. I can't hear myself."

This is our conversation until we hit the park. She demands I keep the others in line while she manages the other half, just like old times, which makes me feel rather proud. I know she does this because she is confidant my worldly adventure was a success. I am even more amazing in her eyes. I am Sam the corgi man, in my element again and doing just fine!

Henry is all over me with questions.

"What'd you eat? What'd you eat? What'd you eat?"

I am polite and dignified, not wanting him to feel I outdid him back when he was homeless. But my success cannot be more obvious. A dog's figure says it all. I outdid him. I tell Henry about the donations, which appears to shock him—not the part about the donation buckets, because he has seen those and had meals there. He is shocked humans donate their food on a regular basis. He had no idea.

"Henry, have you not noticed the donations come out in the morning at the same time spaced the same days apart?"

Henry gets that intense pit bull stare like he's trying to figure out if I am making him out to be stupid.

I quickly add, "Oh, don't worry, Henry. You did not enjoy living with humans here for long, so you were not able to study their social norms. I am sure that if given the opportunity, you would have educated yourself. Don't feel bad, Nellie didn't know. And Nellie doesn't even understand sting collars. She thinks the sting is some type of magic, as if walking over the line your mom tells you not to walk over in the yard makes the universe sting you." I pant and pant, laughing, laughing.

Henry gets his pit bull stare again and says, "I vaguely remember that sting. It doesn't fall from the sky?"

I give up and run after Eric.

So, we run around the park while Bosslady spends her entire time on the box toy all the humans have. She has one up to her ear and another toy on her lap and she is beating it with her fingers the way she did at Nellie's house, back in the day when we slept and she took her treat box back to the far room. This is fine with me as it's been quite a substantial while since I've frolicked with the gang. I am a bit desperate for social time, if you will. I am running through the woods, under bushes, around the empty pond with no mud, across the field, now brown and lumpy. Bosslady has put out a large bowl of water which we all lap up with considerable vigor. Then she pulls out her treat box—same box as before—which makes me wonder if anyone ever found the stick I buried. I make a mental note to conduct a quick search when time and circumstance allow.

Our walk back is not eventful. Sadie sleeps the entire trip and I spend my cerebral energy memorizing the route back just in case I ever get misplaced again. From now on, I want to at least find my way to the park.

However, the routine today is substantially altered. After Bosslady drops Nellie home, I stay in the car, which is fine with me, as I assume this arrangement is simply to allow the ole corgi's quality time with Bosslady.

But after a while it becomes quite apparent I am at risk of transfer again.

Chapter 36

Marcy
Finding. Hiding

"I CANNOT BELIEVE you did this," Lorene shouted at Marcy's open car door. Marcy told her to hush and get in. Lorene sat heavily and slammed the door. "You stole a dog?"

"Elizabeth told me she won't be back until after dinner. She does not know I have stolen the real Sam. It's not stealing, not yet. It could lead to stealing. I want to spend time with him, let him get used to this hotel. I'm thinking of adopting him. If she says I can't adopt him, then OK I'll steal him."

Lorene pulled out a cigarette and lit it, cracking the window. "So after dinner, you have to take him back. I swear, you take the dog back today. I mean it."

Marcy drove toward Exit 14, which led to Leroy avenue, which led to Jones street, where there existed a hotel that allowed dogs. She had brought a large crate, which was still in its packaging box. The room was booked under the name Iliza Nomoor, which reflected the promise she made to herself if she ever got out of this quagmire. She had called Lorene to confess a plan, but if her plan failed, she would of course lose her dog walking jobs. Then, there was always possible jail time. Lorene had told her she would listen, but that was all. She would not participate in whatever scheme Marcy was planning.

"I don't understand the hotel. And is this confusing to the dog? You have something wrong with you. You need to find help. Help."

"Don't talk about insanity, makes me nervous. Of course, I am not sure I disagree with you. Actually, I agree." Marcy put on her blinker and took the turn with vigor. "But they can't get away with this. No way."

"What have they gotten away with?"

"They had this all worked out. All planned."

She looked over at Lorene, who stared back at her with tired and sad eyes. Marcy wondered if that was how her eyes looked to Edward.

"The show depended on finding Sam, and yet we never found him. The sightings were down. He made no appearances on the hidden cameras. And the clock was ticking. I told you about this, remember? I suspect they figured Sam was dead."

"So, you think they, what, they found another dog? Where did they find this other dog?"

"I've got to figure that out."

Marcy pulled into the parking lot of a The Friendly Hotel, a one-story brick building with a large neon sign attached to its roof with the word vacancy flashing in red. Marcy let Sam out without leashing him then retrieved the crate from the back. Lorene took out a cigarette and held between her thumb and forefinger as she followed Marcy into the lobby. The carpet was soiled and the two vinyl sofas smelled of smoke. Marcy spent a moment complaining to the employee at the desk about the smoker smell. The woman at the counter spoke broken English and ignored her. Marcy paid for three days, which came to $180.

"You keep dog in crate. All time. Sign this. It say you keep dog in crate. All time."

Lorene lit her cigarette. "You're going to leave Sam in the crate all day?" she said as she exhaled smoke.

"You just said Sam. See, you believe me."

"Dog. You're going to keep the dog in crate all day?"

"Keep dog in crate. All time. Or fine," the lady said.

Marcy rolled her eyes, picked up her folded crate and marched down the side hall. She told Lorene, who walked fast by her side, that she had no choice but to reserve a backup plan place of residence for Sam, just in case she decided to steal him. She could not keep Sam in her apartment, and she was not going to keep him with Edward and her mother, which would require a confession of sorts. She didn't confess to her mother anymore. Lorene appeared so nonplussed she could not speak or smoke.

It took them a several minutes to put the crate together and make sure Sam stayed inside without barking. Marcy ordered a cheeseburger, then went over the results of her research with Lorene as they all waited for Sam's food. There were two missing corgis—one in upstate Connecticut,

one in Pennsylvania. She did not believe Elizabeth and Ellen would steal
a dog in Connecticut, but Pennsylvania was a possibility. Marcy found
a family that had lost a dog approximately three weeks prior to the
discovery of fake Sam, or what Marcy figured was the fake Sam. The dog
had been in the backyard and had escaped out of the open fence gate.
There had been a few articles on the family, including pictures of the
dog, which looked very much like Sam in coloring and weight. There
had been posters placed round the owner's town and neighboring towns.
All shelters and veterinarians in the state had been contacted. There was
even a Facebook page with forty friends of the owner.

Unfortunately, they did not have the expertise and clout to go national
with the PR. There were no connections with Elda Jeneris. The owner
didn't have a Hollywood agent. They were simply a family with nice
neighbors. Marcy had, fortunately, also downloaded Elizabeth Nelson's
password file back before Sam was lost, and she was in her snooping
mode. That password file was still on her memory stick and it included
the online credit card account password which allowed her to access her
credit charge history. And this is how she found a gas charge in the same
town the corgi was lost. The charge was made two days before the dog
went missing. She left that out of the story she told Lorene. She simply
said she had evidence that indicated Elizabeth Nelson obtained gas at a
station in the Pennsylvania town the same week the dog went missing.

"I cannot tell you anything more than this."

"So, there is no way you know for a fact she was there, so this is
all hypothetical, right? There is no way on earth you will ever be able
to prove this." Lorene lay supine on a small double bed staring at the
ceiling.

The hamburger arrived, Sam devoured it.

Lorene paused to watch Sam eat a moment. "Did the dog have a
microchip? I thought they said they researched all lost dogs in the tri
state area and they all had microchips. This dog had no microchip."

"Yes, the dog had a microchip. I assume it was taken out. I've got to
figure out a way to get the fake Sam to the vet. Not too hard to do. I'll
just make a detour tomorrow on my walk."

"I'm not believing this."

"I have connections in the veterinarian world. I've done things for
them."

"Please don't tell me what you've done for the vets. I like to think of them as pure. Look, let's say they did this. Let's say you really are dealing with corrupt people, which is hard to believe because corrupt people tend to have corrupt lives, right? Like you would find other things they did in the past?"

Marcy smiled, but said nothing.

"Why are you smiling? Do you know something?"

Marcy said nothing.

"You have found something else?"

"This town is so corrupt; you wouldn't believe just how corrupt it is. But, I'm not telling you what I've done, what I have found, because I'm changing. I've decided to be an honest person if I get through this and save Sam. It's a deal I'm making with myself. But I will say this—we are not dealing with angels. And that leads to the final problem. Elizabeth knows I lied about losing the dog. She thinks, however, I asked someone else to walk the dogs and that person engaged in the police chase. I let her believe that. It's best when caught in a lie to let another lie takes its place. I kept my mouth shut, did not confess to anything."

"Jesus, she could call the police. You're willing to go to jail over this?"

"I've kind of been in jail ever since I lost Sam. You've noticed I don't have a social life anymore, right? Chris calls, I ignore the phone. My friends text me to go out, I tell them no. I've been so crazy with guilt. I can't live with guilt anymore. If I go along with this, I'll continue to live in jail. And you know, here is what gets me—while humans scheme and manipulate, dogs simply want to survive."

"Yeah, but really, this is dangerous. And they will find out you lied to them. This is lying to police. Marcy. Hello? This is bad."

"Well, I have an idea about this police officer, a hunch. He lied, too, you know. Us liars don't want to be discovered. It's a thread line between us."

"OK, do what you want, and I'll help if I can. Only if you take Sam back today. You jumped the gun here, sweetie. You should not be taking a dog around like this. Take him back, before Elizabeth comes home."

After Lorene left, Marcy let Sam out of the crate. He jumped on the bed and curled up by her side as she tapped on the lap top and searched Google. The Pennsylvania neighborhood was two hours away according to the Google router. Maybe she will call Edward to help her, then again, maybe not.

Marcy closed her eyes and saw a vision of her innocent brother, lying prostrate in the park field, offering himself to the herder, waiting to be found. He was so bizarre, but in his own way so pure. And what was she now going to do? She had allowed him to get involved and now if she did this and it didn't work, she would be investigated, probably arrested. They always investigated the family of criminals, so they would of course talk to Edward, particularly since he had worked with her.

Her mother would become hysterical. Nothing terrified her mother more than the prospect of Edward confronting the police. Viral internet videos of police shootings always showed the police mistreating a perpetrator who had a low life value. Poor. Minority. Disabled. It was the one predictable thing about those viral videos of police shootings. All victims had lives that society deemed to have low value. And there was one thing Marcy and her mother knew after twenty-four years with Edward—years of inadequate education, constant bullying, community dismissal—his societal life valuation was low. "Don't call police" was a mantra in a family with a member whose societal worth was low. And now she was going to call police.

Marcy called the Windhaven Police Department and left a message for Don Willard. Next, she called Janie, her vet tech friend, asked for a favor.

AFTER SAM WOKE up, Marcy took him to her van and drove slowly to Elizabeth's house. When she let him into the basement, he turned and tried to come back, as if confused by the constant changes. Nellie barked from the sofa, which seemed to annoy Sam and make him more determined to leave with Marcy.

Marcy bent down and scratched behind Sam's ears—something he always liked. He was panting and distracted. Lorene was right, taking Sam for the day was impulsive and probably wrong. Maybe she shouldn't go through with her plan either, which was thought up impulsively, too. She could simply look the other way as they found someone to adopt him. Surely there was a family that would adopt a gorgeous corgi.

"I'm sorry you're going through this, Sam," she said softly. Sam licked her hands. "Oh fuck it all. If this doesn't work, I'm going to steal you. Don't you worry. I'm going to get you one way or another."

Chapter 37

Marcy
The best story is always the true one

THIS MORNING, AFTER Marcy walked the dogs, she drove them all home, except for the fake Sam, or Sam 1. She headed for the vet, where Janie was waiting, but she was held up in the usual I-95 traffic jam.

When her cell phone rang, Sam 1 started barking. The caller I.D. was simply a number, no name. She still answered. The voice was officious, deep, and familiar.

"Is this Marcy?"

"I don't know. Why don't you tell me who you are first?"

"This is Officer Willard, returning your phone call."

"Of course. Yes." She took a breath and let it out slowly. "So, how are you?"

"Busy."

"So, I need to meet with you as soon as possible, like in about an hour."

"Like I said, I am busy."

"You have to meet with me. I have information about a crime. So, you have to meet with me. Soon."

"I'm sorry. Can you tell me what this is about?"

"Hold on a sec." Marcy jammed on the breaks to avoid hitting a car that cut in front of her. She rolled down her window. "You asshole! I've got a cop on the phone!"

"Are you driving a car?"

"Kind of."

"You either are or are not driving a car."

"I have hands off stuff."

"You have a mic? You're talking into a mic?"

"You know, can we discuss something beyond small scofflaws? I am late for a vet appointment for a dog that has probably been stolen from some nice, middle class family. I have a few things to check on. I need to meet you, like at a park, somewhere we can talk, you know, in private. Can we say, ten?"

"If I say yes, will you hang up and not talk anymore on the phone while you drive?"

WHEN MARCY FINALLY made it to the park with only Henry and Sam1, she let Henry out first, leashing him right away, then Sam 1, and they all walked around the circumference until she saw Officer Willard pull into the parking lot. He slowly stepped out of his car, as if tired and frustrated, then slammed the door and looked out over the grounds. He raised his hand at her and started walking.

Marcy watched him lope toward her. His hair appeared more ginger in the sun and his build seemed leaner. Maybe he had lost weight after the concussion, or the stress increased his metabolism. After he arrived by her side, he bent over and pet Sam, who gave him a quick sniff. He regarded Henry but didn't offer him a rub. There was no ring on any finger.

"I see you're walking the pit bull without a tag, again."

"Yes. That's one of many things I wanted to talk about."

"This is why you asked me to meet you? Or is this just where you take your dogs?"

"Yes, I take my dogs here. It's also a great place to meet because no one but the dogs can hear us. I don't trust coffee shops, and I don't want to go to the police station. Let's walk." She unleashed the dogs and they ran ahead of them. Willard picked up a stick and tossed it. Both Henry and the Sam1 ran after it.

"So, is this the infamous lost, now found, corgi?" He stuck his hands in pockets and looked over at Marcy.

"No. My brother found the real one. This is the fake one. There were two lost corgis. Pretty amazing. Life is so full of coincidences and surprises."

"Well, actually, in the police department we have a saying. There is no such thing as a coincidence. Only very bad liars."

"I'm a good liar. You're a bad liar."

He stopped walking and crossed his arms.

"Pardon me?"

"Look, Mr. Willard."

"Don. Call me Don."

"Don, look, I was the one with the baseball hat and the pit bull, who is named Henry, by the way, and is a wonderful stray I found but cannot keep because I am in an apartment complex that does not allow dogs, so he stays temporarily with my brother and my mom. But someday I will live in a place that allows dogs. I'm just buying time. There you go. It was me. And I do not own a gun."

Willard uncrossed his arms and looked at Henry but said nothing.

"And I had to get the dogs home during that storm, as you know, and there was no way except around that are dead tree that somehow justified you guys cordoning off an entire street, which, mind you, is unfair. It was an extreme situation and it called for extreme measures. And I am very sorry."

"I know."

"And before you arrest me and drag me into the police station, I have something that I think will interest you. Some amazing evidence of theft, fraud, and possibly . . . wait a second. When you say, you know, do mean you know I was the person who was in the car, or do you know, like, you know, go on, you know?"

"I've known it was you. But I had gone a little nuts myself. I could always say the gun fell out or something, but then when they found the bullet, it became complicated."

"You shot at me. That's the thing that gets me, OK? Why did you shoot at me?"

"I don't remember shooting. The gun must have gone off when the branch hit me. I think I pulled the gun just to make a statement because you were speeding away. And, I will say, just because you're a woman, doesn't mean you're not to be feared. I've been shot at by women before. Not in this town but back when I worked in New York."

"So what? I can't go to jail, OK? My brother is disabled, like very disabled, in a way that the world will never understand or appreciate.

As you know, there is no place for him to live. He has social security disability that is not enough to keep him eating, much less alive. And Edward is way too sweet to live on the streets. One day, you guys will misunderstand him and shoot him, because he has no value. He will yell something wrong, do something dumb, innocent but dumb, like me, but I am smart and able to weasel out of things. He is not. And amazingly society looks at me and thinks, well, she is a young white woman, so she has value. But Edward? He is deemed to have no value. But Edward has value to me and mom, OK? Just like Henry out there has value to me. My mother has no siblings. Her parents are dead. So when she is gone, it's all me. Edward belongs to me. So I can't go to jail. And, well, OK, I admit I'm pretty stupid. But here is the thing. I want to change. I want to be better. Also, it's better for you not to put me in jail because a trial will bring out all that nasty gun business. Furthermore, you'll be sorry, because, well, I have evidence of illegal activity that is great stuff for a cop. I am telling you—I have a great story. The guilty parties are people whose lives have value so they will fight and the odds are against us. Still, it's a great case, one that will help you with your next annual review. So, we can make a deal. You don't get me in trouble and I will give you good evidence."

Willard remained silent, ran his fingers through his hair, looked around. "That was long. You need to practice editing your speeches."

"I know. I can edit words but when it comes to my mouth, I have a hard time."

"This is interesting. Why don't you summarize quickly what kind of crime we have here."

"In order to tell you what I have, I have to confess to some other crimes. They are nonviolent crimes and I'd like to add that our jails are filled, and our country's incarceration rate is the highest in the world. So, just saying."

Don now had both hands over his face and was slowly shaking his head.

Marcy turned toward the park building where two large concrete benches twisted around a large oak tree.

"Why don't we wait until we are seated for the rest of your story," Don said. "I don't want to stand through all these confessions."

When they reached the benches, he sat heavily, brushed his pants. Marcy wondered if he was thinking how to approach her, whether it was appropriate to talk unofficially, or in a more professional manner. His eyes shifted over in her direction, moved down her legs quickly then out to the dogs. Marcy was glad she had changed into yoga pants.

"What if I were to tell you that my disabled and very confused brother, with the help of another town resident, found the real Sam. He was not found by the famous detective, or certain wealthy and respected women. But, by the time my brother found the real Sam, those women had already stolen another dog to be the stand in."

"Are we talking about Ellen Maher?"

"Possibly, but for sure Elizabeth Nelson. I suspect Ellen was in on it, too."

"And these women would do this because?'

"Because Ellen had found a deal for a TV show. Elizabeth was also an investor, co-producer. The deal sprang out of the publicity surrounding her lost dog. Seems the entire world was enamored with the Find Sam community. I am sure you are aware of all the appearances on the TV shows. Yes? Well, they panicked. They figured Sam had died. Maybe he was eaten by a coyote or hit by a car. Or maybe he had roamed far away from Connecticut. So she found another corgi somewhere in Pennsylvania. I have proof that Elizabeth was out there a day before a corgi went missing."

"Someone saw her car? Someone saw her?"

"Better than that. She made a charge on her credit card a gas station near the family."

"And you know this how?"

"That is where I get into trouble. You simply have to trust me. What you will have to do is get a search warrant for Ellen's computer and bank accounts etc. You have to look into her charge accounts and see if she was there. I suspect she was."

Don sat a moment, letting this sink in. The dogs were chasing each other in the distance. Henry was now trotting over to them, panting heavily.

"People don't just turn into villains. There's usually a track record. For example, you were laid off at your publishing house because you had a rather sharp tongue. And they were downsizing. But also, because you were upset with certain male editors making more money than the females, something you knew about because you hacked into the firm's payroll accounts. They didn't want anyone to know about the salary discrepancy, so they made a deal with you. They would not report that, if you left the firm and stayed quiet."

"And how in the hell did you find that out?"

"I'm a police officer. I looked into your background after that incident, or after I got back my memory of that incident. I figured I'd find some sort of record of misconduct."

"Wow. And they told me it was all quiet. I'd leave and that would be it. You can't trust anyone in life."

"We're talking Chairman of the Board of Education. Nice, involved community citizen, here."

Henry started barking at something, probably a squirrel. Sam 1 ran around the pool. For a moment, Marcy simply let the cold breeze pass over her, toss her hair around a bit. She didn't respond. She wondered where he was going with all of this. Was he going to take her in, then tell her to forget the rest?

"But of course Elizabeth is no angel. Not really," he added.

"No, she's not. You probably know that Elizabeth's son had all kinds of drug problems. He was arrested. Maybe you found out some things about the family, the dysfunctional family, because of his arrest, right? That is probably why you say that. But I know other things. You want to know why your new Police Department building is so overbuilt, expensive, and wonderful? Don't get me wrong. I'm glad you guys got that new building, but the First Selectman, along with Elizabeth, who was on the police commission with him at the time, didn't give the construction job to the lowest bidder. It went to a general partnership. Our First Selectman was a limited partner. And the Nelsons were investors."

"You hacked the town's computer? You hacked everyone's computer. How many computers did you hack?"

"Elizabeth had a great journal. And, well, a very unsecured computer and email. And I used to walk the First Selectman's dog. I have walked other town official dogs, too. There is more, if you'd like me to go on. Look, I'll never do it again. I am changing. I promise. I can be rehabilitated, you know."

Don stared down at his hands for a moment.

"You're a bit guilty, too, you know," she said. "Pulling a gun on an unarmed woman? Profiling a pit bull."

"Yeah, I know. I think it's best to keep the original story. Man. Strong man. Tattoos. I will change it from pit bull to mutt that resembled a pit bull. How's that? But I am not really buying into the dog theft thing."

"That sounds great. The part about you dropping everything, not the part about not believing about the dog theft. OK, so, here is something I'm going to throw out. I took this Sam, Sam1, or fake Sam, to the vet this morning and had them check her to see if it was possible that a microchip was removed. They found this place on the back of his neck that indicated some sort of minor surgery. It is possible the chip was removed."

"So, someone took the dog, removed the chip, and pretended it was the famous Sam from Find Sam?"

"Yep. I've called this family in Pennsylvania that lost their dog. I'm heading out there as soon as I can. You're either with me or against me."

"So, does Ellen know you have the dog?"

"I am borrowing the dog."

"Is there anyone home, like a housekeeper? Let's try to do something legal. I'll get a search warrant, which will cover the dog, then we confiscate property, visit this family."

"This will alert her." Marcy said. "And alerting a criminal that they are being investigated may make things complicated. Elizabeth and Ellen are rich and connected. Lawyers will come running."

Don stood and looked out at the dogs. The corgi was now splayed upon the grass. He shook his head, put both hands over his face again, and rubbed his eyes. Marcy noticed this was the second or third time he rubbed his eyes like this. She found it an interesting habit, kind of boyish and charming.

"I've got some work to do. Why don't you get this corgi back to Ellen Maher's home. Let me see what I can come up with. Meet me at the station in two hours."

Chapter 38

Marcy
Truth is rarely famous

THE LOBBY OF the police station was empty. An officer working behind the window nodded at Marcy after she walked in, as if expecting her.

"Don will be right out," he said.

Marcy sat and stared at the picture on the wall to the left of the office window. A stern looking middle-aged man in a decorated blue police uniform, hands folded in his lap, obviously the police chief, although she didn't bother to get up to check the plaque to confirm. Other than the picture, the walls were clean, just empty, which made her wonder if they simply never got around to hanging pictures or if they intended visitors to simply see nothing but authority. There weren't even magazines on the cheap glass topped coffee table. The bleak nothingness of the room made her think about, well, nothing, but herself, her guilt, all she had told Don Willard and now regretted.

The side door opened and an officer walked in, Sam1 on a leash trotting by his side. The officer introduced himself as Officer Mooney. He handed the leash to Marcy, said something quickly about how good a dog Sam 1 was, but didn't linger or ask any other questions. He left as abruptly as he came, and she was left in the bleak room with Sam1.

The corgi sat, still panting, and stared after the police officer as he went through the side door. Marcy was impressed with the dog's equanimity. He was stolen from his home, placed in a crate, brought before large crowds of humans who laughed and applauded him, fed terrible organic grain dog food, then forced to live in a large home with a busy unloving new owner. And now he was hanging out at a police station. He seemed to simply accept it, as if he figured once in a while a dog gets lifted out of normal life and dropped in the middle of a pack of strange humans. This is the life of a dog.

Within a few minutes, the door opened again and Don walked quickly to Marcy, a bundle of paperwork in his hand. He bent down and petted the corgi

"I called Ms. Maher at work, told her I had confiscated her property, the dog, as part of an investigation. I told I had a search warrant for her computer, which is in the back room. She was angry, of course, asked what this was all about. We have to hurry. She will be getting a lawyer, probably a good one."

"You got a search warrant approved this fast, based upon my word?"

Don leaned into her and lowered his voice. "Uncle's a judge. Not the judge that approved the warrant, but a judge. Everyone knows everyone."

"I should work for the police force."

SCRATH, PENNSYLVANIA WAS not two hours away, it was almost a three hour drive from Westhaven. It was one of those towns with a strip of main street, a few gas stations, and two large grocery stores. Outside of this main strip were a series of treeless neighborhoods that looked as if everything had been cut up with a square cookie cutter. Small rectangular houses, cleanly shaved quarter-acre front yards, some with a few young trees and shrubbery, most covered only with grass, now browning. The family Marcy and Don were visiting lived in one of six houses that lined a small cul-de-sac off a busy four lane thoroughfare. Their white ranch had dormer windows and bright green shades. Two small bicycles, one with training wheels, were parked in the driveway next to a Chevy suburban. A large birdfeeder hung from a naked maple tree limb near the kitchen window.

Marcy and Don climbed the four steps that led to the front porch, where two bright yellow rocking chairs sat, still and empty. Don rapped on the door and a girl who looked about six years old answered. A plump woman with short brown hair stood behind her, her hands resting calmly on the girl's shoulders.

"You're a policeman!" the girl exclaimed.

"Is this the Dalton residence?"

"Yes. Is this about Goldie?" the woman said.

"You got Goldie!" The girl clapped her hands.

"Remember what I said, Lindsey? This doesn't mean this is our dog. OK? It could be someone else's dog. Let's let the officer talk first."

A boy dressed in a hoodie was now at the door. He looked a several years older than the girl and either had an angrier attitude or was more mature and this was how a more mature child behaved—angry. He crossed his hands and sat on one of the rocking chairs. Marcy wondered if the dog had a strong relationship with this boy. Perhaps the boy had been through all the visits from people helping them hunt the dog. Nothing had worked out for them, so now he was frustrated, angry, and skeptical.

After the mother calmed the girl, Don kneeled down so that his eyes were level with the girl's. "We're going to bring the dog to the far end of the driveway. And I want one of you, not all of you, one of you"—He looked up at the mother—"to call the dog, just like you used to, OK?"

"Which of us would you prefer?" the mother said.

The girl raised her hand and jumped up and down. The boy looked at Marcy.

"How about we start with him," Marcy said. "And your name is?"

"Matt."

"OK, Matt. We'll start with you. You call the dog. Then we'll let Lindsey call the dog."

"So, I call him, then what? What if he just walks around, doesn't respond?"

"Well, if the dog doesn't respond, or you look at him and know it's not Goldie, then we leave. But wouldn't you be sorry if we didn't try?"

The boy shook his head and slowly walked down the steps. It was a cold day, and he crossed his arms but refused his mother's offer to retrieve a coat for him. Marcy sat on the steps while Don went back to his car. When he opened the door, the dog that leaped out was different from the one in the police lobby, or the one that had appeared on *The Elda Jeneris Show*, or the one at Find Sam celebration parties, even the one who walked with Marcy and the gang. That dog was shy, calm, sometimes distracted, at times agitated. This dog pounced around the yard, sniffing energetically. Before the boy could call out, "Goldie," he was running full speed. The boy fell to his knees, opened his arms, and received the full force of the dog as it knocked him down, jumped upon his chest, and licked his face. The girl danced around her brother and dog, the mother placed her hands over her eyes.

"Goldie, Goldie, Goldie, why did you run away?" the small girl yelled.

"It's him." The mother wiped her eyes and stood before Don. "I don't understand why there's no microchip, but I know my dog. That is Goldie."

"We think someone may have removed it," Don said.

The children were now running around the yard, corgi nipping at their shoes. The boy picked up a tennis ball under a bush and tossed it in the air. Everyone watched the children. The mother's face suddenly changed.

"You mean someone took him? Did they try to sell him? Why would they take him? Where did they put him?"

"It's a long story. Are you familiar with the Find Sam Movement?" Marcy said.

"Yes, we followed all of it, because Sam looked so much like our Goldie. We actually gave money to the cause because they had done such a good job bringing awareness to lost dogs. Wait."

"Your corgi met Elda Jeneris," Marcy said. "And lived for a short while with a famous public relations executive. He's had a blast while you guys were worried sick."

"So this was an accident? The microchip had to have been removed. So what's going on?"

"I was wondering if maybe you could help us out there," Officer Willard said.

Chapter 39

Marcy
Liars plus money equals lawyers

MARCY HAD ASKED Ellen and Elizabeth to meet her at the apartment, but they had insisted the location be Elizabeth Nelson's house.

"All I want is my dog back," Ellen had said.

They had already hired lawyers and had threatened a lawsuit. But Marcy was not intimidated. Neither were the Daltons, who agreed to show up for the meeting. They had decided to congregate at the end of Elizabeth's driveway to discuss the plan first, then enter as a group. Don wanted to the confrontation organized and peaceful. Marcy's friend, Janie, from the Vet's office also agreed to attend. She had arrived early carrying a folder with x-rays and other evidence of a microchip being removed. Basically everyone's role was to shut up and let Don talk.

They all stood at the front door behind Matt who held Goldie. By the boy's side was his mother, filled with the fury of a mother whose boy had been abused. Right before the front door opened, Lorene's car screeched to a halt on the street. The doors opened and Edward and Lorene stepped out and ran across the lawn. Lorene ran, Edward lumbered. The group waited for Edward, then, after an obligatory welcome by Elizabeth, entered. Elizabeth gave everyone the same smile she used to give Marcy and Edward at the Find Sam meetings—a slight upturn of the lip edges.

"I am a witness," Edward said as he entered Elizabeth's foyer. "I think this trial will need an expert witness. And I am that expert witness."

"Edward, this isn't a trial. But you are a witness," Marcy said. "Sorry, Elizabeth, we're all a bit unorganized. But, well, here we are."

Elizabeth stepped back and let them into the living room. A few barks rose from the basement. Marcy recognized Sam's bark, it was a quick, loud bark that repeated itself over and over, then stopped. Sam did this bark when he wanted out. He was probably already sick of Nellie.

The living room was filled with men in black suits, tailored button-down shirts, silk ties, and Italian loafers. There were five of them and they introduced themselves quickly. Marcy forgot all their names but tried to remember the tie colors. She figured the suit with the red tie was the boss. He was seated by Elizabeth, who said nothing. A briefcase was open on a coffee table and one suit with long arms, wearing a yellow tie with black objects splattered over it, was shuffling through some papers. The rest of the suits, worn by younger men, had dark solid ties. Don had not asked any other police officers to attend. He told Marcy he wanted to witness the reaction of the suspects first. He had backup police in cars a block away. "Lawyers are more dangerous than guns sometimes."

The head suit with the red tie shook Marcy's hands, then Don's hand, calling him Officer Willard. Matt picked up Goldie and held him tight, as if he thought there was a chance they would steal his dog again.

"Well, I see you two have come prepared," Don said. "I was not expecting a deposition here. Just wanted to share with you what we have so far."

"Why don't all of you have a seat," the red tie man said. "Jack, get these ladies some chairs from the dining room."

One of the dark tie men retrieved a few chairs from the dining room then placed them around the room. Everyone sat, except Don and Matt, still holding the dog tightly.

"So, I'm not sure of your purpose, Officer Willard," the red tie continued. "But we are advising our clients not to answer any of your questions until we are sure what's going on here. We understand that the dog walker for our clients seems to think there was a mix-up."

The dogs in the basement started up again.

"Can we bring the other Sam up for a moment?" Marcy said. "I think if we are going to straighten out the dogs, it's important to have the real Sam here."

Don rolled his eyes at her, indicating she was breaking the big rule, which was to shut up.

The lawyer raised his eyes at Elizabeth who nodded and left. They waited until she returned with Sam who ran straight for Marcy, then Edward, prancing around them several times, panting.

"Sam, sit. Be a good boy," Marcy said.

Ellen stared at Sam, then looked away quickly.

Sam sat, still panting, and stared up at Marcy, waiting for additional instructions. Matt's Goldie struggled in his arms, eager to sniff Sam's butt.

"Matt, can you let your dog go so we can at least see them," Don said.

Goldie trotted over to Sam and sniffed. Sam barked and leaped back, as if unsure of the dog's intentions, then looked back up at Marcy and sat. Once together, their differences were obvious. Sam was still a bit hefty from all his hamburger days, and his head was slightly bigger. The coloring was exactly the same—same white patch on the chest, same golden hue. Sam's rear end more muscular. However, the biggest difference was in eye contact. Sam obviously knew Marcy and kept looking up at her, then back at Goldie. Goldie ignored Marcy and seemed more interested in Matt. To anyone who knew dogs, or understood nuances in behavior, it was obvious who the real Sam was.

Marcy stared at Ellen until their eyes met, then kept eye contact until Ellen broke it and looked away. Ellen seemed in control, almost stoic, until Matt picked up his dog and held him tight, looking around the room as if they were enemy combatants. Ellen's eyes filled slightly and she looked down at her hands.

"Since no one is going to answer any of my questions, I will tell you what we have so far. We have some vet technicians here who claim there is a place on this boy's dog, Goldie's neck, that clearly looks to be a scar from some sort of incision. They also suggest that the place on this neck is where microchips are usually placed, and it is highly likely a microchip was removed. We don't know who would do that, certainly not the vets here. We are still investigating that. We clearly have an emotional ID on this dog, as you can see by its reaction to this family. We also have a dog walker who has emotionally I.D.'ed the real Sam."

"My client will contest these suppositions. We will demand her dog returned. I believe you realize we are contemplating a lawsuit. You cannot take someone's dog like this and bring it to this poor family who obviously wants to believe your story."

"This is my dog!" Matt yelled. "And you're not going to steal him again. You can't steal my dog again."

"No one is stealing anyone's dog," Marcy said.

"Well, I will just step in here and say something." Edward stood and shoved his hands into his baggy khakis. "I want this Sam, if the owner is arrested, or whatever is going on here. I want the dog because I found him. You can't return a dog to an owner who never understood his aptitude, his ability to figure out garbage routes. She had no faith in her dog. She probably has faith in our military. Am I right? You probably have faith that we shall overcome the international crises." He stared at Ellen.

Ellen looked at him briefly then back at her hands.

"So, the boy keeps his dog, but I want that dog." Edward pointed at Sam. Sam stared up at him.

"You cannot take our client's dog." The red tie continued looking only at Don, ignoring Edward.

"And as to this dog walker," Elizabeth said, ignoring the lawyer who gave her a stern look. "I have proof that she was here, at my house, two blocks from your little adventure with reckless car driver. Remember? She let another person walk the dogs and he probably wore a Mets hat and had a pit bull. She walks a pit bull, you know. Did you know that? And she lied to everyone about where she was when she lost Sam. She was at my house!"

"Ma'am, we know for a fact the perpetrator who chased me was a large man with tattoos on his neck and upper arms and the dog was not a pit bull. We've discussed this with Marcy," Don said in most officious voice. "So, whatever you suspect is simply not reality."

"I know my files were looked at, too," Elizabeth said quickly. "She hacks computers."

The lawyer waved his hand at Elizabeth.

"Remember?" Elizabeth raised her voice at Marcy. "You confessed to me. You did. We made a deal. You shut up about the damn dogs and I shut up about your lies."

"Elizabeth, that's enough," the red tie said.

Matt started crying. He sat on the floor, holding onto his dog.

"Well, no one is taking any dogs. OK? And, if this were simply a mix-up, we could simply exchange dogs. But there have been crimes committed," Don said. "This boy's dog was stolen. And it is my understanding you had a deal for a TV show that depended upon finding a dog. Right? So, what we think happened is someone informed you of another corgi. Or maybe you noticed this corgi traveling through town. Maybe you saw this dog, once?"

"You cannot prove anything!" Elizabeth said.

"I'm going to have to advise you to let us do the talking here, Elizabeth." the red tie said. "No more outbursts."

"We have some gas charges here in the vicinity of Scrath, Pennsylvania, made by you a day before the dog went missing," Don said.

"Oh and this is proof I stole the dog? I have relatives in Philadelphia. I am always traveling back and forth to Philadelphia."

"Oh, I am sure you traveled through this town before, noticed the dog, how much it resembled yours. But it's not just the charges at a gas station. It seems you enjoy tea lattes at Starbucks. I bet you don't remember Sallie Larkmount? An employee there who happened to be leaving and saw this corgi in the back of a Volvo SUV, all crated up. See, she remembered it because she had this thing about dogs locked in cars, even in the fall and winter. I stopped by the Starbucks because there was a charge for a soy chai latte on Ms. Maher's credit card. Actually, it was two lattes."

Sam jumped up on Marcy's leg and barked. She gently pushed him and raised her finger. He sat, as if waiting for a treat. Edward stared down at Sam, while the rest of the room, except Elizabeth, now whispered to each other. No one said anything. Don took out his cell phone and tapped it briefly, then placed it back in his pocket.

Mrs. Dalton suddenly spoke. "How could anyone be so caught up in anything to steal a family's dog? Goldie was part of our family. You stole our family. Look at your house. Look how you live. All we have is our family. Come on, Matt, this is enough. I can't listen anymore. And you'll never ever take this dog from us again. It would have to be done over my dead body."

Chapter 40

Sam
Survival and world views

I LOVE TROTTING along with Henry, a former homeless dog and therefore a brother. I understand him—that furtive glance, shifty way of strutting along, like any minute he may have to run. I've been there, done that. I get it. I am a worldly corgi now. Henry never stops with the questions, always trying to figure out what the hell happened to me, then after I tell him, he says he has a hard time believing it all.

"You corgis love your big stories. Yous guys with your wandering adventures and tall tales. I'm not getting this story though. Some 'chosens' take Nellie's Mom away?"

"I am telling you guys what I saw, OK? The male humans in uniforms, 'chosen ones,' came in whilst I was trying to determine the trustworthiness of the new dog, who is rather shy and has horrible manners. Ass smells like perfume. I had to practically dance around the asshat to sniff his butt."

"And so you're now with me and Bosslady's bro? Like, what, forever?"

"Bosslady retrieved me after the 'chosen ones' took Mom and Nellie's mom away. I had to stay with Nellie for way too long. Can you imagine staying with Nellie? And his mom also fed us organic grain, same as my old mom. Anyway, now I'm here, so no worry. Bosslady shows up every day. I am thinking Bosslady needs me to stick with the big guy who is not quite right. They always need us to protect certain humans. But, this is not a problem, as this big guy is great. He feeds us donated food!"

Henry yells at me, tells me to shut up, he's sick of talking about everything. He's a moody ole chap, a bit jealous of me, the new competitor for belly massages. But it is quite pleasant chatting with him, as he does love listening to me, interrupting only to ask more questions, allowing me to become quite the raconteur. Occasionally, for no apparent reason, he yells at me. Bipolar disorder. Some of the homeless dogs acquire this disease. I have heard the Bosslady refer to it in regard to a friend, or maybe it was in regard to a family member, I cannot quite recall, but Bosslady is quite familiar with the diseases of the mind.

Henry now yells again, gives me shade, the big guy jerks his leash.

"Look, my fellow canine, what's this all about?" the big guy says. "You going Russian on me or something? Do you want to fight this little midget here? That is what we call bullying and it's not allowed. K?"

The big guy is great, quite naive, but most humans are, all thinking regular dogs, as opposed to corgi dogs, have mastered translation of the English language. I am always translating. I say, "Henry, you're making the big guy frustrated. So stop it or we don't get bacon when we get back home. And don't get him started on another soliloquy about Russia. The man doesn't stop talking about that, OK?" I am working on the Russia word that seems to be a favorite of this big guy. It appears to refer to another location, one with very bad humans, or perhaps misunderstood humans.

Henry grumbles. The big guy jerks his leash again and we're off. We circle the block several times and return to this small grey house, with very little bushes for sniffing and only one tree in the back, all of which is quite uninspiring, to say the least. I do appreciate the big guy's mom. She is a rather gentle soul, kind, albeit with an odor that signals a touch of anxiety. I find her anxiety understandable.

Today when we arrive home, the Bosslady is waiting for us. She bends over and rubs my back, and I lay down to offer my enlarged, yet wonderful belly. She obliges my every wish. Henry nudges his fat face in between her hands and my fur, and she starts on him, which I suppose is only fair. Humans like the Bosslady distribute hand massages evenly.

After our massages, that end too quickly, Bosslady asks the big guy about our behavior. He informs her that we indeed have been, in his words, "OK." They start talking, so Henry, who has never paid much attention to human talk, which of course is why he has never learned the English language, mind you, wanders off. I do not wander off but remain, intensely focused on all human discussion, because, well, this is what I focus on. I stare at Bosslady's eyes because they always tell me what is inside the human words. I see her eyes slide away as she tells the big guy she has to tell him something. So off they go to the chairs. I follow.

"Edward, Don and I've been talking. About where the dogs will live?"

"Sam can't live in the jail with his crooked owner," Edward says. "You aren't going to send the dog to jail with her."

"OK. First, Elizabeth probably won't go to jail. She's claiming she found Sam. She has a good lawyer. She is rich and white. The world won't put her in jail."

"So, where are they going now? Where will you put the dogs now?"

The big guy, Edward, looks worried. I am worried. It appears we will be moving again. Henry could very well reject the move and run off, the way a few of these ex-homeless dogs do because they enjoy the danger, the adventure, of lost-ness. I do not want to live lost and wandering again. I do not want to live in the free world, work in the free market. It would be nice to have a permanent place, a regular schedule, a warm bed, food, a human who massages regularly. I succeeded, yes, but in so many ways socialism worked for me.

"I was thinking this house is not really big enough for you and two dogs."

I trot off to tell Henry there will be yet another change. He says, "Fuck this, I'm running away." Pit bulls have toilet mouths.

"Look, Henry, you got to stop the distrust. You can't just think all humans are the same if they look alike or smell alike." He cusses again, I return to my listening position.

"So, Edward, here is my new plan," I hear Bosslady say.

"Your plans are changing faster than Russia's cyber maneuvers."

They walk out the door, when a car pulls into the driveway and I cannot hear their plans anymore. I have no idea who is there and what they are discussing. Henry lies down, then passes out. I stand guard by the door and wait for whatever life will be presented to me. I am not too concerned. I have a new way of looking at life, a new way of being, if you will. Once you have been out and about, learned how to live with primal types, survived on donated food, your world view is a bit altered.

Nothing will destroy me without a fight. Sometimes you don't know this until life changes and settled ways of living become past ways of living. But if you have the right attitude you can stray, but you'll never be lost.

Chapter 41

Marcy
The officer and the voyeur

MARCY LOVED THIS English pub, known for its hamburgers and fries. But she didn't like the long drive. They always had to take long drives when they wanted to eat out. Windhaven gossip had to be avoided for now. She sipped her pint of Guinness. She ate only half the hamburger.

"I know why you're not eating the entire hamburger," Don said, before he shoved a chunk of fried fish into his mouth.

"I will eat the fries."

He shrugged then rubbed his face with his palms, as if wiping away something messy in his brain. This small gesture had sparked her attraction. She loved the metaphorical act of wiping his face with his dirty palms. It made her wonder what he was wiping away in his mind. Which led to the other trait that attracted her—his humanity.

"Hamburgers make dogs fat," Don said.

"It's just half a hamburger. I don't want him running away to get good meals. He's slimming down. Edward does a great job walking him and Henry. And you do a good job taking care of them, too."

"Yeah, well, I don't mind them, as long as you come by every day to look after them. OK. Look—" He rubbed his face again. "I was thinking. We can't keep running out of town to eat, sneak into each other's place. I realize it looks bad, the guy who arrested dog thieves has an affair with an important witness. But everything's been plea bargained by this big shot New York lawyer, and Elizabeth Nelson has even moved away. I think we need to go public, be transparent. Really, I'm beginning to feel dirty."

There was something about a guileless man that made Marcy want to put her arms around him, bring him into her body. She reached across the table and grabbed his hand. Of course, the main attraction was the dog he saved. Well, two dogs, if one counted Henry. Sam and Henry were moved to his home because Edward and Marcy's mom had been through some hiccups related to skipped meds. For now, Don was the new temporary home, until Marcy found a place that accepted dogs.

"So, I was thinking. Just thinking. About a lot of stuff. Edward has to travel to my house to walk stressed dogs. Stressed because you're not there all the time."

"You want me to walk the dogs. This is about me letting Edward walk them, isn't it? I told you all Edward has to do is walk by Sam. Henry will obey Sam. And he's getting better with the bus routes."

"No. Really. I like the guy. Weird, but so are you, and I kind of like you. Plus, it's good you found me, 'cause I know how to keep people out of trouble. Edward needs help staying out of trouble."

"Yes, sleeping with you has side benefits. I have free police protection for my disabled brother, or at least an advocate in police department. Maybe you can make sure he gets the same treatment as, say, a rich, famous public relations executive armored with expensive lawyers."

"That's a sensitive topic for me. Come on, Marcy." He let go of Marcy's hands and rubbed his face again. "I hate how you change the subject. Always back to the Nelson case. Look, yeah, she had lawyers, she's wealthy, but there was no proof she stole the dog. The gate was left open, the dog wandered away, she picked him up."

"And the judge just believed it! That she found the dog, thought it was Sam, put it in the trap for effect. Oh please."

"No proof of that. At all. Look, I know this is like abduction of a child, but the law sees it as theft of property, not children. The law also requires more proof than your word, particularly since, well, there is a history there with you. We need to stop going there. Every time we eat, you mention this. You got Sam, be happy, move forward."

The Daltons had settled their civil suit against Elizabeth and Ellen, quietly. So they were successfully silenced. The settlement had included transfer of Sam to Marcy.

"Move in with me and the dogs."

"So, I move in. Everyone talks. What happens to my business?"

"It expands. Nothing better than having a police officer's girlfriend walk your dogs. You got added dog security."

"I want to keep Edward as a walker. It's the only job he's ever done effectively. Probably because the dogs don't care about his lectures on Russia. I think Sam actually likes Edward's speeches. And he's doing a good job, don't you think?" Marcy took another bite of her hamburger, mostly the bread, leaving the meat for the doggy bag.

"Yeah, he's OK. Maybe you can unload some of your client's dogs on him. Your list is way too long. All you do is walk dogs."

Marcy's business exploded after she solved the Find Sam case. She now walked over twenty dogs. She no longer had much time for editing projects, although she was working on a few at Don's house. She loved his emails from Midwestern family members. They all had exclamation marks.

"What I was going to say before you went off on me—"

"I don't go off. I have kept my cool pretty well during these past few months. I've been behaving. Don't you agree?"

"Move in with me."

"That's too overwhelming. Moving is overwhelming enough. All my clothes, toothbrush, deodorant. My stuffed animals? And then there are my flowers, furniture. Hamburgers and fries."

"Computer, tennis shoes, and wine?"

"And what about my extended family? Lorene will visit weekly, you know. But let's not get carried away with that."

"I don't care."

Marcy felt her heart rate increase, her face grow warm. This was a man who profiled her pit bull, demanded its identification in a storm, then when she sassed him and screeched away, pulled a gun on her. He could have ruined her life if he came forward with her sins and lied about his own. Like they all do, she had thought. Protect their own, even if it means screwing another. This flawed man with deep set green eyes, thick arms, freckled hands now reaching for hers assumed she was a reformed liar, a reformed hacker, and was giving her a second chance.

"Give me six months. I need more time to know everything about you," Marcy said.

"How dumb do you think I am? How the hell did you figure out my email password anyway? I thought you were changing?"

"I only read the ones from your family. I don't read friends or work. That's a start."

"How many starts do you get?"

"Two. Three. Three is my final offer. And do not use your birthday for the key number to your password application. That is really lame."

"Where were we?"

They were nowhere, but the beginning of somewhere. Marcy knew she would break promises. She would hack computers again, read mail, discover personal notes, journals, comments. She would take her dogs back to client's for afternoon naps. Maybe she would lie about it, maybe not. Edward would come over at night to share his latest theory on some breaking news event. He'd stay too late, promise to stay away, but then come around the next morning. And why not? He was lost. Like Marcy. And Don. And Sam.

The Styrofoam container arrived for Sam's hamburger, which would be shared with the strays. They wrapped their arms around each other and headed back to Don's home, knowing they would see Sam at the window—a small silhouette of two oversized furry triangles rising from a thick head. His bark would bring Henry, both tails wagging freely, happy to be here, happy to be found.

Epilogue

Facebook page: Find Sam!

We couldn't find anything for Find Sam!

Twitter: @FindSam

No results for @FindSam!

Debbie Ann Ice was born, raised, tolerated on a sultry, green island on the coast of Georgia. She worked in New York city for several years and ended up in New England, where she studied writing while managing her two very special sons and her canine daughters (English bulldogs).

Her stories have been published in numerous online and print publications. She has written a few novels, all set in either low country Georgia, New York, or New England.